ETERNAL PATRIOTS

THE CRUSADE FOR A MORE PERFECT UNION

Neil Perry Gordon

For William - Who inspires, challenges, and enlightens, constantly guiding me to discover the best within myself. This book is a tribute to the strength of your influence and the depth of our friendship.

Contents

CHAPTER ONE
THE SINCLAIR TAVERN

As evening settled over Yorktown, Virginia, the Sinclair Tavern stood defiantly, its structure a testament to the town's resilience and brooding anticipation. Inside its walls, thick with the scent of smoke and storied pasts, were the murmurings of rebellion. Eliza Sinclair, with her fiery red hair that echoed the embers in the hearth, was the lifeblood of this establishment.

The tavern's atmosphere was dense with the tang of pine tar and river salt, crackling with the energy of a people pushed to the brink by harsh British rule. This was a town scarred by the unforgiving hand of war, mourning the deaths of young sons and valiant fathers, each loss a theft of innocence that time would never return.

Within these walls, the patrons' voices wove a tapestry of resilience and sadness, speaking of the scars they bore, some visible upon their skin, others hidden deep within their souls. They recounted stories of the fallen, of the broken, of silenced childhoods. They spoke of the women—mothers, daughters, wives—who had endured insults no victory could erase, their dignity torn asunder, leaving a trail of silent sorrow.

It was into this sanctuary of shared grief that a British officer entered, his red coat slicing through the muted confines of the room like a freshly opened wound. His arrival was like a sudden chill that precedes the frost. His request for ale hanging in the air met with a silence that felt as heavy as the hand of judgment.

Jeremiah, the blacksmith whose presence was as formidable as his forged iron, broke the hush. His voice was a low, dangerous rumble. "You have the gall to wear the blood of our kin and ask for our ale?" His hands, already coiled into fists, itched for retribution.

With the boldness of those accustomed to authority, the officer claimed his right. "I am a soldier of the Crown and entitled to the hospitality due to me in any British establishment."

Mary, a widow whose heart had been shattered by the red tide of war, let out a cry that cut through the tension. "What hospitality? The kind that left my children fatherless?"

The room's mood turned sour, a tide ready to crash down upon the solitary redcoat. Then Jeremiah let his anger spill over, propelled by too much ale and a fury he could no longer restrain. His hand, guided by a sense of justice that had been denied too long, found the grip of his knife and, in a swift motion, plunged it deep into the officer's ribs. The man's gasp was a sharp note against the tavern's sudden outcry. Chaos erupted, the patrons aghast, as the red of the officer's coat darkened ominously with his own blood.

Eliza, her command once unchallenged, now faced a tempest that threatened to engulf all she stood for. "No!" she shouted over the clamor, her voice ringing with authority, but the deed was done. "This is not our way!"

The spark had been struck, and flames of consequence began to spread. Once merely burdened with the sorrow of oppression, the patrons were now participants in an act of rebellion that would not be easily quelled. The officer, who had sought only a moment's respite, had become the fulcrum of a conflict that would extend beyond the tavern's weathered walls. The incident in the Sinclair Tavern would soon become the talk of the town; a rallying cry for some, and a symbol of shame for others. For Eliza, it would begin a tumultuous chapter that threatened the fabric of her already fragile world.

Jeremiah stepped back, the knife slipping from his fingers to the floor, his chest heaving with the weight of what he had done. The room, filled with the collective breath of its occupants, seemed to brace for the repercussions of his act.

The officer's life hung in the balance, his fate in the hands of those he considered his foes. Eliza, a heart heavy with foreboding, realized the gravity of the situation. This act of violence was more than a mere outburst; it was a declaration, a spark that could ignite the powder keg of revolution within the peaceful limits of the city.

As the dying soldier was hastily attended to, whispers of the coming struggle filled the room. This incident would not pass quietly into the night. It would grow, gain momentum, and soon enough, the whole of Yorktown would find itself at the center of a conflict that had been simmering for a long while.

Once a beacon of camaraderie and colonial merriment, the Sinclair Tavern fell silent, its joy extinguished by a solitary act of violence. Eliza, the proprietor whose presence once danced like a flame among her patrons, now faced the direst predicament of her life. In the tavern's subdued glow, the body of a British soldier lay on her floor, his blood seeping into the battered wooden floorboards.

With a heart burdened by dread, Eliza knew there was but one person who could help, though it pained her to admit it. Swallowing the bitter pill of necessity, she slipped out into the night, the cool air of Yorktown doing little to ease the heat of panic that flushed her cheeks. The streets, lined with the slumbering homes of her neighbors, were silent witnesses to her urgent passage toward the headquarters of General Charles Cornwallis.

There she found Captain Thomas Reddington, where she knew he would be, steadfast at his post, his form as resolute as his oaths to King and country. "Thomas," she began, her voice a whisper of the storm raging within, "there's been an incident at the tavern. I need your help."

Seeing the distress etched upon her features, Thomas felt the old embers of their past love stir within him. "Eliza?" he inquired, a frown creasing his brow. "Tell me, what's happened?"

Without another word, Eliza beckoned him to follow. As they traced her steps back to the tavern, the silence between them was a chasm filled with the echoes of love that was once vibrant, now overshadowed by duty and war.

Upon entering the tavern, the gravity of the scene before them struck Thomas soberly. An officer of his rank, his comrade, lay slain. His duty was clear, his course of action defined by the red coat that draped his shoulders. Yet, as he looked into Eliza's eyes—those deep wells of emerald that had once reflected their shared dreams—he read her silent plea. She hoped against hope that he would, for old time's sake, for the remnants of a bond that once held them close, keep this quiet.

"Eliza," Thomas began, the conflict within him giving rise to a tremulous voice, "you know I cannot conceal this." His words were the final nails in the coffin of her fleeting hope.

"Please, Thomas," she implored, reaching for his hand, a gesture driven by desperation. "For what we once had, do not let this spark a greater fire."

Thomas gently withdrew his hand, his duty an unyielding chain that bound him. "I am a servant of the Crown. The King's law must be upheld," he said, his words a quiet declaration of his intent. "Whoever did this must be tried, and if convicted, will hang. I'm sorry, but there's no other way."

As Thomas gave orders for the blacksmith's arrest, the tavern's patrons watched in a silence fraught with the understanding that their world was changing irrevocably and inexorably. Jeremiah, the blacksmith, stood defiant yet resigned, his fate sealed by a soldier's duty.

With her tavern now a stage for tragedy and her heart a battleground of love and loyalty, Eliza watched as Thomas stepped back into the night, a specter of the order he upheld. As the door shut behind him, leaving her amidst the shards of a life she once knew, Eliza Sinclair braced herself for the dawn of a new chapter in the history of Yorktown—a history now stained with the blood of a soldier mingled with the tears of a Patriot.

CHAPTER TWO
THE TRIAL

The courtroom, a mixture of anticipation and dread, fell into a heavy silence as Jeremiah, the stout-hearted blacksmith with hands accustomed to the forge rather than fetters, was brought forth. His usual countenance of warm determination had given way to a stoic resignation, knowing full well the gravity of the circumstances.

General Cornwallis, clad in the emblematic red that had come to symbolize the might of the British Empire, made his entrance with an austere solemnity that befitted his rank and reputation. His decision to preside over this trial was a departure from the norm, spurred by the victim's military status and his personal acquaintance with the deceased. A whisper of controversy had preceded him, murmurs of whether martial law had indeed stretched its arm to supplant civilian justice.

The general settled into his seat, the wood groaning under the weight of his authority. He stilled the undercurrent of whispers with a perfunctory sweep of his gaze. "Proceed," he commanded, his voice cutting through the thick air, imbuing the overcrowded courtroom with a sense of gravitas that only a military leader of his stature could command.

The Crown's lawyer, a stern man with a hawkish nose, stood first. "Your Honor, esteemed General Cornwallis, we present before you a man, Jeremiah Collins, whose actions have not only taken a life but have also struck at the heart of British law and order in this Virginia colony," he began, his voice carrying to the back of the room. "We shall prove beyond doubt that he is guilty of murder—a crime most vile, deserving of the highest punishment."

The lawyer appointed to represent Jeremiah, a local solicitor named Edwards, rose shakily to his feet. He was no orator, his suit ill-fitting, his face the image of a man out of his depth. "Your Honor," Edwards stammered, "my client, a respected member of this community, acted, alas, in a moment he immediately profoundly regretted. It was not premeditated malice but a response to provocation. We plead for clemency, for understanding, for—"

The general cut him off with a wave of his hand. "Let's move on with the witness testimonies," he commanded, a note of boredom lacing his words. The proceedings were a mere formality to him, the verdict a seemingly foregone conclusion.

The courtroom was an ocean of tense faces, a gathering of the people of Yorktown who had come to see justice done—or perhaps to enjoy the spectacle. The solicitor for the Crown looked over the sea of potential witnesses, his eyes lingering, questioning, accusing. Not a soul stirred; these were townspeople bound by a common cause and an unspoken pact of silence. Jeremiah, the blacksmith, was one of their own, and though his hands had dealt a deadly blow, they could not bring themselves to condemn him. The air was thick with their collective reticence, a silent show of solidarity for the man who had toiled at the anvil, whose sweat had mingled with the soil of their land.

Eliza wrestled with inner turmoil under this heavy cloak of communal loyalty. Her tavern had been the stage for the act that brought them all here, and the players, now silent, looked to her for an unwelcome encore. Standing just within her line of sight, Thomas gave her an almost imperceptible, subtle nod. It was enough to stir the resolve within her. Eliza knew what must be done. Her testimony could tip the scales for Jeremiah, and as the blacksmith's eyes met hers in a silent plea, she felt the weight of his life in her hands.

With a slow, determined breath, Eliza rose from her seat. The wooden legs of her chair scraped against the floor, the sound cutting through the hush of the courtroom like a verdict in itself. She made her way to the stand, each step a heavy drumbeat in the march toward an uncertain future. She passed the patrons of her tavern, each averting their gaze, their silence now a burden she alone must lift.

As she took the stand, the room drew in a collective breath. When it finally broke the silence, Eliza's voice was clear and strong, though the hearts of all who heard it knew the cost of her words. She spoke of the night that had changed everything, her words painting the picture that none other would offer, sealing the fate of a man they all held dear. Eliza stood before the imposing polished wooden desk of the general, her red hair a fiery contrast to the drab backdrop of the courtroom.

Poised off to the side, Thomas watched her with a complex mix of admiration and trepidation.

"Miss Sinclair," prompted the Crown's lawyer, "I assume you can tell us what transpired on the night in question."

Eliza's voice was steady. "The officer … came for a drink. Words were exchanged with Jeremiah, harsh words."

"And then?" probed the lawyer.

"He was killed," Eliza said softly. "Jeremiah acted in a flash of anger, not of calculated intent."

The room fell silent as her testimony hung in the air, a damning declaration of guilt.

General Cornwallis leaned forward, steepling his fingers. "Is there anyone who can corroborate this testimony?" His voice echoed in the stillness. No one stirred; the loyalty of the townsfolk to Jeremiah was steadfast.

"Very well," the general said, leaning back with an air of finality. "I've heard enough. The evidence presented is sufficient. Jeremiah Collins, you are found guilty of murder and are hereby sentenced to hang at the gallows in the public square this afternoon at two o'clock sharp."

The courtroom erupted in murmurs of disbelief and despair, but the general seemed unaffected by the emotional tumult. He rose, his judgment delivered, and left the courtroom with the same air of detachment with which he had entered.

The public square of Yorktown, once vibrant with the hustle of trade and the laughter of kinship, now bore a somber structure. At its heart stood the gallows, a harrowing monolith of dark timber that pierced the afternoon's gloom. Its shadow of death stretched long and ominous across the stones, marking the path that all souls must eventually tread. With its crude beams and stark platform, the hastily constructed scaffold seemed to groan under the burden of its grim purpose.

The townspeople, a patchwork of stoic resolve and seething anger, filled the square. They stood mingled with the red-coated soldiers, embodying an empire that seemed more distant with every passing moment. The air was charged, a volatile blend of fear and defiance, as the lines between neighbor and occupier blurred and sparked.

As the hour of reckoning neared, the crowd's simmering unrest threatened to boil over. Accusations flew like arrows, and the press of bodies teetered on the brink of chaos. The armed soldiers, their faces as stern as their duty, formed a bulwark around the gallows, a barrier against the tide of rebellion that could break at any moment.

It was in this crucible of raw emotion that the blacksmith appeared. Bound yet unbowed, he walked with a dignity that belied his grim fate. The crowd fell into a suffocating silence as he ascended the steps, each footfall a dirge that echoed in the collective heart of Yorktown.

And then Eliza emerged. The woman who had been the heartbeat of the Sinclair Tavern, the town's confidante and friend, now bore the weight of their collective scorn. The crowd's murmurs turned to a roar of betrayal; the woman who had spoken the truth was now marked by their anger as the bringer of Jeremiah's doom.

Eliza's approach to the gallows was a gauntlet of vitriol and disdain. "Traitor!" a voice cried out, sharp as a knife's edge. "It's your fault," shouted another. The words stung, a cacophony of blame that sought to drown her spirit.

Facing the sea of anger, Eliza stood firm. "We all saw what happened," she declared, her voice rising above the tempest of condemnation. "I, too, am saddened and angry, but that does not justify failing to abide by the law and God's will to speak the truth."

For a heartbeat, the square held its collective breath. Eliza's plea reached out, an appeal to their better angels. Jeremiah's eyes locked with hers, a silent exchange that carried the weight of unspoken forgiveness. She stepped back, her piece said, her soul exposed.

The executioner, cloaked in the somber garb befitting his grim vocation, stood as a sentinel of death beside the newly erected gallows. His movements were precise, devoid of hesitation, each step and action part of a macabre dance he had performed countless times. The noose, looped with a ghastly efficiency, was a stark symbol of finality—a twisted cord that bound the mortal coil to the inexorable verdict of the Crown.

As the executioner set the rope around Jeremiah's neck, the rough hemp grazed against his skin, a tactile reminder of the life he was about to leave behind. The crowd moaned, the moment suspended in time like the fog clinging to the Yorktown fields. With the solemnity of a priest administering last rites, the executioner's hand moved to the lever. His grip was firm and resolute as he became the arbiter between the living and the dead. Then, in a motion as sudden as it was expected, he thrust the lever downward.

In the aftermath of the sudden drop, time itself seemed to pause, its passage halted by the grim finality of the scene. The townspeople, frozen by the shock of the spectacle, stood as statues in the square, the echo of the platform's fall reverberating through the silence like a somber bell tolling the end of an era. The air, once filled with the clamor of dissent and the palpable tension of impending loss, now hung heavy with the reality of the moment.

It was a silence that spoke louder than any cry of outrage or sorrow could, a collective intake of breath that held within it the stark truth of mortality and the cost of justice in tumultuous times. Eyes that had been wide with anticipation now looked downward, unable to meet the sight of the lifeless form that swayed gently in the afternoon breeze, a stark reminder of the frailty of existence.

As the minutes stretched, the crowd began to disperse, each person carrying the weight of what they had witnessed. Quiet conversations bubbled up, tentative testing of the waters of normalcy, but the words felt hollow, the routine gestures of departure imbued with a new sense of gravity. The square, once a bustling center of community and life, was now a theater of memory, the final act of which had left a space that could never be filled.

Slowly, the witnesses to Jeremiah's final moments retreated into the familiarity of their lives, the rhythmic pattern of footsteps on cobblestone marking the return to a reality forever altered. Yet, the residue of the event lingered, an indelible stain on the town's fabric, the ghost of Jeremiah's presence a specter that would haunt the people of Yorktown for generations to come.

After the body was taken down and removed for burial, Eliza remained alone, her figure etched against the tableau of loss and consequence. Her gaze, fixed upon the gallows that bore Jeremiah's ethereal shadow, was a silent testament to the heavy price of truth in a time of tumult.

As the remnants of the crowd dissolved into the labyrinth of Yorktown, the public square lay bare, haunted by the echoes of a tragedy that would reverberate through history, remembered in hushed tones and heavy hearts.

CHAPTER THREE
THE SPY

As weeks turned into whispers of late summer into early autumn, the Sinclair Tavern slowly regained its former cadence, the heartbeat of Yorktown, its warmth from the hearth spread through the room, casting a gentle glow that softened the edges of recent memories. With a grace born of resilience, Eliza moved among her patrons, her laughter once again a familiar melody in the wood-beamed hall.

The hanging of Jeremiah, though a raw wound, had begun to turn into a scar over which the passage of time gently brushed. Eliza's role in the affair, a maelstrom that had brewed bitter resentment, faded to a reluctant acceptance. She was, after all, a daughter of Yorktown, her loyalty to the revolution as steadfast as the ancient oaks that lined the cobblestone streets.

Her rugged and battle-weary patrons had not forgotten that night, but their anger had dulled. They appreciated her kindness, open door, and especially the ale that quenched the dust of hard-fought days under British rule. Eliza was one of their own, and their shared desire for freedom from the Crown's tyranny bound them in a patchwork of grudging forgiveness.

Yet Eliza knew the precarious nature of her position. Trust, once fractured, demanded careful tending. She understood that her actions henceforth must be beyond reproach. A second misstep would shatter the fragile truce time had bought. So, when the door opened to admit a stranger on an otherwise ordinary evening, Eliza felt the undercurrent of apprehension ripple through the room. The newcomer's silhouette was tall and commanding, the cut of his coat unfamiliar, yet the purposeful manner in which he surveyed the room demanded her attention.

As the man's gaze settled on her, a stillness to his bearing spoke of unseen horizons and untold stories. Eliza approached him, her poise as much a shield as it was an invitation to conversation.

"Good evening, sir," she greeted with a blend of wariness and the hospitality that was her trademark. "You've found yourself at the bosom of Yorktown's hearth. I'm Eliza Sinclair, the keeper of this establishment. May I know the name of the man who brings new tales to our door?"

The stranger offered a courteous nod, his demeanor marked by an air of enigmatic assurance. "James Ardmore," he introduced himself, and though the name was not known to her, there was a sense that it carried weight and a significance.

Eliza's eyes narrowed slightly, assessing the man who bore a name yet to be etched into the narrative of their struggle. "Mr. Ardmore, you are most welcome," she said, her tone balanced between the candor of an ally and the caution of a woman who could not afford the luxury of blind trust. "The patrons of the Sinclair Tavern are friends of liberty and solace seekers. Which, I wonder, brings you to our door?"

In the flickering light, as the tavern's life swirled around them, a dance of shadows and murmurs, Eliza stood ready to discover whether James Ardmore would be a chapter of unity or a verse of discord in the continuing saga of the Sinclair Tavern.

The stranger's dark and discerning eyes swept the room. They paused on Eliza, and she felt an inexplicable connection in that brief exchange. This was a man who knew the art of observation and thus understood the language of silence.

"Am I under obligation to share my purpose except to say I desire ale, supper, and a private room?"

"A private room?" Eliza replied, offering a pained smile while pouring the stranger a pint. "That would cost you."

James patted his coat pocket. "I've got coin."

Eliza nodded as the tavern's atmosphere settled back into a rhythm of jovial banter and the clinking of tankards, the kind of evening that whispered of normalcy. Eliza, her nerves a silken thread stretched taut, returned to her duties with a watchful eye on the new arrival. James Ardmore's presence was an enigma wrapped in the quietude of the room, his allegiance a question hanging unanswered in the smoky air.

Her patrons, a loyal brood born of revolution and camaraderie, eyed Ardmore with a blend of curiosity and distrust. The memory of Jeremiah's fate was a bitter draught that still lingered on their palates.

"Not again," their glances seemed to say, a silent chorus of caution that Eliza understood all too well.

Yet, as she conversed with James, there was an undeniable pull, a connection that sank roots into some unexplored part of her being. It was an alchemy of spirit that she could neither deny nor comprehend, a chemistry that seemed to rewrite the very air between them.

Despite her patrons' murmurs, Eliza's intuition guided her hand. She served James a meal, poured him some more ale, and prepared a room where he could rest. With each word exchanged, the night deepened, and the tavern's walls bore witness to their growing rapport.

As the last whispers of the day receded and the embers in the hearth settled into a warm, comforting glow, the tavern's once cheerful clamor surrendered to a hushed stillness, save for Eliza and the enigmatic stranger, James. With the departure of the final patron, their solitude was sealed within the weathered walls of the timeworn establishment. The silence of the tavern stretched out before them, a vast expanse for secrets to be tentatively trodden upon.

Moonlight spilled through the leaded glass panes, casting elongated shadows that danced across the room, setting the stage for a night woven with veiled intentions and unspoken promises. James, now merely a shadowy figure ensconced in the tavern's darkened recesses, seemed a specter of intrigue. His voice, when he spoke, was a blend of resolve and restraint, betraying the significance of the hour.

"There are … things at play, larger than us," he began, his tone laced with a deliberate caution as if his words were costly. "I find myself here, under a mantle of secrecy, for the sake of a cause much greater than my own." He paused, glancing toward the door as if half expecting it to swing open. Assured of their isolation, he leaned in closer, his whisper barely rising above the crackling of the dying fire. "I serve the Continental cause, Eliza. This is not just idle wanderlust that guides my steps, but the silent drum of rebellion, the urgent beckoning of liberty. I gather … whispers, shadows of intent, for an impending confrontation at Yorktown, under the direction of General Washington himself."

His revelation hung between them, as delicate and precarious as the cobwebs that adorned the shadowy corners of the room, each word a thread in the intricate web of revolution.

Eliza froze, her hands mid-motion on the countertop, the tray she had been holding almost slipping from her grasp. Her eyes widened, reflecting a storm of shock and the sudden, heavy burden of a confidante. "Yorktown?" she repeated, her voice tinged with disbelief, an undercurrent of awe lacing her words. "But … that's impossible. The British stronghold is impregnable; the Chesapeake Bay teems with warships. How could the Patriots possibly hope to breach such fortifications?" Her mind raced, grappling with the audacity of the plan.

James met her gaze, the illumination of the candles highlighting the resolve etched into his features. "That is why I've come, seeking you out," he said, leaning closer. "Your insight, your … connection with the townsfolk. I've been told with great confidence you can be trusted and aid our cause."

Eliza's hands, still gripping the tray, her focus entirely on the man before her. The full moon's light cast James's face in sharp relief, a solemn duty and earnest plea tableau.

"Your uncle in Philadelphia, a man deeply entrenched in the Patriots' war effort, spoke highly of you." James continued a step, closing the distance between them. "He assured me of your loyalty, your unwavering commitment to our cause, and the trust you inherited from your father's legacy."

Eliza inhaled sharply; mentioning the name of her father's brother—a revered and distant figure in her childhood memories—stirred a well of emotions. "Uncle Samuel?" she whispered, her voice laced with a blend of respect and surprise. "He's … he vouched for me?"

James nodded affirmatively. "Yes, he did without hesitation. He spoke of your intelligence and courage and how those traits run strong in your family. He believes that you hold the key to navigating the intricate social weaves of Yorktown, and with your help, we can turn the tide."

Eliza felt the weight of her lineage, the unspoken oath to uphold the ideals that had cost her family so much. She squared her shoulders, accepting the mantle her uncle's faith had placed upon her. "Then let us ensure that his trust is not misplaced," she said, her voice now steady. "But you've heard of the fate of the blacksmith Jeremiah," she stated, not a question but a shared knowledge of past events. "Would that not give you pause to trust me?"

James's hand reached out, tentative yet filled with a silent plea: "I have heard word of what transpired, yes. But I also see the resolve in your eyes, Eliza—the fervor for our cause that past events have not dampened. You seek redemption, and we find common ground in that pursuit."

Eliza placed her hand atop his, a silent vow passing between them. "I can be trusted, James," she affirmed, her voice now steady with renewed purpose. "I stand with you and with the cause. Tell me what must be done."

James met her gaze, the gravity of the situation reflected in his eyes. "It's a formidable task, indeed," he acknowledged. "Cornwallis has made Yorktown his own citadel, confident in its natural defenses. The bay protects it by sea, and the York and James Rivers guard its flank like watchful sentinels."

Eliza's expression shifted from shock to a strategic focus as James laid out the broader strokes of Washington's daring strategy. "It's a bold plan," she said, her mind racing through the implications.

"Indeed," James agreed. "The French fleet under Admiral de Grasse has already set sail north with the intention of securing the bay with force if necessary. British ships will be unable to provide aid or offer escape."

"And what of Lafayette?" she probed, displaying her knowledge of the French general.

James nodded admiringly at her quick grasp of strategy. "Lafayette has taken the reins of an American force in Virginia," he explained. "He's curtailed British freedom to roam and resupply with a cunning campaign. His moves are less direct and quieter, yet they're pivotal. Think of him as the sturdy anvil awaiting the decisive blow of de Grasse's hammer from the sea."

"And what of the Continental Army?" Eliza asked, her gaze never wavering.

"They will be the decisive strike. Washington's plan was to march with Rochambeau's forces, not toward New York as the Brits believed, but to Yorktown. They will join Lafayette and, with the French naval blockade in place, will lay siege. It's a coordinated effort designed to close every avenue of support or escape for Cornwallis."

"Rochambeau?" Eliza asked, unfamiliar with the Frenchman.

"Commander-in-chief of the French expeditionary force."

"And when will this occur?"

"Within weeks. That's all I can say for now."

Eliza absorbed the plan, her mind visualizing the movements of armies and warships like pieces on a chessboard. "And what is to be my role in this?" she inquired, already anticipating the answer.

"You will continue to listen, to observe. The officers and soldiers still talk, even if not in the tavern. You will pick up on their morale, their plans, and any sign of them catching wind of the true threat. And you will feed them misinformation, keep their eyes fixed on New York. Every false report you help circulate is another step toward ensuring the success of the siege."

James watched as Eliza processed the gravity of her role. "I understand," she finally said, a resolute edge to her voice. "We must keep the British blind to Washington's real plan. Perhaps Yorktown could be the battle that decides the war."

"That's our hope," James acknowledged, "and with your help, Eliza, it's a hope that burns all the brighter."

Eliza's eyes wandered, absorbing the words of a man she had just met earlier that day. "But what if the French fleet fails to arrive on time?"

James nodded somberly. "Such is the gamble of war. But we have faith in our allies and our generals. Victory at Yorktown could turn the tide and finally compel the Crown to petition for peace."

Eliza realized the weight of what James and his compatriots were undertaking. It was a daring play, a bid for a decisive victory that could dictate the thirteen colonies' future. And here she was, at the center of it all, her tavern a nexus for the threads of war and espionage that wove together the fate of nations.

As the moon disappeared behind blackened clouds, Eliza moved a lantern closer, casting a soft light that seemed to touch James with an ethereal glow. Eliza watched him, this man who had come like a specter out of the mist, who spoke of war and liberty with equal fervor. His eyes, filled with quiet admiration, met hers; in them, she saw a reflection of her commitment to the cause. "I knew I was right to trust you," James said, his voice a low timbre in the quiet early morning. "Yorktown will be our proving ground, where the chains of tyranny are finally broken. And we will be here together to tip the scales toward freedom."

Moving by his conviction, Eliza felt a surge of allegiance to this man's quest—perhaps something more. There was a familiarity in his presence, a resonance deep within her that she could not quite place. It was as if she had known him before, as if their paths had crossed in some distant, forgotten way.

"I will stand with you," Eliza affirmed, her words carrying the weight of her newfound resolve. "This tavern, these people, are all part of the struggle. You're not alone in this."

James reached across the bar, taking her hand in a comradely and intimate gesture. "Nor are you," he replied. "We're threads in the same tapestry of destiny."

As he spoke, a sense of profound change enveloped Eliza, a sensation that the very course of her life was shifting beneath her feet. The battle for Yorktown, the climax of a long and arduous struggle, loomed on the horizon, its outcome uncertain. Yet, with James's hand in hers, Eliza felt a surge of hope.

The dawn heralded a new day, and as its light bathed the Sinclair Tavern, Eliza stood on the cusp of history, her destiny entwined with the enigmatic spy and the cause that had become her own. The promise of a nation's birth hung in the balance, and with it, the chance for something more—a connection that defied explanation, a bond that felt as old as time itself.

CHAPTER FOUR
THE SEER

The mid-morning sun filtered through the canopy of Yorktown, casting a dappled pattern on the path that led up the hill to the Sinclair Tavern. Amidst the familiar bustle, a solitary figure made her way toward Eliza, her movement fluid, almost ethereal. It was Agatha Wren, a woman as enigmatic as the twilight mists that clung to the town's outskirts. Accused of witchery by those who misunderstood her gifts, Agatha possessed a spiritual wisdom that seemed to transcend the earthly plane.

Her reputation for uncanny foresight was as well-known as the tranquil acceptance that graced her features, a serenity undisturbed by the town's whispers of disapproval. She approached Eliza with an intense gaze that suggested an urgent purpose.

"Eliza." Agatha's voice was a whisper, yet it carried the resonance of a distant bell. "A moment of your time, if you please."

Recognizing the gravity in Agatha's tone, the two made their way toward the woman's modest abode, which felt removed from the town's clamor. Inside, the air was cool, scented with herbs and the earth's faint, underlying tang. It was a sanctuary where the veil between the seen and unseen felt noticeably thinner.

Agatha's eyes held Eliza's, a knowing look hinting at untold secrets. "Tell me of the stranger, the guest at your tavern," she implored.

Eliza nodded, a sense of apprehension knitting her brows. "Stranger? How do you know?" she said.

"Shhh," Agatha soothed, her hand raised in a gentle gesture for silence. "I have seen his arrival, though not with these eyes. The connection between you two is no mere chance encounter. It is a design woven by the fates, a tapestry that spans lifetimes."

Eliza felt a chill, though the room was not cold. "Lifetimes?" she echoed, skepticism warring with the curiosity that Agatha's words ignited. "What does that mean?"

Agatha moved to a small table, where a deck of tarot cards rested among scattered parchments. "Our souls are old, Eliza, older than this earth we stand upon. The cards speak of a labyrinth you and this man navigate—a maze that ties your past incarnations to a destiny unfolding."

Eliza nodded slowly. "There's been a stranger who's recently graced my tavern."

Grasping the deck of cards, Agatha offered a smile. "Yes, this is that man."

Eliza listened, a part of her resisting the notion, yet another part—the part that had felt an inexplicable bond with James—was inclined to believe. "And what is this binding destiny that you speak of?" she asked, her voice barely above a hushed tone.

"It is a confluence of events, pivotal moments that will shape your future as well as the birth of a nation." Agatha pushed back a lock of her silver hair, her gaze fixed on Eliza. "Your roles are interlocked. The choices you are about to make will echo through the ages."

A surge of restlessness encouraged Eliza to stand, the weight of Agatha's revelations pressing upon her. She thought of James, the spy who had come like a shadow into her life, bearing dangerous secrets and a past now claimed to be intertwined with her own.

"But what about the present, Agatha? The war and the battles to come?" Eliza's question was a plea for something tangible to grasp amid the swirling eddies of Agatha's prophecies.

"This war is but one thread," Agatha murmured, her eyes now distant as if peering into realms unseen. "But indeed, the battle here is crucial," she said, pressing a finger on the cloth-covered table. "Be wary, Eliza. The path ahead is perilous, yet it leads to a dawn of great promise."

With those cryptic words, Agatha fell silent, leaving Eliza to ponder the enigmatic tapestry of her fate—a fate that seemed not solely her own to weave. Eliza remained motionless, her mind a swirl of incredulity and intrigue. "What is this you speak of—past lives?" she said, the concept foreign yet oddly resonant. "Do you mean lives before this one? As if our souls have walked other paths before we came to be in this time and place?"

Agatha nodded, her eyes reflecting the depth of her knowledge. "Precisely," she began, her voice carrying the timbre of ancient wisdom. "The soul's journey is vast and complex, beyond the span of a single lifetime. We are the latest vessels of an enduring essence seeking knowledge, growth, and, eventually, enlightenment."

Eliza found a chair and sank into it, her practical nature battling with the profound implications of Agatha's words. "But how can that be? How does a soul … continue? And why do we not remember our past lives?"

Agatha clasped her hands together, the light from the window illuminating her translucent blue eyes. "The soul, Eliza, is eternal, ever-learning, ever-evolving," she explained, her gaze fixed somewhere beyond the walls of the earthly realm. "Each life is a chapter in a much grander story, each experience a lesson that shapes the essence of who we are."

Eliza considered this, furrowing her brow in thought. "And James and I—our souls have known each other before?"

"Yes," Agatha said and moved closer, her presence somehow both grounding and otherworldly. "The connections we forge are not bound by time as we know it. They stretch across the expanse of many lives, drawing us together for reasons that serve the soul's greater purpose."

"And what is my greater purpose?" Eliza's skepticism was waning, the certainty in Agatha's voice chipping away at her doubts.

"Oh, that is to be determined," Agatha replied, her words painting a picture of a journey that transcended mortal understanding. "Some are here to guide, others to heal, some to lead, and many to love. Each life offers a piece of the puzzle, a step closer to the soul's ultimate destiny."

Eliza sat in silence, absorbing the seer's revelations. The notion that her connection with James was something more than chance, that the journey of their souls preordained it, was both unsettling and oddly comforting.

"And what of this war, Agatha? This struggle for our freedom?" Eliza asked, her thoughts turning to the immediacy of their plight. "Is it also part of the soul's journey?"

Agatha's expression was serene, yet there was a fervor in her eyes. "This war is a crucible, not just for the nation, but for the earthly souls within it. It is a defining moment where the choices made will ripple through time, influencing humanity's path far beyond what we can imagine."

Eliza rose from her chair, a sense of determination taking root. "Then we must choose wisely," she said, the scope of her role in the tapestry of history dawning on her. "For the sake of this life, and perhaps, for the lives that are to come."

Agatha smiled, a knowing, enigmatic smile that seemed to acknowledge the vast, unseen tapestry into which they were all woven.

As the noonday sun began to crest, casting long streams of light across the room, Eliza felt the weight of her next words. "And our choices must be our own, must they not? Free from the bonds of expectations of those around us?"

"Indeed," Agatha replied, her voice seeming to echo the wisdom of ages. "To choose freely is the greatest power bestowed upon us by the

Divine, and often, it is in the quiet stirrings of our heart that we hear the archangel call for our true destiny."

Eliza pondered this, her gaze drifting toward the window where the sky was ablaze with the rising sun. The fiery skies seemed to mirror the conflict raging beyond their haven, a silent testament to the turmoil and passion of human endeavors.

"In the face of war, love may seem like a delicate flame, easily snuffed out by the winds of chaos," Eliza mused aloud, her thoughts drifting to Thomas. "But perhaps love is the fiercest warrior, fighting its way through the darkness to ignite hope where none exists."

Agatha nodded, her eyes alight with the reflection of the flames. "Yes, love is the ember that, once kindled, can set a whole field ablaze with its power. It is the anchor and the compass, grounding us and guiding us through the storm."

The room fell into contemplative silence, broken only by the soft crackle of the fire in the hearth. Eliza knew that the war, with all its shadows and light, was not just a battle for territory but a struggle for the very essence of what they held dear. In this moment of quiet revelation, she understood that the heart of the conflict lay within the hearts of those who fought it.

With a new resolve, Eliza turned to Agatha, and her decision was clear. "Then let us tend to our flames, come what may, and trust that the light we nurture will guide us through the darkest of times."

Agatha reached out, her hand clasping Eliza's with a strength that belied her fragile form. "So be it," she whispered. "For in the end, the light of our souls will outlast the cannons' roar and the battle's fury. It is that light which will define us, now and forevermore."

CHAPTER FIVE
THE MISSION

In the waning twilight, the harbor of Yorktown transformed into a reflective haven for Thomas Reddington. Surrounded by a diverse fleet of the British Royal Navy, including imposing ships of the line, agile frigates, nimble sloops, and various support vessels, he stood contemplating. His gaze lingered on the HMS *Dauntless*, a majestic sight against the evening sky. Amidst this maritime display of power, Thomas found his thoughts caught in the relentless tide of his unwavering loyalty to the Crown and his deep, undying affection for Eliza Sinclair. Eliza was not only the love of his life, but also a passionate supporter of the Patriot cause. This conflict set his heart adrift in a sea of turmoil as he grappled with the dichotomy of his duties and desires.

Their shared history in Yorktown, once a tapestry of innocent dreams and youthful love, had unraveled under the strains of war. The echoes of their last encounter, where convictions clashed and hearts were laid bare, reverberated in Thomas's mind. Eliza's impassioned plea against his allegiance to the Crown reopened a wound that time had not healed.

Before their breakup, Eliza and Thomas had shared many heartfelt conversations, each laying the foundation for their eventual parting.

One particularly poignant exchange remained etched in Thomas's memory, a defining moment in their relationship.

It was a cool evening, and they had met under the tallest oak along Main Street, where they had spent countless hours dreaming of their future together. The air was thick with the scent of autumn leaves, a prelude to the coming change. "Eliza," Thomas began, his voice hesitant. "I've been offered an opportunity: a commission with the King's army. It's a chance for a great future for us."

Eliza's expression shifted, her eyes reflecting a turmoil of emotions. "A future with the Crown? Are you serious, Thomas?" she scoffed. "Turning your back on your own people, on everything we believe in?"

"It's not about turning my back, Eliza. It's about choosing a path that ensures a secure and stable future. We could have everything we ever wanted," Thomas had tried to explain, his own conviction waning in the face of her resolve.

"But at what cost? How can I possibly share a life with a man who chooses chains over freedom, over his own heart?" Eliza's words were impassioned, starkly contrasting to Thomas's pragmatic approach.

Thomas had reached for her hand, but she pulled away, a physical manifestation of their growing distance. "Our love can withstand this, Eliza. I'm doing this for us, do you not understand? It's for our future."

"Our future?" Eliza's voice had broken with emotion. "There's no future where I share my life with a man who does not stand with his people, who does not fight for what is right. This war is about more than just us, Thomas. It's about our country, our freedom."

That night had ended with tears, accusations, and a chasm growing between them, widened by war and conflicting ideologies. Their paths diverged from that moment, setting them on courses that would define their lives. Thomas's choice to join as a Loyalist and Eliza's unwavering support for the Patriot cause marked the end of their romance, a love overshadowed by the tumultuous backdrop of revolution.

Despite Thomas's certainty six years ago, his faith in the cause had waned. The once-indomitable British forces, symbols of power and order, now seemed less formidable in the face of these resilient Patriots. This shift in the tides of war stirred doubts within him, casting a shadow over his envisioned future.

Thomas's solitude was gently interrupted by the approach of a familiar figure. It was Michael Dunn, a fellow Loyalist and a dear friend from days long past, his presence an unexpected comfort. "Thomas!" Michael called out with a warm grin, closing the distance between them. "I thought I might find you here, staring out at the sea."

The corners of Thomas's mouth lifted in a half-smile at the sight of his old comrade. "Michael," he greeted, clasping the other man's outstretched hand. "It seems the sea is the only thing vast enough to hold all my thoughts these days."

Their handshake turned into a firm pat on the back, a silent exchange of camaraderie. Alight with the kindling of old friendship,

Michael's eyes carefully studied Thomas's countenance. "You look like a man wrestling with the weight of the world."

Thomas sighed, his gaze drawn back to the darkening waters where the silhouettes of mighty warships bobbed in the twilight. "I suppose I am at that," he admitted, a shadow passing over his features. "The choices we've made in these times of war, they seem to cost more with each passing day."

Michael's voice was soft but clear as he responded, "We've all paid a price, Thomas. But tell me, is it the war that burdens you so, unless it's too personal to share?"

The question struck a chord, and Thomas nodded. "It's Eliza," he said, the name filled with a mixture of fondness and pain. "Our separation was … harsh. She chose her cause, and I chose mine, but the heart does not heed the call of duty quite so easily."

Michael nodded in understanding, his gaze sympathetic. "I remember the fire between you two. Even now, it's clear she's still on your mind."

"Indeed, she is," Thomas murmured, his voice barely above a whisper. "But she stands with the rebels now, and I remain loyal to the Crown. It's as if our love was doomed when the first shots at Lexington and Concord were fired."

The two men stood silently for a moment, allowing the sea breeze to carry away the heaviness of their words. Then, gathering a quiet resolve, Thomas said, "And despite it all, I hold onto hope that when this war ends, we find a way back together."

Michael placed a reassuring hand on Thomas's shoulder. "If love is true, it endures, Thomas. War may test us, but it does not have to define us—not completely."

Their dialogue tapered off as the last light of day surrendered to night. The gentle creaking of the ships and the distant call of the sea birds filled the silence between them. They parted with a nod, each lost in thought—Thomas with a heart full of questions about love and loyalty and Michael with the quiet, unconditional support only a childhood friend could offer. The harbor, once a place of innocent dreams, now bore witness to the complex tides of a world at war and two men trying to navigate its uncertain waters.

The dusky twilight of Yorktown's harbor slowly gave way to the deep blues of the approaching night as Thomas, lost in his ruminations, barely noticed the approach of General Charles O'Hara, General Cornwallis's stern-faced deputy. Without preamble, O'Hara beckoned Thomas to follow him, his demeanor brooking no argument.

They navigated the cobbled streets, lit sporadically by the flickering lights from windows, reaching the headquarters where Cornwallis operated. Inside, the air was thick with the tension of war strategy and anticipation. Cornwallis, a figure of formidable authority, sat poised behind his impressive mahogany desk that seemed to embody the might of the British Empire.

His command reverberated within the confines of the war room, every syllable underscored by the urgency of the intelligence reports strewn across the table. Maps of New York and its environs were marked with arrows and notes, indicating the Continental Army's recent movements, which had become increasingly bold and strategic.

"Captain, the dispatches are clear," Cornwallis began, a finger tracing the map's routes. "The rebels are mobilizing. They've managed to elude our patrols and spies, moving closer to New York City with each passing day."

Standing rigidly at attention, Thomas let his eyes scan the documents, absorbing the gravity of the situation. The intelligence spoke of Washington's army amassing in the shadows, a prelude to an assault that could pivot the war's momentum in favor of the Continental cause.

Cornwallis carefully shifted his gaze to Thomas, seeing the resolve settle upon the young officer's features. "You've been chosen, Captain, not merely for your skill in the field," he explained, his tone shifting to reluctant admiration, "but for your unique understanding of the Colonial mindset. Before your allegiance to the Crown, your upbringing here provides you with an insight we foreigners lack."

Thomas nodded slowly, the memories of his early years in Williamsburg rising unbidden. He was of this land, yet now stood apart from it, sworn to a distant king. The dichotomy was not lost on him, nor was the strategic advantage it presented.

"Your reconnaissance is crucial, Captain," Cornwallis emphasized. "You must infiltrate their ranks, discern their strategy, and relay their plans. New York must not fall. It is the linchpin to the colonies, and its capture would sever the lifeline between us and the North."

A flicker of hesitation crossed Thomas's stoic facade as he processed General Cornwallis's command. "General, if I may," Thomas ventured cautiously, the weight of his question as heavy as the musket he bore. "Would not General Clinton in New York have sufficient men for such espionage? Men who are already familiar with the territory and its intricacies?"

Cornwallis paused, regarding Thomas with a calculating gaze. "The dispatches, while centered on New York, indicate a broader strategy at play. It seems the rebels may be attempting to draw our attention there, to stretch our forces thin," he explained, his finger hovering over the map's intricate web of routes between Yorktown and New York. "They've been too quiet in the regions between here and there, and such stillness often precedes a storm."

Thomas's stance remained unchanged, but his mind was alive with the implications of Cornwallis's words. He understood that in war, the surface often belied the lurking depths.

"The intelligence we've gathered is sporadic, incomplete," Cornwallis continued. "Scouts report a series of clandestine meetings in taverns, coded messages intercepted between couriers, and stockpiling of supplies in outlying villages. This suggests that the Continental Army may orchestrate something far more intricate than a direct assault."

Cornwallis leaned in, the urgency in his voice compelling. "This is why you, Captain, will journey north, not merely as a spy but as an observer of the land and its whispers. You have a keen sense of subterfuge and the subtleties of rebel tactics. We need to understand the full scope of their plan, from Yorktown to New York. If there's a ruse to be unveiled, I trust you to uncover it."

Thomas absorbed the weight of his new charge. It was not just about gathering intelligence; it was about piecing together a puzzle that spanned hundreds of miles. Every hamlet and crossroad could hold the key to the rebels' true intentions.

Cornwallis's gaze held firm. "You must keep our positions here safe from misdirection. Your mission is to ensure our defenses are a step ahead of any ruse the rebels may present. Do I make myself clear, Captain?"

Thomas met Cornwallis's stare with a newfound intensity. "Perfectly, sir. I will discern their strategy, map their movements, and expose any feint they dare to attempt. New York will not fall, nor will the rebel's diversions mislead us."

With a decisive nod, he accepted the general's orders, his thoughts already racing ahead to the covert operations that lay before him. Stepping out from the office, Thomas understood the full breadth of his mission settling upon his shoulders, as pivotal to the war as any battlefield engagement.

With his orders engraved in his mind, Thomas felt the sharp sting of the challenge ahead. New York, a bustling hub of Loyalist support and military might, was rife with spies and counterspies. It was a labyrinth of allies and enemies, where the line between friend and foe was as thin as the paper bearing the secret messages he would soon seek to discover.

Thomas's resolve hardened as he exited the stifling atmosphere of Cornwallis's office and stepped into the cool evening. The night air did little to alleviate the heat of the burden he shouldered. Eliza's face flashed before him—a reminder of the personal cost of this war. Yet, he steeled himself, the Patriot's passion for freedom clashing with his own allegiance to the King and country.

With a silent prayer that his actions would steer the course of history toward a swift and honorable end, Captain Thomas Reddington set forth toward New York, toward the heart of the impending storm. His footsteps were measured, his mind a whirlwind of tactics and countermeasures. The war's fate hinged on the intelligence he would gather, and he was all too aware that the slightest misstep could tip the scales irrevocably.

CHAPTER SIX
SPYCRAFT

James found solitude and secrecy in his private chamber at the Sinclair Tavern. His quarters were a luxury not afforded to many, a testament to his ample purse of sterling and the clandestine nature of his mission. The room, though modest, was a strategic sanctuary where his role in General Washington's elaborate ruse would unfold.

Eliza discreetly arranged for James to have this space, which was normally meant to sleep up to four, understanding that his work was pivotal to the Patriots' cause. She understood that the information James gathered could tilt the scales of war in their favor. The room was sparse, with two sturdy beds, a wooden table, four chairs, and a single curtained window overlooking the bustling streets of Yorktown.

With the only sound of the scratching of his quill on parchment, James leaned over the sprawl of maps and documents strewn across the table. Each paper, each inked line, held a piece of an intricate puzzle that, if assembled correctly by the redcoats, would spell doom for the Colonial cause. But James was the master of misinformation, a role he embraced with the gravity it deserved.

He picked up a map, tracing his finger along the New Jersey side of the Hudson, where the feigned Colonial Army encampments dotted the landscape. In the quiet of his room, he rehearsed the lines he would feed the unsuspecting British officers. "Yes, the preparations are nearly complete," he would whisper over a pint of ale. "The assault on New York is imminent." The lies flowed easily, a necessary deceit.

James meticulously folded one of the forged dispatches, his fingers steady despite the mission's gravity. His thoughts rested upon the Sinclair Tavern; its rich history of Patriot assembly now bore an invisible barrier to the King's men. Since the night the local blacksmith's anger spilled over into violence, culminating in the stabbing of a British officer, a palpable tension had settled over the establishment. The enemy now saw the once welcoming doors of the Sinclair as a threshold to dissent and peril—a sentiment fueled by whispers of that night's bloody outcome. Though the law afforded them the right to claim hospitality within its walls, no officer in a red coat dared to challenge the silent decree from the townsfolk's collective disdain.

The proprietress Eliza had not barred them explicitly, but the incident had forged an unspoken pact among her patrons. Once filled with the raucous laughter of men and women from either side of the conflict, the tavern's air now carried a somber note, a reminder of the cost of war and the chasm it had created between former comrades.

In this newfound sanctuary of his private quarters, James found an unlikely advantage; here, he could strategize and forge his missives without fear of prying eyes. Yet, as he sealed an envelope, he could not help but sense the echoes of the past that lingered in every corner, a ghostly reminder of the violence that had torn through the fabric of this small community.

In the quiet of his private chamber, James's quill moved with deliberate strokes, the ink bleeding his plans onto paper with a rhythm as steady as his heartbeat. The room was a fortress where strategies could be conceived, and plots could be hatched away from the vigilant eyes of the outside world. Each fold of the counterfeit dispatches was a whisper against the oppressive silence, a tangible piece of the resistance that, if successful, would build strength day by day.

As James sealed the final envelope, he paused, allowing himself to imagine the Sinclair as it once was—a bustling crossroads of ideas and camaraderie. Its atmosphere was tempered by caution and the unspoken understanding of the stakes at play. It was within these very walls that Eliza had become an unwitting sentinel, her acumen an asset that James could not afford to overlook. As he understood, her talent for discerning the truth behind the masks people wore was more than just intuition; it was a weapon in its own right. He had learned that her ability to extract whispers of significance from idle chatter was impressive and vital. The days when uniformed soldiers thronged her tavern were gone, but James harbored the hope that the hidden ones, those shrouded in secrecy, would still fall prey to Eliza's network. Her purported knack for identifying those susceptible to manipulation would serve as the linchpin in James's mission to sow seeds of deception among the British officers.

James felt the weight of the war upon his shoulders, but he also sensed the stirrings of hope. With each letter, each word he crafted, he was drawing an unseen battle line—and Eliza, with her sharp wit and sharper instincts, was poised to play a pivotal role in the days and weeks to come. James hoped that Eliza's interactions throughout the town would afford her an intimate knowledge of their ranks. He would rely on her to identify those key officers susceptible to his deceits. Her ability to subtly direct conversations and glean intentions was an art he was briefed she possessed—a skill that could turn the tide of war if implemented correctly. Eliza would be his ally in the intricate dance of espionage, and her insights would guide him through the masquerade of loyalty he was about to perform.

James laid out the intricate web of deceit he was to spin. At the heart of his covert operations was the grand ruse of an imminent assault on New York—a charade conceived by General Washington himself. James, cast as the clandestine conductor, would subtly affirm these fictitious preparations in his discourse, planting the seeds of this grand illusion in the minds of any listener.

With a network of double agents threaded through the British ranks, James was tasked with crafting a narrative so compelling that even the most skeptical would be drawn into its snare. He would breathe life into the empty encampments sprawled across the Hudson, their convincing facade a testament to the Patriots' cunning.

The orchestrated movements of Washington's forces, a meticulously choreographed deception, relied on James to affirm false sightings and reports. These whispers of troop advances, meticulously seeded, were intended to misguide British eyes northward, obscuring the true objective of Yorktown. In the clandestine game of war, James was a master of the unseen, his every action shrouded in secrecy. He knew the value of timing and the art of misdirection. General Washington's strategy shifted dramatically with the revelation that Admiral de Grasse was steering his French fleet north toward the Chesapeake Bay rather than New York Harbor. James kept a vigilant watch, understanding that within weeks, the Allied forces would commence their march toward Yorktown. They aimed to encircle Cornwallis's forces there, where they had established it as a British stronghold. Yet, all hinged on the French command of the Chesapeake—a fact James safeguarded with meticulous care.

The air thick with the scent of ink and parchment, James's concentration was a fortress against the outside world. His mind was a whirl of clandestine plans and false leads. The knock at the door was soft and unobtrusive, yet it broke through his focus with the subtlety of a new melody woven into an ongoing symphony.

"One moment," he called, pushing back his chair and hurrying to the door. Slowly, he cracked it open and saw Eliza bearing a tray that held a late-night meal—a modest offering that belied the care she took in its preparation. "Oh, it's you," he said relieved, and held the door while she entered.

"I thought you might need sustenance for your evening's endeavors," Eliza said, her eyes scanning the documents littering the table.

James met her with a smile of genuine appreciation, the homely meal she brought a soothing balm against the intricate, knotted plans sprawled before him. "Thank you, Eliza. Your care is … fortifying."

Yet as Eliza placed the tray down, her eyes were not on James but on the array of maps and missives scattered before him. With the acumen of a seasoned tactician, she surveyed the crafted chaos—myriad marked trails and marshaled troops, all a masquerade of military maneuvers. Where others would see authentic orders, Eliza read the subtle signs of subterfuge. "You intend to mislead," she observed, her voice a mirror of her discerning gaze.

James's hand stilled, hovering above the papers as if to shield them from further scrutiny. The air between them thickened with the weight of unvoiced secrets and shared conspiracies. "Yes," he confessed, a soft echo of resolve in his tone. "The general's plan is but a specter, a ruse laid bare to veil our true objectives."

"And I assume you will need me to discern the officers who can be … persuaded by your fabrications?"

"Exactly," James affirmed, impressed by her quick grasp of the situation. "Your insight into the townsfolk, your ability to navigate their truths and lies—it's invaluable."

Eliza nodded firmly in response, her expression reflecting her determination. "Consider it settled. We each have our duties in this endeavor, James. I shall not shy away from mine."

James nodded, silently acknowledging the depth of the deception at play. But before they ventured further into the night's covert undertakings, a question hung in the air, one that James found himself compelled to ask. "Eliza, how did you come to be the owner of the Sinclair?" he inquired, his gaze softening with genuine interest.

Eliza's expression blended pride with a touch of melancholy. "The Sinclair is more than an establishment; it's a family legacy," she began, her eyes reflecting the flicker of candlelight. "After the pox took my parents, the prospect of the tavern's doors closing loomed over me like an unforgiving storm. But I saw beyond the grief—a chance to honor their memory and to uphold the values they had fought for. They had turned this tavern into a haven for free thought and fellowship amongst those who dared to challenge tyranny. So, I took up their mantle to serve ale and meals and forge a stronghold for our cause. This tavern is my heritage, my battlefield, and my sanctuary."

James nodded in reverence, his eyes alight with recognition of Eliza's true stature. She was not merely the keeper of the Sinclair but a staunch defender of the freedoms they all sought. Her spirit was entwined with the cause that stirred the hearts of men and women across the colonies.

James met Eliza's searching gaze, the solemnity of his own loss mirrored in his eyes. "Much like the cruel hand of fate that visited you, Eliza, I, too, was touched by tragedy," he confessed, his voice a quiet reflection of shared heartache. "The tempest of life swept me up and cast me upon this threshold."

His posture, relaxed yet imbued with a certain latent tension, suggested a narrative heavy with the burden of the past. "My own odyssey commenced in the grasp of grief when I was but a boy of ten. It was a chill dawn when the scourge of the King's brutality extinguished the loving light of my parents. In the cold silence that followed, my purpose was forged—not in the fires of vengeance, but in the unyielding strength of resolve and the pursuit of something greater than myself."

Eliza's compassion bridged the distance between them, her touch a balm to the raw edges of his remembrance. "The courage that lives within you is a beacon, James," she offered, her voice steady and sincere. "In your journey, from the ashes of despair, you've kindled the flame of a future where hope outshines sorrow."

The moment stretched between them, laden with unspoken understanding and shared resolve. James found comfort in the flicker of connection, his spirits buoyed by Eliza's presence. "It was amidst the silent sentinels of knowledge within Philadelphia's hallowed libraries that I discovered my true calling. There, where the whispers of liberty and justice echoed through the stacks, I vowed to champion a cause beyond retribution."

With the past unfurling in his mind's eye, he continued, "As a spy, I am the quiet whisper in the darkness, unseen but ever vigilant. My conviction is as unwavering as the ancient trees that stood guard over my childhood, their roots entrenched in the same earth that now fuels our struggle for independence."

The silence that followed was filled with an unspoken understanding, a mutual recognition of the sacrifices their roles demanded. In that quiet, James watched Eliza move with purpose, her silhouette a testament to the enduring strength that defined her. At this moment, as she turned to leave, James felt an unfamiliar pull—a stirring of admiration not just for the Patriot she was but for the woman who carried such burdens with unyielding grace.

A spy's life was one of solitude, a solitary path in the name of freedom, where the enormity of the cause often quelled personal desires. Yet, as Eliza's presence filled the room, so did the idea of something more—a connection beyond camaraderie. The very thought was as dangerous as it was alluring, a flame that could ill afford to be kindled in the midst of the revolution's chaos.

"Eliza," he called softly, the name like a vow upon his lips, and she paused at the door. "Your partnership in this … it means more than you know."

She looked back at him, a knowing smile on her lips, a spark of something indefinable but potent in her gaze. "We're in this together, James. For the cause." With a nod, she stepped through the doorway, leaving James in his thoughts. As the door shut with a gentle click, the echo seemed to resonate with the finality of their unvoiced feelings. James's gaze lingered on the space she had vacated, the ghost of her presence both a comfort and a torment.

The notion of romance would have to remain just that. Like his loyalty, his heart was dedicated to American independence, to the dream of a nation unfettered by tyranny. And yet, as he sat down to his meal, Eliza's image haunted him, a tantalizing whisper of what might have been in a world not torn asunder by war.

CHAPTER SEVEN
WILLIAMSBURG

As the familiar outlines of Williamsburg took shape on the horizon, Thomas reined in his horse, allowing for a slower approach. It was not just another stop; this was the land of his genesis; the very soil held the whispers of his name. Williamsburg, with its brick-laid streets and bustling markets, was also home to his parents, who remained ensconced in the town's daily rhythms, blissfully unaware of their son's clandestine return.

Thomas steered clear of the paths leading to his family's doorstep, the weight of his deception heavy in his chest. His parents, staunch supporters of the Colonial cause, would be a risk to the veil he had carefully drawn over his identity. Recognition by anyone who knew him was a danger he could not afford. Every nod in his direction, every lingering gaze, could unravel the threads of his covert mission.

The air of Williamsburg, laden with the scent of wood smoke and earth, now carried an undercurrent of risk for Thomas. He absorbed the noise of the town's industrious spirit, a spirit steeped in revolutionary fervor, a fervor he was tasked to dissolve from within. Amidst the cries for liberty, Thomas's heart drummed a silent beat of treachery, his every step a calculated dance on the knife edge between two worlds.

The rhythmic cadence of his horse's hooves against the cobbled streets provided a backdrop to his ruminations. He noted the mix of genteel townhouses and bustling taverns, the animated conversations of townsfolk and students from the nearby College of William & Mary spilling out into the streets. Each word, each snippet of rebel sentiment, was a thread in the larger tapestry of war he was tasked to unravel.

As he approached the House of Burgesses, the horse's breath clouding in the cool air, Thomas caught sight of the crowd. A sense of curiosity pricked at him, a spy's instinct to blend in, to listen, and to observe. This was the stage upon which the politics of revolution played out, and he was a clandestine actor in its unfolding drama. The House of Burgesses itself stood resolute, its brickwork a silent chronicle of the colony's transformation from loyal subjects to ardent dissidents. Here, men had dared to dream of self-determination, and in that bold dreaming, they had sparked a conflict that now consumed the continent.

In the shadow of this edifice of Colonial self-rule, a crowd had gathered, their faces turned toward a small wooden platform erected in the space before the twin towers of the building, a makeshift stage for the day's oratory. Thomas dismounted, his heart a pendulum swinging between duty and doubt, as he prepared to merge with the Patriots. He tethered his horse to a nearby post, its flanks heaving slightly from the journey, and edged closer to the assembly.

His gaze flitted over the crowd, an amalgam of earnest faces and eager whispers. Nudging the elbow of a man beside him, Thomas inclined his head toward the platform and queried, "Who is the gentleman we're to hear speak?"

The man, clad in the simple attire of a tradesman, glanced at Thomas, his eyes alight with a mixture of respect and excitement. "That, sir, is our former governor—Patrick Henry. A staunch voice for liberty and a brilliant mind," he said, his voice tinged with pride. "If there's a man who knows the heart and the course of our cause, it is he."

Thomas nodded, his expression schooled to neutrality despite the pulse of interest the name sparked within him. He understood that Henry was a key figure in Virginia politics and likely privy to the plans and intentions concerning New York. The speech would surely be a rallying cry, but it could also veil subtler hints of strategy, insights Thomas could not afford to miss.

Thomas maintained an expression of impassivity, though his mind raced with keen alertness. Henry's oratory would surely be a clarion call to the cause, but he also bore the heavy knowledge of being a target for British forces. Each declaration he made in public was fraught with peril, every syllable potentially dissected by British spies and informants, such as Thomas himself, he thought with a satisfying smirk.

When Henry ascended the platform, a collective silence descended upon the assembly. The throng, a mosaic of the colony's populace, stood united in solemn attention, underscoring the significance of what was to come. Thomas, discreet in his position among them, attuned himself not only to Henry's inspiring address but also to the nuanced subtext woven throughout, intended for those astute in the language of covert resistance.

"Fellow countrymen, I stand before you today to recount a moment of extraordinary valor and pivotal triumph in our fight for liberty. On the frostbitten morn of January the third, in the year of our Lord seventeen hundred and seventy-seven, our Continental Army, led by General George Washington, faced the uncertainties of war upon the fields near Princeton."

He paused, allowing the weight of his words to settle among the listeners.

"The air was taut with the anticipation of battle and the acrid scent of gunpowder. Our soldiers, fatigued by combat yet unyielding in spirit, prepared once more to engage with the British forces that lay in wait."

Henry's gaze swept over the crowd, meeting the eyes of his constituents as if to draw them back through time to that fateful day.

"General Washington, astride his mount, looked upon the faces of his men—faces etched with the toils of war but not yet devoid of hope. And with a voice that cut through the silence of dread, he spoke. 'Brave patriots!' he called, 'This day, we stand on the precipice of destiny. Our cause is just, our hearts steadfast, and victory beckons us forth!'" Henry's voice echoed the conviction that Washington might have wielded.

"With sword drawn and pointing toward the enemy, our general rallied the spirits of his men. 'We have braved the icy grasp of rivers and weathered the harsh pangs of hunger. Yet, we have not faltered; we shall not yield!' His resolve became their beacon."

Henry lifted his hands, a storyteller evoking the drama of history. "As General Washington led the charge, the sun seemed to honor his courage, casting a golden aura around him. 'Today, we turn the tide!' he proclaimed. 'Today, we demonstrate to the world that the flame of liberty, once ignited, shall never be smothered!'"

The crowd was hanging onto Henry's every word as he recounted the tale. "The men, once shackled by doubt, now stood emboldened, their resolve fortified by the general's impassioned speech. With cries of freedom, they advanced, a symphony of valor and the unyielding desire for independence."

Henry's oration was nearing its crescendo. "The Battle of Princeton, my friends, was not just a victory of arms but the triumph of an indomitable will. It was a testament to the spirit of a leader who, in the face of overwhelming odds, spurred his men from despair to determination, from fear to fortitude."

A hush fell upon the gathering as the former governor concluded. "The valor shown on that day, the bravery and sacrifice, are the very sinews that bind our quest for liberty. Let us never forget that it was not merely a strategy that secured our victory; it was the undying spirit of a people resolved to shape their destiny. A destiny of freedom, a path of independence, forged by the will of those who would not be subdued."

As the speech drew to its conclusion, Henry elevated his voice, offering not just a narrative but a clarion call: "And so, my fellow countrymen, as we stand here in the birthplace of our revolution, let us take up the mantle laid before us by those valiant souls at Princeton. Let us, too, continue the fight for our liberty, for our right to determine our own destinies!"

The crowd erupted in a chorus of agreement, their spirits lifted by Henry's rousing words. As the applause died down, Thomas used the opportunity to subtly probe the bystanders, seeking murmurs or indications of Patriot troop movements toward New York. His questions were cautious, his ears attuned to the faintest whisper of intelligence that might aid his mission.

Finally, as the assembly thinned and Henry's advisers afforded him a moment of respite, Thomas advanced with calculated casualness. "Governor Henry," he began, extending a hand, "your words have captured the essence of General Washington's leadership and kindled a fervent desire within me to take up the cause alongside him."

Henry's keen gaze appraised Thomas, a slight nod acknowledging the compliment. "Then it is passion such as yours that fuels the very spirit of our cause," he replied, his voice still carrying the remnants of his public address.

"I am bound for New York," Thomas continued, his voice earnest, "eager to lend my abilities to General Washington's campaign there. As you so vividly described, his strategic mind is the key to our victory."

Henry's expression was one of intrigue, possibly assessing Thomas's fervor. "New York will be a crucible," he said thoughtfully. "Washington will need every loyal patriot at his disposal."

With his carefully chosen words and convincingly earnest demeanor, Thomas had laid the groundwork for his ruse. He had fashioned himself as an ardent supporter of the cause, seeking only to draw closer to the heart of the Continental strategy.

Thomas leaned in slightly, lowering his voice to a conspiratorial murmur. "Mr. Henry, might you have knowledge of when hostilities are to commence? I wish to arrive in New York with ample time to join the ranks before the first strike."

Patrick Henry regarded Thomas with a measured gaze, the weight of leadership evident in his discerning eyes. "Young man, the winds of war are unpredictable," he responded cautiously. "Plans shift with the tides, and secrecy is our ally. Your zeal is commendable, but specifics of an attack, should there be one, are closely guarded."

Thomas nodded, understanding the need for discretion. "Of course, sir. I only seek to ensure that my journey is timely and that my efforts to support General Washington are not in vain."

Henry's eyes held a spark of respect for Thomas's apparent dedication. "Your eagerness to serve will be well received," he assured him. "Make haste, but also make certain that you are prepared. The path to New York is fraught with challenges, and the enemy is ever watchful."

With a final, firm handshake, Thomas expressed his gratitude and took his leave, his mind alight with the nuances of the conversation. He had obtained no specifics, yet the interaction had provided him with a subtle affirmation of the urgency of his mission. He mounted his horse, the information—or lack thereof—fueling his resolve as he set off toward New York, a lone figure against the sprawling canvas of revolution.

CHAPTER EIGHT
THE DIVINATION

With a heart gripped by the need to decipher her fate, Eliza stood once more before the weathered door of Agatha's abode. Pushing open the door, Eliza entered the dim-lit chamber, a sanctuary of secrets, where the mingled aromas of ancient herbs and the leather of timeworn tomes seemed to hold the whispers of the past.

"Agatha," Eliza began, her voice steady yet betraying a flicker of the turmoil within, "you have unwoven threads of a destiny that entwines me with James, yet the full pattern eludes my grasp. Can you provide more for me so I can understand?"

Agatha's form, a blend of shifting light and deep shadow, beckoned Eliza to the table, swathed in cloth. Seated opposite, Agatha's hands, gnarled as ancient roots, reached with graceful intent toward the deck. Each movement held a thousand clandestine whispers shared in confidence with the passage of time. With a practiced flick of her wrist, a card sprang forth, its emergence carrying the weight of ages, resonating with the silent music of history itself.

"The Hierophant," Agatha intoned, her voice echoing with a timbre that seemed to reach back through the annals of time, "represents the sacred bridge between worlds." She gestured to the card, where the figure, garbed in the regalia of the holy office, sat enthroned, his demeanor a balance of authority and tranquility. "See here, the triple crown upon his brow," Agatha continued, finger tracing the image. "It symbolizes his connection to the conscious world we dwell in, the subconscious layers beneath, and the superconscious heights above—binding the vast realms of experience."

Eliza leaned in, her gaze intent upon the card as Agatha pointed to the two pillars framing the Hierophant, like guards to the temple of wisdom. "These pillars stand for the dualities we navigate—the spiritual and the material, the inner and the outer. And yet, he sits between them, a testament to balance and unity."

Agatha highlighted The Hierophant's raised hand with a reverence that spoke of deeper understanding. "His blessing is an act of transmission, of bestowing the cosmic knowledge that pervades all existence." Her eyes then moved to the scepter in the other hand. "And the scepter," she elucidated, "affirms his role as the sovereign of spiritual laws that govern the cosmos and the soul's awakening within it."

She leaned back, allowing the full import of The Hierophant's image to settle over Eliza. "This card, this Hierophant, is the custodian of esoteric teachings and sacred rites, a guiding light to those who seek ancient and ever-new knowledge. His authority commands the mystical traditions that weave individual destiny to the universal fate of all beings."

Agatha's words hung in the air, a sacred mantra that connected Eliza to a lineage of seekers past and present. "His appearance in your reading," Agatha concluded, "heralds a profound connection to the universal truths, a sign that your quest is intertwined with much greater narratives that unfold in the tapestry of humanity's spiritual odyssey."

Agatha's fingers caressed the edge of the next card before turning it over to the flickering candlelight, which seemed to imbue the image with a secretive life of its own. "The Seven of Swords," she began, her voice a hushed whisper that carried the weight of unspoken lore, "embodies the realm of the unseen mover, the silent strategist."

Her eyes, reflecting the flicker of the flame, fixed upon the card's portrayal—a solitary figure tiptoeing away with five swords, leaving two behind. "Observe the bearer of the blades," Agatha directed, ensuring the card's tale captured Eliza's full attention. "He treads quietly, extracting valuable insights, truths not meant for his possession, yet seized by his cunning."

A shiver of recognition coursed through Eliza. "James," she breathed in a whisper.

Agatha's lips curved into an enigmatic smile. "Yes, perhaps," she acquiesced. "The bond you share with James is woven into this prophecy's very sinew, a confluence ordained by the stars themselves to illuminate a truth buried by time's relentless march."

Agatha returned her gaze to the card and traced the imagery, her fingertip gliding over the remaining abandoned swords. "The two left untouched signify the knowledge that is yet to be discovered, or perhaps the wisdom that one chooses to leave behind, for reasons only the heart knows."

She looked up at Eliza, her gaze piercing through the shroud of mysteries enveloping them. "This card whispers of the delicate art of discernment and discretion. It is the dance of the mind with shadows, the secret plans and hidden motives that move silently beneath the surface of more overt actions."

Eliza absorbed the mystic's explanation, the card's meaning seeping into her understanding like a shadow slowly stretching at dusk. "The Seven of Swords challenges you to look beyond the obvious, to perceive the subtleties of intentions, and to guard against the unseen thefts of truth," Agatha concluded, her voice trailing off as if allowing the secrets themselves to settle into the silence between them.

Eliza leaned forward, her gaze intent upon the arcane symbols. "What revelation do these bearers of mystery hold for us? For the path that James and I are to walk?" she pressed, her words like tendrils reaching into the mist.

"The cards, my child, whisper of what may come," Agatha replied, her eyes reflecting an ancient knowledge. "They cast light into dark corners but do not dictate the journey. Yours is the hand upon the tiller, yours the course to chart."

A sigh of exasperation escaped Eliza, "But why must you enshroud vital truths in such an enigma? Can you not clear the mists that cloud our way?"

Agatha's fingers stilled, her touch upon the cards gentle as if to quiet unseen spirits. "The oracle speaks in riddles, for not all truths are ripe for harvest. They must be sought, pondered, and only then embraced," she counseled, the timbre of her voice a woven blend of solace and mystery.

Eliza's attention, sharpened by a quest for understanding, refocused on the spread before her. Agatha's hands, seasoned in the language of the tarot, beckoned forth the image of the High Priestess. The card shimmered in the candlelight, revealing a figure shrouded in an air of mystique seated before a thin veil decorated with pomegranates. The High Priestess's eyes were deep pools of knowledge, her countenance etched with the tranquility of one who holds the keys to hidden wisdom.

"Behold The High Priestess"—Agatha's voice rose like a soft hymn—"keeper of the sacred scroll, a manuscript woven with the very threads of destiny." Her finger traced the columns of Boaz and Jachin flanking the Priestess, symbols of the pillars of Solomon's Temple, representing the duality of nature and the passage to sacred knowledge. "She sits at the gateway of the subconscious, a silent sentinel guarding the secrets that lie beyond. Her wisdom speaks of unity and the transcendent truths that bind all existence."

As the High Priestess's enigmatic gaze held Eliza's own, Agatha unveiled the next card: The Devil. In stark contrast, this card bore the image of a satyr-like entity, Baphomet, an embodiment of temptation and material bondage, its massive wings spread, casting a shadow over two figures enchained below. "And here, The Devil," Agatha intoned, her voice a somber note, "captures the vision of enlightenment in his snare, twisting purity with deception, binding free will with the chains of illusion."

The Devil's eyes glowered with a cunning light, a false prophet of freedom. The figures at his feet, a man and a woman, stood, their shackles loose enough to be slipped off, suggesting that the power to escape the entrapment was within their own grasp. "This card warns of enslavement to the material, of losing one's way on the path to spiritual liberation," Agatha explained, her eyes locking with Eliza's. "It is a reminder that the shackles that bind us are often of our own making, and liberation lies in acknowledging our own power."

The juxtaposition of The High Priestess and The Devil in the reading spoke to Eliza of a profound struggle between the revelation of hidden truths and the seductive pull of darker forces. Agatha's steady gaze implored her to understand the gravity of the cards' message: in her journey with James, the balance between enlightenment and shadow, freedom and bondage, would be pivotal.

The Wheel of Fortune rose next from the deck under Agatha's deliberate touch, its grandeur unfolding before Eliza's wide eyes. The card was a vivid tapestry of complex symbolism, the wheel itself center stage, encircled by the alchemical symbols for mercury, sulfur, water, and salt—the building blocks of life and the four states of matter. Mythical creatures perched at the wheel's quarters, each a guardian of the cardinal points and the cyclical nature of change.

"At the heart," Agatha elaborated, "is the wheel of destiny, ever spinning, ever shifting the fortunes of men." She gestured to the regal figure atop the wheel, robed in the garb of ancient nobility, rising with the turn of fortune. "This king's ascent marks a time of favorable outcomes and progression. Conversely"—her hand then indicated the figure descending on the opposite side—"this fallen one warns that what goes up must also come down. The wheel is impartial and relentless in its rotation, a reminder that change is the universe's only constant."

Eliza, her mind adrift in the revelation of the wheel, turned to Agatha, her expression etched with a plea for clarity. "What does this portend for James and me?" she implored, seeking a beacon in the tumultuous sea of prophecy before her.

"Your union with James"—Agatha spoke with a resonance that seemed to echo the very spin of the cosmos—"is entwined with this cosmic wheel. Together, you are called to reclaim the light ensnared by shadows, to turn the wheel away from an age of deceit toward an era of enlightenment. This task will test the very fibers of your beings, forging a new world from the crucible of the old."

Eliza's face mirrored the complex weave of emotions within her, the interplay of confusion, resolve, and the dawning realization of the magnitude of her role in this grand design. "Is our purpose, then, to find something lost, a blueprint for what the world may yet become?" she asked, her voice tremulous in the stillness of the hovel.

Agatha's response was a tapestry of the cards' enigmatic wisdom: The High Priestess, a sentinel of sacred truths; The Devil, a symbol of the illusions that bind; and now, The Wheel of Fortune, the emblem of inevitable change. "These are but echoes of what may come to pass," she intoned. "To decipher the full meaning, to navigate the labyrinth of fate, you must unite your efforts with James. Only together can you pierce the veil that shrouds this profound enigma."

With the mystery still cloaked in the shadows of the unknown, Eliza knew that her next steps were inexorably linked to James. She must find him to unravel the secrets of the cards, for in their combined strength and wisdom lay the key to altering the very fabric of their destiny.

CHAPTER NINE
GLORY AT SEA

Amid the port's clamor, James stood, his figure resolute against the chaos. His eyes, wide with a mix of awe and strategy, were fixed on the HMS *Dauntless*. Despite her current vulnerability, the size of the vessel and the formidable array of cannons lining her decks spoke to her latent power. Shipwrights swarmed her hull, their repairs urgent and rhythmic, a testament to her importance to impending conflicts. The wounded yet still imposing warship lay against the tranquil river—a prize of French opportunity in the shadow of British might.

As James pondered the scene, his heart buoyant with anticipation, the air suddenly filled with a chorus of shouts. He turned, and his breath caught in his chest. There, cleaving through the azure canvas of the sky, were French sails—a sight as exhilarating as foreboding. The formidable armada emerged as if conjured by the very spirit of the sea, a promise of the tumult to come.

Securing a small dinghy, James, armed with the intelligence of the *Marsillois*, Admiral de Grasse's flagship, made his stealthy departure from the shore. He glided through the water with each stroke muffled as if to mask his intent from the sea itself. His information had been clear: the *Marsillois* was the heart of the fleet, where the admiral would command.

As he rowed, James found his rhythm in harmony with the sea's own cadence. He could not help but pause for a moment, gazing out across the waters that bore the silent sentinels of France's naval might. Over two dozen warships lay anchored, their masts like a forest of resilience against the horizon. The *Marsillois*, especially, commanded the view, her decks bristling with the readiness of war and the quiet promise of support to a nascent nation's cause. It was a sight that stirred a mix of awe and solemnity in James; here floated the embodiment of an alliance, the tangible proof of a shared commitment to liberty.

He took a deep breath, letting the salt air fill his lungs, reinforcing his resolve. Then, with a nod to the gravity of the mission that lay ahead, he returned to his oars with renewed vigor. As James approached the towering vessel, a rope ladder draped casually over the side offered a silent ascent. With purpose and caution, he climbed aboard, his presence yet unnoticed in the vessel's vastness.

The deck of the *Marsillois* was a mosaic of sailors, each a thread in the fabric of naval life, oblivious to the spy in their midst. Admiral de Grasse emerged without fanfare, his presence formidable and obvious, his uniform a rich tapestry of power, golden epaulets catching the sunlight, his polished boots reflecting the seriousness of the hour.

With a composure born of necessity, James approached. "Admiral," he began, his voice betraying none of the urgency that hammered in his veins. The admiral cut him short, his tone an icy edict against supposed trespassers. Undeterred, James revealed his identity.

"Admiral, I am Captain James Ardmore, dispatched by General Washington with intelligence of critical import." Skepticism shadowed de Grasse's eyes, but James's steady gaze and the sealed letter he produced spoke of his authenticity. To James's relief, the admiral spoke English fairly well, easing the conversation, since James knew only a little French. This unexpected ease allowed him to press on with greater confidence.

The admiral scrutinized the letter, the creases of suspicion on his brow softening as he grasped its significance. *"Capitaine*, this way, please."* He beckoned, gesturing for James to follow him. They moved to the strategic sanctum of his quarters, a realm where coastlines etched across maps whispered of fates yet unsealed.

James stood firm inside the admiral's strategic sanctum, focusing on de Grasse. "Admiral, the British fleet is en route from New York. Their intent: to breach the Chesapeake and aid Cornwallis," he declared, the map beneath his fingers bristling with an imminent threat. "We must seize control of the Bay. With Washington and Rochambeau closing in on Yorktown, securing the Bay now is critical—it will cut off Cornwallis's only path of retreat and ensure the siege's success."

The admiral's eyes, unwavering, absorbed the cartographic sprawl before him. "I am aware of my duty. We will dominate the Chesapeake," he declared resolutely, the weight of the upcoming siege of Yorktown heavy in his words.

As the day unfolded, the sun's passage was a mere backdrop to the fervent planning within the flagship's timeworn walls. James and the admiral, entrenched in tactical exchange, were architects of tomorrow's warfare.

*

In the tense interlude of waiting, the days stretched endlessly, each sun cycle blending into the next, with the shadow of conflict ever-present. For three days, the allied forces watched the horizon with a predator's focus, the anticipation of engagement as constant as the tide. Rest was an elusive dream as the specter of the British fleet's arrival cast a long shadow over the encampment. The men, caught in a limbo of readiness, were bound to their posts, the possibility of confrontation an unspoken promise hanging in the still sea air.

On the fourth morning, the world was awash with the amber hues of dawn, a tranquil facade that belied the tension gripping those who stood watch. In this uneasy peace, the call they had been waiting for finally shattered the silence, slicing through the morning haze like a blade. "Sails on the horizon!" the lookout cried, his voice the harbinger of the long-awaited storm. It was a proclamation that severed the last threads of pause, thrusting all into the throes of reality, where months of meticulous planning would be put to the test against the British prowess at sea.

The French fleet swiftly maneuvered into battle formation under Admiral de Grasse's keen command. With deft precision, the twenty-

71

eight warships positioned themselves, their broadsides bearing down on the approaching British. On the opposing waters, the British fleet, though battered from earlier engagements, presented a formidable front with their line of nineteen warships ready for combat.

Like titans of the sea, the two fleets faced each other—a mere expanse of water separating their imminent clash. Numbering in the hundreds, the French guns were primed and aimed, their crews standing by in tense anticipation. With their own cannons readied, the British awaited the command to unleash their firepower.

A profound silence enveloped the space between the calls to arms, a momentary calm before the storm of iron and fire. Then, as if on an unspoken cue, the stillness fractured with the thunderous roars of the first volleys. The battle for control of the Chesapeake—and indeed the nation's future—had begun in earnest.

For over two hours, the sea became a theater of destruction. The French fleet, steadfast in adversity, withstood the British assault with disciplined resistance. The *Marsillois* herself bore the fury of the battle, her cannons' resounding reply to each British salvo a fierce declaration of defiance.

James, perched precariously on the deck of the *Marsillois*, became an infinitesimal fragment in the grand and violent mosaic of war. The air was thick with the roar of cannon fire, an orchestra of destruction that resonated in the very marrow of his bones. Cannonballs tore through the sky with a monstrous hiss, sculpting ruthless arcs of devastation in their wake. The retaliatory fury of the French fleet's cannons erupted in thunderous explosions, a symphony of annihilation that vibrated through the souls of men. Amidst the chaos, the clash of metal, and the anguished shouts of battle, it was the deep, resounding boom that dominated—a relentless drumbeat punctuating the end of lives and the splintering of ships, composing the dreadful score of the sea's most unforgiving dance.

All around James, the reality of battle was laid bare: the acrid stench of gunpowder, the sickening spray of human blood that mixed indistinguishably with seawater, and the piercing screams of pain from the wounded. The decks were slick with the lifeblood of officers and seamen alike, a grisly mosaic of severed limbs and lives cut short.

In the midst of this pandemonium, James narrowly escaped death himself. A cannonball whistled past, so close he felt the brush of its deadly trajectory, a hairsbreadth from severing his head from his body. He witnessed the carnage, the relentless exchange of artillery, each blast a reminder of mortality's fragile thread.

As the *Marsillois* roared with the thunder of her guns, James witnessed humanity's dual faces—the valiant hearts beating against the tide of war and the savage dance of destruction that claimed the brave and the fearful alike. The battle raged, a harrowing ordeal of endurance shaping the very course of history with each passing moment.

James felt the reverberations of the cannonades as if they were chiseling away at the foundations of his mind amidst the chaos. The violence of each exchange between the fleets was heard and felt—a relentless vibration that threatened to splinter the soul from the body.

As the sun dipped toward the horizon, its waning light bled into the canvas of the sky, an artist's final stroke on a day marked by the tumult of battle. Once resolute and unyielding, the British found their spirits fracturing under the relentless barrage from the French fleet. Their signal to withdraw was not merely a white flag against the blood-red skies but the closing of a chapter written in the language of cannonade and courage.

On the deck of the *Marsillois*, amidst the acrid tang of gunpowder and the pungent odor of charred wood, James stood, his body and soul marinated in the residue of war. The ship, a valiant beast that had thundered with the roar of its guns, now quieted, its sides still warm from the heat of battle. The smoke that had once choked the air began to dissipate, revealing a horizon streaked with the colors of victory and survival.

The French sailors, illuminated by the fading sunlight, erupted into a chorus of jubilation. Their voices, harmonious in victory, starkly contrasted the day's echoes of despair. With a heart thundering as fiercely as the guns had, James felt a surge of kinship with these men, his brothers in arms. The joy of triumph swelled within him, a buoyant force that lifted the weight of fear and fatigue that had, until now, been his constant companions.

Around him, the deck was a tableau of both desolation and resilience. Men embraced, their laughter mingling with tears, releasing the pent-up tension gripping them. Others attended to the wounded, their steady hands and soft words a balm to the injured who had borne the battle's brunt. Some moved silently among the fallen, their somber duty to honor the sacrifices that had been made, ensuring that the cost of this victory would not be forgotten amidst the revelry.

The admiral, a stoic figure throughout the fray, allowed a rare smile to grace his lips as he observed his crew's exultation. His eyes met James's, and in that glance was an unspoken acknowledgment of the ordeal they had endured, the strategy that had been validated, and the future they had secured. Together, they had steered the course of history, their fates intertwined with the fate of nations.

As nightfall draped its cloak over the scene, the *Marsillois* bore her scars with dignity, her damages a testament to her valor. The sailors, their duty done, turned to the task of repair and recovery, their spirits unbroken, their resolve strengthened by the knowledge of their achievement.

James, amidst the tapestry of aftermath and anticipation, felt a profound connection to the moment and the men who shared it. The triumph was not just of battle but of the enduring spirit, the unquenchable desire for liberty, and the bond forged in the crucible of conflict. This was the essence of victory—not just a momentary conquest, but the forging of a legacy that would echo through time.

CHAPTER TEN
CONTINENTAL CONGRESS

Exhaustion was Thomas's constant companion, his limbs heavy with the toll of a fortnight's journey on the unforgiving roads from Williamsburg. As Philadelphia's skyline came into view, hope flickered in his weary heart—this burgeoning hub of industry and rebellion promised a brief respite in the form of a tavern's modest comforts and the simple luxury of a bath to slough off the road's dust.

Nearing the city's pulsing center, Thomas navigated the cacophony of life that thrived amidst the cobblestone streets. The symphony of commerce and the rhythmic dance of horse-drawn carriages painted a vivid contrast to the serene life he had known before war cast its long shadow. He moved among the throngs; his purpose masked by the casual drift of a traveler.

Then, amid the crescendo of the city's bustling energy, a figure of undeniable authority appeared. General George Washington, a living legend sculpted by the hands of valor and controversy, rode forth on a chestnut steed that cut a formidable silhouette against the throng. With each measured step of the horse, the air grew still, the very essence of the nation's struggle and hope reflected in the man's piercing gaze. With his mission smoldering inside him, Thomas felt the weight of history burning like flames in the general's eyes, understanding the true magnitude of the moment unfolding before him.

His aura was magnetic, an invisible force that drew everyone's attention and whispered of victories and sacrifices etched into the annals of time. Thomas, mere paces from this living legend, felt the weight of history pressing upon his shoulders. His task to delve into the secrets of the opposing force now felt as tangible as the knife tucked under his cloak.

As he edged closer, a keen sense of trepidation surged within him, his pulse a frantic drumbeat heralding the proximity of danger. He was a whisper away from the heart of the revolution, from the architect of the plans he was sent to dismantle. His nerves danced like a taut bowstring, the excitement of his proximity to Washington battling with the imperative to remain unseen, a ghost amongst the city's revelry.

In this extraordinary moment, cloaked in the cacophony of Philadelphia's embrace, Thomas was a silent observer of greatness. He grappled with an inner turmoil that gnawed at his facade of indifference; he was inwardly ablaze, a tempest of apprehension and thrill. For here stood Washington, not just the fulcrum of war, but a figure of mythic stature, now rendered in the flesh and commanding blood before him— a man of such formidable presence that even the brick structures lining the boulevard seemed to acknowledge him.

With each thunderous beat of his heart, Thomas was acutely aware of the delicate balance he must maintain—a Loyalist spy ensnared within the storm's eye, the revolutionary tempest that was General George Washington. Amidst the ebb and flow of the crowd, Thomas watched as Washington, the living symbol of the revolution, dismounted with a poised urgency from his horse. Flanked by his security detail, the general moved with purposeful strides toward the State House, their silhouettes sharp against the city's muted palette. Without ceremony, Washington and his entourage crossed the threshold of the heavy oak doors, the future of a nation in their wake.

Disguised in plainness, Thomas merged seamlessly into the throng of the chosen congressional delegates, his senses sharpening as the moment's gravity pulsed within him. With the members' heated discourse as his cloak, he bypassed the sentries and entered the sanctum of revolution, an undetected observer of the nascent threads of a nation's fate.

With a practiced subtlety, he found solace among the trusted advisers, a silent witness amidst the architects of war. He listened intently as General Washington, with a firm and hushed voice, outlined the contours of an audacious operation. The words "siege" and "Yorktown" hung in the air, each utterance a deliberate note in the symphony of strategy being composed before him. Cloaked in the chamber's shadows, Thomas sensed the war's story being woven into the tapestry of history.

Ensconced in the penumbra of an alcove, Thomas's breath was a whisper, his form nothing more than a wraith to the illuminated minds around him. Washington's voice, the undercurrent in the murmur of patriots, navigated the complexities of revolution with the precision of a master tactician. His discourse, a delicate balance between candor and cunning, was the loom on which the fabric of a country's destiny was being delicately woven.

Washington's gaze swept across the room, locking eyes with each delegate as he spoke, his voice carrying the weight of imminent history. "Gentlemen," he began, the resolve in his voice as solid as the oak that lined the chamber, "if we are to seize the flame of victory from the clutches of this prolonged struggle, Yorktown must be our crucible. The British, entrenched there, believe themselves secure, their attention diverted north. But a successful siege would sever their lifeline, cripple their southern strategy, and signal to the world that our cause is not only just but unstoppable."

He paused, letting the magnitude of his words settle like cannon smoke after battle. "A victory at Yorktown," he continued, "would be more than a military triumph. It would ignite the fires of hope in our people and send a clear message to Parliament and King George that we are a force beyond their subjugation. It would compel recognition of our sovereignty and may well bring an end to this war." The general's words echoed in the hallowed space, a declaration of a future written not by fate but by the audacious will of a people united for independence.

As the pieces fell into place, Thomas's understanding deepened. He was privy to a pivotal moment, the crafting of an attack that would shape the very future of the nation. He knew he must commit every detail to memory, the nuances of the plan etched into his consciousness. For now, he was more than a mere spectator; he was a silent guardian of a secret that held the power to define the outcome of the revolution.

Time seemed to stretch and warp around Thomas as he absorbed the gravity of Washington's plan, but the subtle change in the room's energy pricked his senses—the shift of a gaze, the narrowing of eyes. Someone had taken notice of the man who did not belong.

Whispers threaded through the gathering, a murmured undercurrent that grew in volume and suspicion. "Who is that man?" one delegate asked, his voice cutting through the clandestine hum. "Why does he lurk so in the shadows?" another inquired, his brow furrowed.

Thomas felt the walls closing in, the eyes of the past and future of America upon him. In an instant, his cover was compromised. With the reflexes of a cornered animal, he turned on his heel and bolted for the nearest exit, his heart thundering like cannon fire in his chest.

The clamor of the room exploded into chaos as he dashed through the door, the sound of his own heavy breathing accompanied by the shouts of men and the commanding voice of Washington's order, "For God's sake, stop that spy!"

Gunfire erupted behind him, bullets whistling past and embedding themselves into the plaster with deadly intent. Once outside, Thomas weaved through the labyrinthine streets of Philadelphia, his every step a gamble between life and death. His mind was a whirlwind of escape routes and desperate plans.

As he turned a corner, a bullet grazed his arm, a searing testament to the perilous thinness of his evasion. He could hear the pounding footsteps of his pursuers, the guardians of secrets he now possessed. The night air was split with the sounds of his flight and their pursuit, a symphony of survival and the cost of freedom's fight.

The city became a blur as he ran, the revolutionary fervor that once filled his heart now replaced by the raw instinct to survive. Thomas's daring had set him on a path with no return, a fugitive's flight on the precipice of history.

His escape from the State House had been narrow and fraught with peril, but Thomas knew his mission was far from over. With the knowledge that the true target was Yorktown and not New York—a ruse to mislead and outmaneuver—the imperative to deliver this intelligence to General Cornwallis was paramount. Every lost second could spell disaster for the British hold on the colonies.

Adrenaline fueling his every step, Thomas navigated the treacherous pathways that led away from the epicenter of his near capture. The cloak of the night was both ally and enemy, offering concealment and treacherous shadows in which his pursuers could hide. The sound of his heavy footsteps echoed against the cobblestones, a stark reminder of the urgency of his flight.

He went to the city's outskirts, where Loyalist sympathizers lay hidden. Securing a horse, Thomas set off under the cloak of darkness, the pounding of hooves syncing with the pounding of his heart. The journey to Yorktown would be long and perilous, but the fate of the British forces depended on his swiftness.

Thomas pushed forward through dense woods and across rivers whose surfaces reflected the tumultuous skies. As dawn broke, painting the horizon with streaks of crimson and gold, the significance of his mission became ever clearer. Washington and the French General Rochambeau's armies were converging on Yorktown, and the element of surprise was their greatest weapon. The weight of his message bore down on him with each mile traversed. It was a warning that could alter the course of the war, a message that held the lives of thousands in its words.

Upon arrival, his message would be simple yet earth-shattering: New York was a feint. The combined forces of the Americans and French were marching south to lay siege to Yorktown. His warning was the key to the British's chance to fortify, prepare, and perhaps fend off the decisive blow the enemy forces hoped to deal. Thomas rode hard, knowing that the future—his and that of the nation yet unborn—hinged on the success of his desperate endeavor.

CHAPTER ELEVEN
JAMES AND ELIZA

The Sinclair, cradled by the stillness of Yorktown's waterfront, became a sanctuary of calm for James. The echoes of cannon fire had faded, leaving him in a contemplative silence. This brief interlude of peace starkly contrasted with the recent sea battle, where he had faced the grim dance of war, death, and espionage.

Eliza's soft knock and entry into his quarters was like a gentle wave lapping at the edges of his solitude. The tray in her hands bore simple nourishments, yet the unguarded look in her eyes truly fed him. She crossed the room with an elegance that belied the turmoil surely raging within her, just as it churned inside him.

"Thank you," he said, nodding and accepting the tray. Then, as he stared out the small window toward the sea, he whispered, speaking his thoughts, "I still hear the cries of men over the waves."

Eliza met his gaze, her eyes reflecting the depths of the ocean. "I cannot fathom the sights you've seen, James," she replied, her voice steady but tinged with concern.

"The French fought bravely," he continued with a long sigh. "But it's not the thunder of guns I recall most vividly—it's the silence that followed. It's haunting … yet here, now, the quiet seems different with you."

"The solitude here speaks of life, not loss," Eliza observed, moving a step closer. Her presence was a balm to the raw edges of his spirit, her proximity both a comfort and a kindle to the flame that had sparked between them since their eyes first met.

He glanced outward again, the horizon a blur where the sky met the sea. "The cries … they were the worst part," James confessed. "It's not the clash of swords or the roar of cannons that haunt a man; that's exhilarating." He paused. "It's the aftermath."

"You carry those sounds with you," Eliza said, understanding more than she wished to.

James nodded slowly, the weight of his role as soldier and spy—an amalgam of honor and deceit—bearing down on him. "Yes, but in this quiet … with you … the cacophony dulls. It's as if your presence chases away the ghosts of the *Marsillois* and all those other French and British warships."

Eliza inhaled sharply, the air seemingly charged with his admission. "I wish I could silence those ghosts for you entirely," she murmured, her voice a tender vow.

He turned to her fully now, the gap between them charged with a current neither had anticipated when their day began. "Perhaps you already do, Eliza. Perhaps you are the calm in my storm."

Their eyes locked, and that gaze played out myriad possibilities. Each shared look, each spoken word, was a careful step on a tightrope of burgeoning intimacy.

She took another step, now close enough for him to feel the warmth radiating from her. "And what of your ghosts when I'm not here?" she asked, her voice low, barely over the whisper of the wind whistling through the gaps around the window frame.

He reached out, his hand hesitating in the air before settling on her arm, his fingers lightly grazing the fabric of her sleeve. "I think I will carry this moment with me now, a remnant of peace amidst the echoes of war."

His touch lingered, a gentle claim that spoke volumes, bridging the quiet with an intimacy that words could not. His admission hung in the air, a soft testament to the moment they had created together—a haven in the tumult of war. In this brief interlude, this pause between breaths, the world around them seemed to recede, leaving only the truth of what stirred quietly in their hearts.

"What I hunger for," James continued, the timbre of his voice deepening, revealing layers of emotion he had kept veiled until now, "goes far beyond what's served on a plate." His hand, which had paused in its journey to the tray, found the warmth of Eliza's touch instead. And in that simple contact, a flame was kindled, casting light on the depth of their unexplored bond.

Their hands met, not merely in touch but in silent dialogue, each fingertip whispering of the longing they felt. In that prolonged contact, words were unnecessary; their very souls seemed to converse, understanding and replying in kind. With a natural, almost gravitational pull, they found themselves leaning closer, their faces drawing near with the inevitability of two stars caught in each other's orbit.

As their lips brushed, the world around them softened into a blur, and every sense focused on the gentle pressure and soft warmth. It was a kiss that spoke of beginnings, paths converging, and two hearts recognizing their counterparts. The kiss deepened, each movement a dance, each breath shared a pact of mutual yearning and hope, long harbored and now set free.

This kiss was a vow, a daring step into a dance as old as time, yet fresh and vital as if they were the first ever to partake. James, the ever-diligent spy, found his discipline unraveling, replaced by an urgency to live in the moment, to seize this joy that had been so unexpected. The stoic soldier's exterior melted away under the gentle assault of Eliza's passion, revealing a man who yearned for connection, for the touch of another soul that understood the shadows and the light of his existence.

As they broke away, breathless and hearts racing, the world beyond Sinclair's walls could have been a lifetime away. Here and now, there was only Eliza, a bond that had been sealed with a kiss—a promise of hope amidst the backdrop of war, a defiant act of living in a time when each day could be their last. The world had narrowed to the space between them, the soft sound of her sigh and her skin's glow. Then, the knock came, jolting them back to reality, and a voice. "Eliza?"

"Brenda?" Eliza's voice was a breathless echo. "What is it?"

"I'm sorry to bother you, but a man is asking for James." Brenda's voice filtered through the door, laced with concern. "He insists it's urgent."

James felt the echo of Eliza's touch lingering on his skin, starkly contrasting with the call of duty that now beckoned him. Reluctantly, he untangled himself from their embrace, his senses still awash with the warmth of their newfound intimacy. With each step toward the door, he felt the tangible shift from private tenderness to the stark reality of his role in this war—a protector and a harbinger of hidden truths.

Stepping away from Eliza's enveloping warmth, James reluctantly traversed the Sinclair's creaking wooden stairs. Each groan underfoot reminded him of the world's demands, pulling him back from the stolen tranquility into his role as a guardian of secrets.

As James pushed open the door to the ground floor tavern, the raucous symphony of life greeted him—a stark contrast to the quiet he'd left in his quarters. The air was thick with the scent of ale and the musky tang of sweat, an aroma that spoke to the earthiness of its patrons' everyday struggles and joys. Men and women from all walks of life mingled together: tradesmen in their sturdy clothes, women donning dresses stained by the rigors of household duties, all united under the warm glow of flickering candles and the hearty taste of life at its most raw.

James's eyes adjusted to the dim light and found Harrison, a familiar face amidst the crowd of weathered faces and laughter-lined eyes. The fellow spy's stare cut through the tavern's haze, an anchor of solemnity in a tide of merriment. Their eyes met, sharing a silent communication that spoke of urgency and understanding.

"Harrison Johnson," James uttered, his tone a measured blend of cordiality and caution. His voice was nearly lost in the lively hum of conversations and the rhythmic thud of tankards on wood.

"A discreet chat?" Harrison intoned softly, his voice a ghostly whisper against the backdrop of boisterous life enveloping them.

James leaned in, his next words cloaked in the cacophony. "Stroll out front in a spell, then circle 'round to the back stairway. It's less traveled," he said with a conspiratorial edge. "I will meet you upstairs."

Harrison melded into the bustling crowd, each step deliberate, a silent waltz of espionage among the tavern's patrons. James savored a last moment amidst the throng, the tavern's robust aromas of malt and hops striking a stark contrast to the delicate fragrance that lingered in his mind, the essence of Eliza that seemed to follow him. He glanced back again, eyes sweeping over the lively scenes before him—each face, a story; each laugh, a tale untold.

With the weight of the impending secret meeting, he turned and began the ascent. The stairs sensed him; their groans were a chorus to the pulse of his quickening heartbeat, each step upward drawing him away from the cacophony of life below and toward the gravity of what awaited.

Upon entering his quarters, James found Eliza, her presence starkly contrasting with the raucous tavern. The room seemed to hold its breath as Harrison entered, his eyes flickering with a spy's caution. "She should not be here," he murmured, the shadows of his trade darkening his words.

James's response was immediate, unwavering. "Eliza stays," he declared, his voice leaving no room for argument. Her determined nod was all the confirmation Harrison needed, and with a resigned sigh, he let the matter drop.

Harrison, with the practiced stealth of a seasoned operative, reached into the inner pocket of his coat and withdrew a sheaf of papers, each creased with the care of countless foldings. As he unfolded them on the table, the dim light caught the intricate sketches and symbols, the outline of a book etched alongside notes in a cryptic shorthand only those in their line of work could decipher.

"It's a manuscript called the Solum Codex," he whispered, his eyes not leaving the papers as if they were as precious as the document they referenced. Eliza leaned in, her curiosity piqued by the mystery unfurling before her.

James and Eliza watched as Harrison's finger traced the sketches. "Actually, it's more than a manuscript," Harrison continued, his gaze lifting to meet James's. "It's the culmination of a society's highest aspirations, and it could very well be the blueprint for our nation's future."

Tapping a finger on the paper, James asked, "But where does this come from?"

Harrison's tone shifted, taking on a somber hue as he delved into the lore surrounding the Solum Codex. "As I was told, its creators were a lost people," he said. "Their way of life was so advanced, so inherently peaceful, that it threatened the powerful rulers of neighboring lands."

Eliza leaned in, her eyes reflecting the flicker of the candlelight. "A society destroyed because it chose harmony over dominion?" she asked, her voice tinged with sadness.

"It appears so," Harrison confirmed. "Armies, fearful that such ideals would undermine their own power, conspired to eradicate them from history. Their city was razed, and their wisdom obliterated, except for this one thing that endured."

"The Solum Codex," James said, frown creasing his forehead. "It's a legacy of a civilization that could have changed the world."

"Indeed," Harrison interjected. "It's said that the Codex surfaced centuries later in Western Europe, where it came to the attention of French Enlightenment thinkers. And from them, it was passed to one of our own—a man who himself dreamed of liberty and knowledge."

"Jefferson?" Eliza ventured, her intuition connecting the historic dots.

Harrison nodded, a look of admiration crossing his features. "Thomas Jefferson, yes. It's believed he was entrusted with the Codex by his French contemporaries, who recognized a kindred spirit in his philosophies."

"The irony," James mused aloud, "that a document from a destroyed utopia could potentially save another striving to be born."

Harrison spread his hands, a gesture encompassing the gravity of their situation. "And that's why we must act. The Codex is more than history; it's a blueprint for a future we're on the cusp of realizing."

The room's air seemed charged with the weight of centuries, the echo of a dream that had once been silenced yet still clamored to be heard. Here they stood, the bearers of a torch that could light the way to a new dawn or be extinguished in the darkness of ignorance and fear. The Solum Codex was their responsibility—it was the voice of the past, beckoning to the future.

Eliza, though silent, absorbed every word, her presence a testament to the trust James had placed in her. She was no longer merely an observer but part of the unfolding drama that could reshape their world.

"So where is this Solum Codex now?" James asked.

Harrison leaned closer, the flicker of a nearby candle casting dancing shadows across the earnest faces gathered in the room. "It was stolen."

"Stolen?" James repeated.

Harrison's voice hushed to a whisper that carried a mix of admiration and ire. "The pilfering of the Codex was nothing short of a clandestine triumph," he confided. "A Hessian spy managed to purloin the tome in the chaos of twilight."

Eliza's eyes widened, the intrigue of the tale weaving a complex tapestry before her. James's jaw set firmly, his mind racing with the implications of such a breach within their nascent government's stronghold.

"The spy knew exactly when the State House would be most vulnerable during the chaos of a citywide celebration," Harrison detailed. "While everyone's attention was turned toward the festivities, he slipped through the shadows. He understood the night watchmen's layout and routines."

James clenched his fists, the betrayal stinging like a fresh wound. "And this spy… delivered it where?" he asked, the words tasting bitter.

"Here," Harrison said, pointing out the window. "Into the hands of Cornwallis."

"Are you serious?" James questioned, grabbing Harrison's forearm. "Does he know of its significance?"

"Indeed," Harrison confirmed. "Cornwallis is aware of its potential to unify a nation and now seeks to keep it, lest it fall back into rebel hands and seal the fate of the British control over the colonies."

The room fell silent, each person grappling with the enormity of the task at hand. It was not merely a mission of retrieval; it was a race to preserve the very essence of what their struggle for independence stood for—a chance to reclaim their future from the ashes of betrayal.

In the hush of James's quarters, the weight of history pressed close, the air heavy with the importance of their task. Once a simple refuge, the room now held the promise of destiny. The Solum Codex was not just stolen; it was a beacon that had gone dark, and it was up to them to rekindle its light. James felt the gravity of the mission settle upon him. "We must retrieve it," he stated, a new fire igniting in his chest. "We cannot allow its destruction, not when it promises peace and prosperity for every soul in this land."

"And how would we do that?" Eliza asked.

Harrison nodded, his face a mask of grim determination. "Before the siege commences, we must infiltrate Cornwallis's headquarters and retrieve it."

Eliza's hand found James's, a silent vow of her own commitment to the cause. "Then we will," she said, the strength in her voice belying the gentle touch of her fingers. "We will bring back the Solum Codex."

James met Harrison's gaze, an unspoken agreement passing between them. Once filled with the warmth of a budding romance, the room now set the stage for a daring operation—a quest for not just the heart but also the soul of a nascent nation.

CHAPTER TWELVE
ON THE RUN

With his heart hammering against his ribcage, Thomas urged his steed through the dense underbrush, the animal's labored breaths mirroring his own. Behind him, the persistent sound of pursuit grew louder, a discordant symphony to his flight. A branch snapped a mere stone's throw away, a stark signal that the enemy was gaining ground.

Suddenly, a shot rang out, shattering the forest's precarious silence. Thomas felt the deadly rush of air as a musket ball sliced through the foliage, narrowly missing his head. He ducked, pressing himself closer to the horse's heaving flanks, becoming one with the creature in their desperate bid for life.

Adrenaline surged through his veins as he scanned ahead, spotting a narrow ravine offering a sliver of salvation. With a sharp tug on the reins and a whispered plea, he guided the horse into the treacherous descent, loose stones and dirt cascading. The rush of the river below muffled the sounds of pursuit, promising a fleeting hope of cover. Together, they plunged into the river's churning grip, the shock of the rough waters stealing his breath while his horse struggled against the current.

Thomas cast a glance upstream, his eyes catching the glint of moonlight on steel as a soldier's silhouette appeared. He was exposed, vulnerable in the open water, but fate favored him—a sudden cloud veiled the moon, casting them both into darkness.

Drenched and panting, Thomas urged his steed up the muddy bank, the dark waters closing behind them like a curtain on their narrow escape. His searching eyes quickly discerned the silhouette of a barn in the distance. With resolve, he guided his horse toward the sanctuary of its shadowy confines, the welcoming scent of aged hay and weathered wood a modest solace in the night's chill.

With muscles wound tight, Thomas led his laboring horse into the stable, the beast's sides still heaving from the river's chill embrace. Amidst the occupied stalls, one lay open—a haven in the dim light where he hoped the soldiers would not cast their gaze upon the trembling, soaked creature. Moving with silent haste, he dismounted and ushered his horse into the solitary refuge of the stable, the air heavy with the scent of hay and the equine musk. Thomas hurriedly climbed to the loft, tucking himself away in the rough hay, which pricked his soaked skin far less than the fear of discovery.

Below, the heavy tread of soldiers' boots resounded, each step a measured beat of the impending threat. Their voices, a hushed rumble beneath him, carried the promise of danger. Thomas lay motionless, scarcely daring to breathe, as the telltale mist of his breath dissipated in the cold loft air.

The ominous thud of boots approached, each step a drumbeat of danger. The soldiers' voices were a low murmur, their words indistinct but their intent clear as they searched the barn. Thomas lay still, every muscle tensed, his presence betrayed only by the faintest cloud of breath in the chill air.

Under the cover of night, the search party moved on, their torches casting long shadows but finding nothing. Thomas allowed himself a moment's relief, his mind racing. His training as a soldier for the British had honed his instincts for such moments—when to fight, when to hide, and when to run.

And run he did, once the danger passed, slipping from the barn like a wraith, a ghost in the war-torn night. His escape was a patchwork of such close calls and daring maneuvers, a testament to his will to survive, to carry on despite the question that gnawed at his resolve: was his cause just, or had he been a pawn in a game where the stakes were as high as the birth of a nation?

In those moments of acute danger, a torrent of doubt suddenly assailed him. Had his loyalty to the Crown been a misguided allegiance? The question gnawed at him, a persistent whisper that mirrored the rustling leaves, speaking of lost causes and misplaced faith. The war, his love for Eliza, and the life he'd known seemed as distant as the fading echo of a dream upon waking.

As Thomas approached the threshold of his childhood home, the sense of loss was overwhelming. The physical exhaustion from his harrowing journey paled in comparison to the emotional toll. The ideals he'd held, the choices he'd made, everything was now cast in the grim light of a war that seemed far from the British victory he once took for granted.

As he dismounted, his legs nearly buckled from the grueling ride and the weight of realization. Perhaps he had chosen the wrong side in this historical tide. Perhaps he had lost everything—Eliza, his family's respect, and possibly his life in the coming days.

Yet, there was no time for reflection, not when the lives of others hung in the balance. Duty propelled him forward across the land where he'd once played as an innocent child, toward the house where his father's scorn awaited, and beyond to a destiny as uncertain as the nation's war-torn future.

Thomas's horse was spent, its flanks heaving as he stopped in the familiar surroundings of his parents' Williamsburg homestead. The journey, normally a stretch of eight grueling days, had been a relentless five-day blur of dust and danger. He had not visited his parents since the war's drums began their ominous beat six years ago.

The son they had known had chosen a different path, leading him away from the burgeoning call of revolution and into the ranks of the Crown's Loyalists. His father's last words, harsh with betrayal, still rang in Thomas's ears, yet desperation drove him back to this doorstep.

With the threat of Washington's soldiers close enough to feel their breath on his neck, Thomas had no choice but to seek refuge. His arrival was met with his mother's gasp and a stony silence from his father.

He recounted his plight, his voice ragged with fatigue, detailing the imperative that he reach Yorktown to warn Cornwallis of the imminent attack. His father listened, his expression growing darker with every word, the old wound of their ideological rift reopening.

"You bring betrayal to our door," his father said, voice shaking with anger. "Your loyalty to the Crown has blinded you, but it will not blind me."

His mother's pleas were a desperate symphony, begging her husband not to forsake their son. But Thomas's father was resolute, his sense of Patriot duty overshadowing familial bonds. Without another word, he left to summon the authorities, leaving Thomas with a mother's tearful embrace and a father's curse.

Thomas felt the tears she shed dampen his shirt. "I'm so sorry, Mother," he muttered, his voice barely above a whisper.

"There is nothing to forgive, my love. Just survive," she choked out, her hands cupping his face for one last look, an image to hold close as he fled into the gathering dusk. With the distant sound of approaching soldiers, like hounds baying for the hunt, Thomas tore himself from her arms. He moved with the silent swiftness of a shadow, disappearing into the dense embrace of the Virginia woods, even as the first redcoats appeared on the horizon. The game was afoot again; the chase, a dance with death he knew all too well.

*

As dawn painted the sky with the first strokes of light, Thomas arrived at Yorktown, his appearance worn and layered with the dust of urgency. The town was still quiet, unaware of the coming day's peril. With critical information at hand, Thomas urgently sought out General Cornwallis.

Escorted into the general's austere command space, a room humming with the echo of battle, Thomas found Cornwallis amidst the strategic chaos of maps and plans. The general, though showing signs of fatigue, radiated an intense resolve. The officers, battle-hardened and resolute, focused their attention on Thomas as he began to relay his message. Despite the wear of his journey, his voice bore the gravity of his urgent tidings.

"Sir." Thomas's voice cut through the tense air. "Philadelphia has sent me with news that brooks no delay." Cornwallis motioned for him to continue. Without pause, Thomas shared his dire findings. "New York is a feint, sir," he declared. "The true strike will come here, at Yorktown. I have witnessed the enemy's tactics, the covert preparations—this is where they will converge."

As Thomas revealed what he had learned, the silent maps before them seemed to pulse with life, forecasting the imminent battle. The officers, their skepticism now replaced by concern, listened closely. With the acumen of a seasoned leader, Cornwallis began to thread this new intelligence into the weave of his defensive strategy.

Once a stronghold of control and command, the chamber teemed with palpable urgency. As dawn's light began to chase away the shadows of the night, Cornwallis stood resolute. The battlefield of Yorktown lay spread out before them, a tableau on which the destiny of empires and dreams of freedom would soon clash.

Cornwallis, his posture rigid with resolve, broke the moment's meditation. "The ruse was executed flawlessly," he conceded, a hard edge to his voice betraying the sting of betrayal he felt. "Yet it pales in comparison to what we face now. This siege …"

Thomas, his expression somber, responded. "It has shifted the course, General. Here is where history will turn." As Thomas unfolded the layers of his intelligence, the maps before them seemed to take on a new dimension, signaling the site of an imminent confrontation. The officers, once dubious, now bore the look of men facing a somber reality as Cornwallis's mind spun the new information into his strategy.

The esteemed general's eyes, hard with the resolve of a commander who had seen many horizons, fixed on the expanse outside. "This ground, this Yorktown, it's where dreams of liberation meet the harsh light of day. Our empires might be tested against the fervor of freedom," he mused, the weight of history in his tone.

His mind raced with the strategic implications of the French naval presence, now dominating the Chesapeake Bay, severing any hope of maritime retreat or reinforcement. "The French control the Bay," he acknowledged grimly, "cutting off our escape by sea and blocking support. Washington, with Rochambeau, will soon march on Yorktown. We find ourselves on the anvil of war, with the hammer poised to fall." A silent moment stretched on as Cornwallis faced the reality of their isolation, the sea no longer a route of escape but a barrier sealing their fate.

With this contemplation hanging heavy in the air, Cornwallis finally broke the silence. "Reinforcements," he declared. "We must call upon Clinton's men to come from New York. Without them, our situation here is perilous."

Thomas studied Cornwallis, noting the subtle shift in the general's demeanor. "And if they do not arrive in time?"

The general turned, his hands tracing the lines of a map, every movement reflecting strategy and silent desperation. "Then we stand and fight with what we have. We know the task at hand." Cornwallis paused, his fingers over the map, his resolve clear as he met his officer's gaze. "Prepare the men. Our will shall be the bulwark against this onslaught."

The abrupt cry from the lookout pierced the dawn. "To arms! The enemy approaches!" And with it, any lingering hope dissipated like mist at sunrise. The silhouette of the Continental Army stretched across the horizon, a formidable force of thousands awakening to the call of liberty and justice.

As the commands echoed across the field, resonating with grim determination, the once steadfast voice of the empire seemed to quiver with uncertainty. Thomas, surrounded by the crescendo of war, felt the resurgence of a doubt that had first taken root during his narrow escape from Philadelphia. It had lain dormant, a subtle disquiet, but now it burgeoned into full view, with the revelation of Yorktown as the focal point of conflict.

The booming of the cannons not only signaled the beginning of a siege; it tolled for the end of an epoch. The smoke from the gunpowder, meandering between the heavens and the earth, served as a backdrop to the deepening of Thomas's profound realization. The courage that once defined him, which had propelled him through the dangers of espionage, now wavered in the face of immense change. Once entwined with royal allegiance, his identity was now being torn asunder, thread by thread, by the very reality he had helped to unveil.

Cornwallis's orders reverberated in the air; yet for Thomas, they were like the distant rumble of thunder, overshadowed by the storm raging within him. The approaching Continental Army no longer appeared as the enemy but as the harbingers of a new era. This realization struck Thomas with an acute poignancy as the battle lines were drawn.

This internal battle had been simmering within Thomas since his escape, and now, as the physical battle for Yorktown commenced, his internal conflict reached its zenith. Every cannon shot that shattered the air mirrored the collapse of his previously unwavering loyalty to the Crown.

In this moment of tumult, the memories of Eliza and the life he had left behind intermingled with the smoke and the sounds of war. His regret, a quiet companion since his departure from Philadelphia, now roared loudly in his heart. Thomas grappled with the possibility of redemption and the hope of recovering the love he had lost. As the battle for Yorktown unfolded, so too did the battle for Thomas's soul, a man caught between the dying light of an old world and the uncertain dawn of a new one.

CHAPTER THIRTEEN
IT BEGINS

The Sinclair had been their cloistered haven since the arrival of Harrison, but the sudden surge of commotion heard outside drew Eliza to the window. Her breath fogged the glass as she watched the transformation of Yorktown's streets from tranquil lanes to arteries of urgency, alive with the British soldiers' frenetic movements. Rain cascaded down, a drumming torrent against roofs and cobblestones, yet Brenda's alarm shattered the silence within. "It's happening—Washington's forces have been sighted!" she announced through the door, a tremor in her voice that mirrored the shiver cascading down Eliza's spine. The words carried a weight heavier than the deluge that battered the town outside.

James and Harrison exchanged glances that spoke volumes. The time for planning had passed; action beckoned—the time to steal back the Codex was now. "We go," James insisted, his voice resolute despite the uncertainty that lay ahead. "With the confusion, we enter Cornwallis's headquarters and find the Codex." His eyes met Eliza's, and she read in them the danger and necessity of their mission.

Harrison, his features set in grim agreement, nodded. Their plan was a gamble that would have them navigate the maelstrom of a besieged city to reclaim a treasure that could alter the very fabric of America's future.

Eliza stepped forward; her resolve as unwavering as the men before her. "I'm coming with you," she declared, the quiver in her voice betraying none of her inner turmoil.

"It's too dangerous," James countered immediately, the protective edge in his voice belying his own fears for her safety.

But Eliza would not be dissuaded. The Sinclair Tavern, once a place of refuge, now felt like a cage. She could not bear to wait in the shadows while destiny was seized outside her doorstep. She was a part of this now, bound to the Codex and the men who sought its secrets.

As they outlined their perilous journey to the heart of the British stronghold, Eliza's mind turned to the broader tapestry of war being woven around them. "What's Washington's plan?" she asked, seeking to grasp the larger strategy at play.

Harrison detailed what he knew of the Continental Army's movements, explaining the construction of siege lines, gabions, and fascines even as British artillery thundered, seeking to disrupt the Patriot's efforts. Eliza pictured the soldiers, including those she knew, laboring under fire to lay the groundwork for what would be a long, grueling siege.

As the first cannon volley thundered across the sky, the Sinclair Tavern's bones groaned under its might, a grim prelude to the chaos unfolding. Within its walls, Eliza's heart mirrored the building's tremor, a visceral echo of the war raging at their doorstep. The once sturdy refuge now felt as vulnerable as the flesh and blood within it.

War's discordant symphony filled the air, a relentless surge of sound that spoke of an imminent, uncertain future drenched in peril. In this crucible, Eliza discovered an uncharted reservoir of fortitude, a steely resolve that surged through her veins with a fervor she had never known. Beside her stood James and Harrison, comrades not just in a cause but in the essence of their beings, united in a bold quest that transcended the mere retrieval of a document. They were pursuing a legacy, the Solum Codex—a key to the dawning of an illustrious future.

Together, they would plunge into the heart of the adversary's lair, a triad bound by destiny's unyielding threads woven from the fabric of bravery and an insatiable hunger for a brighter epoch. Each step they took was a step away from the world they knew, toward an odyssey that could forge the foundations of a civilization reborn from the ashes of conflict.

Cloaked in the solemn hues of the encroaching dusk, Eliza, James, and Harrison became phantoms against the desolation that had descended upon Yorktown. The acrid smog of gunpowder hung in the air, a spectral shroud that veiled their passage through the once tranquil streets now gasping under the pall of war. With each careful step, they wove through the town's carcass, their silhouettes dissolving into the swirling mists and smoke that embraced the beleaguered stronghold.

Headquarters loomed before them, a hive thrumming with frenzied activity as the siege's drumbeat reverberated through its walls. Here, the chaos of war was magnified—a stark contrast to the trio's silent approach, their hearts as much a battleground as the killing fields that stretched beyond. They slipped past the distracted guards, mere shadows flitting through an opening in the tempest, unnoticed and unchallenged.

Inside, the pandemonium was palpable. Orders barked like thunderclaps, couriers dashed like scattered leaves in a storm, and the clatter of hurried preparations echoed the desperation of a force bracing against the tide of revolution. The three interlopers moved with purpose, their cloaks now not just a guise but a mantle of purpose, each fold whispering of the covert mission they bore.

In this place where the urgency of defense had eclipsed all else, Eliza, James, and Harrison were but wraiths amidst the tumult, their quest for the Solum Codex a silent thread in the tapestry of bedlam that Cornwallis's headquarters had become. Their journey would be perilous in the heart of consternation and command.

They found themselves in the dimly lit corridors of power within British headquarters. The outer chambers of the general's office loomed before them, shrouded in secrets and strategy. Cornwallis's commanding, tempestuous voice filled the space, leaving no doubt of his presence.

They drifted through the shadows, their breaths held tight, their movements a choreography of stealth. The urgency of their quest pulsed through them as they merged with the darkness, waiting for a sliver of opportunity. When, at last, the general was called away, his authoritative voice trailing off into the distance, they seized the moment.

The office door creaked open to reveal a room bristling with the tension of war. With bated breath, they scoured the space, fingers probing the depths of drawers, eyes scanning the shelves lined with maps and missives. Time was a luxury they could not afford, and as they searched, the Codex remained elusive, a ghost within the annals of the room.

Eliza's intuition caused her to whisper, "We must go now," with an urgency that cut through the silence. James heeded her call, the echo of their footsteps a fading murmur as they withdrew. But Harrison, driven by a blend of desperation and determination, tarried, his hands rifling through the general's desk in search of the invaluable manuscript.

Then, without warning, the door swung open, and Cornwallis's imposing figure burst into the room, his fierce eyes igniting the space. As the guards flooded in behind him, a palpable doom filled the air, suspending Harrison in a silent tableau. In that frozen sliver of time, Eliza and James became shadows; their presence diminished to near-nothingness against the siege's roar. They seized the fleeting chaos, slipping unseen through a rear exit into the building's labyrinthine corridors. They navigated the dimly lit passageway with haste and quiet urgency, searching for the stairwell that would spill them onto the streets.

Soon, Eliza and James emerged, the cacophony of war enveloping them like a cloak of confusion. They moved swiftly, their silhouettes blending with the throngs of frantic townspeople and the occasional soldier too preoccupied with the unfolding siege to notice their hurried passage.

The Sinclair called to them as they dodged debris and the more perilous gazes of British patrols. They clung to the shadows and became one with the smoke that rose from smoldering embers, their every move a silent plea to remain unseen, to return to the sanctuary that was now a mere illusion of refuge.

The Sinclair stood as it always had, yet its facade was marred by the scars of conflict—windows that once held light were now shattered, and its front door was hanging, a testament to the turmoil that had invaded. Eliza and James exchanged a fleeting look of relief mixed with apprehension as they slipped through the compromised entrance, their senses heightened to every sound—the distant cries, the near misses of cannon fire that seemed to chase them.

"Let's take cover in the cellar," Eliza whispered, her voice steady yet tinged with the strain of their plight. "We can plan our next move." They navigated the dimly lit corridor, feeling their way to the hidden depths of their temporary haven. In the muted silence of the cellar, they found a pause in the relentless storm, a space to catch their breath and steel themselves for the uncertain path ahead.

In that damp and dimly lit refuge, the distant booms of cannonade resonated through the stone and earth, a constant reminder of the chaos above. Here, in the close air of the cellar, Eliza and James clung to the shadows, their minds fraught with images of Harrison's capture. The sounds of the siege, each explosion a dirge for the day's defeat, were a relentless overture to their anxiety and the haunting possibility of their own discovery.

Amid the cellar's oppressive gloom, Eliza's voice cut through the silence, a whisper laden with worry. "Do you think Harrison will speak of the Codex under … under duress?" Her eyes, wide with the gravity of their situation, sought James's in the dim light.

James, his back against the cool stone wall, shook his head with a conviction bolstered by years of shared dangers. "No," he asserted firmly, the words carving certainty in the heavy air. "Harrison's loyalty is ironclad. He's weathered more intense storms than this. They will not break him."

Their mission now lay in embers at their feet. The Codex, their precious key, was in their narrowly escaped maelstrom, and Harrison, their comrade whose resolve was as steadfast as the ancient stones that surrounded them, was now in the enemy's clutches. The tightness of their escape, every moment laced with the threat of death, pressed upon them, a constant, heavy cloak that neither could shrug off.

Amidst the cacophony of the siege, Eliza and James huddled closer, their spirits tethered to the slim hope that they would yet find a way to turn the tides. But for now, they were like phantoms in the dark, holding onto each other, their resolve as brittle and steadfast as the Sinclair itself, which seemed to groan under the strain of the relentless bombardment.

In the cellar's shielded quiet, the reality of their situation became as tangible as the dirt-caked walls surrounding them. Every thunderous impact above was a stark reminder of their vulnerability and the precariousness of the revolutionary cause they deeply believed in.

As the first light of dawn began to seep through the crevices above, lending a pale glow to their hideout, the gravity of their situation settled in the silence between them. They were two souls, momentarily spared yet bound to an uncertain future. The cause they held dear was interwoven with their survival, as uncertain as the smoky horizon awaiting them outside the Sinclair's aged walls.

CHAPTER FOURTEEN
THOMAS'S LAMENT

In the dimming light of Yorktown, Thomas stood ensconced in the shadows of twilight on the upper deck of the officer's quarters. His gaze focused through a spyglass and observed the gathering of Colonial soldiers out beyond the outskirts. The blue of their uniforms, some stained and tattered, others pristine, starkly contrasted with the impending chaos. They were digging trenches, sculpting the landscape of a battle that would paint the sky with the fury of artillery.

As the evening breeze whispered secrets of the impending siege, Thomas's mind was adrift in a sea of regret and revelation. He remembered the pride he once felt wearing the red coat, the weight of the musket in his hand, symbolizing his loyalty to the Crown. But now, those memories were tainted with a bitter realization. He was a traitor, not to the Crown, but to the very soil of his birth, to the ideals of liberty and freedom that his childhood friends, now his adversaries, so valiantly fought for.

Eliza's strong and resolute image emerged like a beacon in his storm of uncertainty. From his vantage point, the Sinclair residence, he could envision her home vulnerable under the looming threat. His heart, which had been hardened by the rigors of war and allegiance to a distant king, now ached with concern for her safety.

As the night deepened, the resumption of the rumblings of cannon fire broke the stillness. Each explosion was a stark reminder of the inevitable destruction that awaited Yorktown. The booming cannons, the streaks of fiery light tearing through the darkness, were not just harbingers of destruction but also, in a twisted sense, symbols of hope for a new nation, a hope he had denied himself by clinging to his loyalty to the Crown.

Each cannon blast unraveled Thomas's allegiance, exposing the depth of his internal conflict. He realized that the empire he served was crumbling under the relentless push for independence. The ideals of freedom and self-governance, which he had once dismissed, now resonated within him with a piercing clarity.

In the chaos of the bombardment, as the walls of Yorktown trembled and the air was thick with gunpowder and desperation, Thomas's thoughts were consumed by Eliza. The fear of losing her, of her suffering amidst the chaos he had helped bring upon them, was unbearable. He knew then that he had to find her, protect her, and atone for the choices that led him to this moment of reckoning.

Thomas descended from his perch with a newfound determination fueled by his fears for Eliza and shifting loyalties. He was ready to brave the treacherous, cannon-laden paths of Yorktown. It was a desperate quest not just to save Eliza but, in doing so, perhaps find redemption for himself and align with the ideals he had come to embrace.

As he stepped into the maelstrom, Thomas clung to a fragile hope that in finding Eliza, he might also find a new path, one that would lead him away from his past and toward a future where he could stand true to the land of his birth and the woman who had captured his heart.

Thomas navigated the streets of his childhood. Once filled with the laughter of friends and the simple joys of colonial life, they now overflowed with the frenetic activity of soldiers. The air was thick with the scent of gunpowder and the sharp tang of fear. Thomas could not help but draw parallels with the stories he had read about European castles under siege. Those ancient fortresses, surrounded by enemies and cut off from the world, mirrored the desperation now gripping Yorktown. He pondered the tales of gallant knights and brave defenders, wondering if their thoughts had been as tumultuous as his own in their final hours.

Reaching the Sinclair, his heart pounded with a mix of dread and urgency. Once a bustling hub of camaraderie and laughter, the tavern stood eerily empty, its front door dangling on one remaining bent hinge. The tables were littered with remnants of hurriedly abandoned meals, now fodder for the rats that scurried across the wooden floorboards. Thomas called out for Eliza, his voice echoing through the empty halls, but there was no response.

With a growing sense of desperation, he rushed upstairs, his boots thudding heavily against the steps. He flung open the door to Eliza's chamber, his eyes searching frantically. Like the rest of the tavern, the room was deserted, a stark, empty shell devoid of life. The realization that Eliza was not there, that she might be lost to him, struck Thomas with a force greater than any cannon blast.

Leaving the Sinclair, Thomas plunged into the labyrinthine streets of Yorktown. His eyes darted from face to face among the soldiers and townsfolk, searching for any trace of Eliza. Each empty glance, each shake of the head from those he queried, only deepened the pit of despair in his stomach.

He moved through the city streets, driven by a blend of fear and hope, each step a mix of determination and dread. Overhead, the sky flashed with the violent bursts of cannon fire. The booming of cannons and the cries of command from British officers formed a grim soundtrack to his search. The streets seemed alien, twisted by the cruel hand of war. The ground shuddered with each impact as clouds of smoke rose like specters above the rooftops, and debris rained down in a macabre dance.

As dawn approached, painting the sky with the first light of morning, Thomas found himself at the edge of Yorktown, his search fruitless. The realization that Eliza might be beyond his reach, perhaps even beyond saving, settled upon him with a crushing weight. He stood there, grappling with the harsh truth that his change of heart might have come too late.

The thunderous roar of cannon fire continued to shake the foundations of the once peaceful town as pillars of smoke snaked into the awakening sky. At that moment, Thomas understood the true cost of his past choices, the price of loyalty to a cause that now seemed so distant. He had lost more than just his allegiance to the Crown; he had lost a part of himself, and perhaps, he feared, he had lost Eliza forever. As the first rays of sunlight broke over the horizon, casting long shadows on the battered streets of Yorktown, Thomas stood resolute in his newfound conviction but heartbroken in his loss.

CHAPTER FIFTEEN
THE RESCUE

In the dank confines of the Sinclair's cellar, the distant cannon fire rumbled as a grim backdrop to James and Eliza's hushed whispers. "We cannot just leave Harrison to his fate," James said, his eyes reflecting a flicker of resolve in the dim candlelight.

Eliza, her face etched with concern, nodded. "Neither him nor the Codex. But how? The city is a fortress, and the streets a gauntlet."

James paced the small space, his mind racing with spycraft. "We wait for the cover of darkness, then we move. Chaos is our ally."

Eliza paused, her gaze lingering on the shadowed cellar walls before returning to James. "That's fine," she said, her voice a calm counterpoint to the booming artillery. "While we wait, tell me of the sea. What does Admiral de Grasse's victory mean for the war?"

The flickering candlelight casting a contemplative glow on James's features. He turned to face her, the gravity of the situation reflected in his eyes. "The French triumph at sea has indeed turned the tide against Cornwallis," he explained. "De Grasse's fleet has severed any hope the British had for escape or reinforcement. Once the predators of these waters found themselves encircled, their might dwindled to that of cornered beasts."

"But how precisely?" Eliza pressed, seeking the threads of understanding in the complex tapestry of war.

James sighed, the strategic implications clear in his mind. "The blockade … it's absolute. No British ship can breach it, meaning Cornwallis is isolated. Without the sea routes, he's as good as stranded."

"So, it's a defeat for the British?" Eliza grasped the situation keenly.

"More than that, it's a blow to their very spirit. The British pride themselves on their Royal Navy. To lose at sea is to shake the foundation of their empire," James replied, his voice a mixture of admiration and regret.

"And now, with the seas and the land closed off, Cornwallis is trapped," Eliza concluded, the strategy unraveling before her.

"Exactly. The siege is underway. The British are hemmed in. This," James gestured vaguely toward the ceiling, "is the beginning of the end for them."

Eliza's hand found James's. "And for us, it's just the beginning. We have much to do."

With a determined nod, James squeezed her hand. "Once the cannons fall silent, we act. For Harrison, for the Codex, for the future."

Above them, the relentless pounding of artillery continued, but beneath it all, two hearts beat with the rhythm of a nascent nation on the brink of birth.

*

Dusk had given way to the inky cloak of night, leaving only the faintest slivers of moonlight to dance through the gaps in the cellar door. Inside, the solitary candle cast long shadows, stretching like specters across the dusty floor where James and Eliza huddled, plotting their perilous course. Time had dissolved into the muffled booms that trembled the earth above them, each blast a grim metronome of the siege's irregular heartbeat.

The assault's cruel hand had reshaped Yorktown's familiar visage into a landscape marred by violence and ruin. As James and Eliza ascended from the shadows of their hideout, they were greeted by war's unforgiving advance. Buildings that once stood proudly were now scarred by cannon fire, their facades crumbling, their innards spilled out into the cobblestone streets like the entrails of some great felled beast.

The air was heavy, not just with the acrid bite of gunpowder that clawed at their throats, but with the dust of destruction that hung in the air like a mournful fog. Here and there, the flames of unattended fires flickered ominously, casting a hellish glow that gave the smoke-choked night an eerie semblance of daylight. Amidst this chaos, the wounded's cries struck a discordant chorus with the silence of those beyond help, a chilling reminder of the cost already paid and the price still to be rendered.

James and Eliza moved with deliberate stealth, their footsteps quiet amidst the chaos. Every shattered window and blasted door they encountered bore witness to the day's fierce clashes. Navigating through the devastated core of the town, their determination was palpable yet tinged with an air of vulnerability, mirroring the smoldering ruins that surrounded them. Their path led to the jailhouse, a solitary light of hope in a night overwhelmed by darkness, where their fellow fighter awaited rescue.

The chaos of the ongoing siege had turned the lock-up into a ghostly husk. The guards who once patrolled with vigilant eyes were summoned to the front, leaving the cells and their captives in hushed, eerie neglect. James and Eliza crept through the dim corridors, the silence of the abandoned jail broken only by the distant rumble of cannon fire and the soft whisper of their footsteps. The keys, carelessly left in the door, a sign of the guards' hurried departure, were a stroke of luck. With careful hands, James turned them in the lock, the click of the mechanism sounding impossibly loud in the stillness.

The cell door swung open with a groan of protest, revealing Harrison, who rose from the shadows with the weary dignity of a man who had made peace with his fate. His eyes, reflecting the flicker of their single sputtering candle, spoke volumes of gratitude and relief. No words were exchanged as he stepped out, a silent understanding knitting their fates together again.

The window of opportunity was narrow—a fleeting gift from the gods of war and chaos, and they moved, a trio of shadows slipping back through the jail's maze, a testament to the enduring flame of hope, even as the world burned around them.

Eliza, James, and Harrison stealthily infiltrated the stronghold of their adversary, Cornwallis, driven by the mission to secure the Codex that had plunged them into peril. They entered his office, a shadowed, deserted chamber where the only sounds were their own movements as they frantically searched through documents. The room was empty, with only distant echoes of conflict seeping through the walls. Eliza and James feverishly rifled through the contents of the desk, Eliza's fingers a blur and James glancing anxiously toward the door with each shuffle from the corridor, alert for any signs of danger.

Suddenly, the door swung open with a crash. Cornwallis appeared, disbelief etched on his face, which swiftly contorted into a mask of rage. "Explain yourselves!" he demanded, rage vibrating in every syllable as his hand found the grip of his sword.

The clash was immediate and ferocious, as British officers accompanying Cornwallis unsheathed their swords with a lethal grace born of rigid discipline. In unison, they advanced, a phalanx of red coats and steel, toward Harrison, James, and Eliza.

Harrison, gripping his borrowed sword with a mixture of fear and determination, met the onslaught head-on. His blade clashed with that of a lieutenant, sparks flying from the collision of wills as much as steel. James, his own sword now drawn, parried and thrust with a dancer's agility, turning desperation into an art form as he engaged another officer.

With her smaller knife, Eliza moved amidst the chaos. She was a whirlwind of focused survival, her strikes swift and targeted. Each movement was a statement of defiance, her eyes alight with the fire of someone fighting for more than just her own life.

The room became a maelstrom of combat, every surface echoing with the din of battle. Cornwallis's initial shock gave way to a commander's composure, and he directed his men with sharp commands, his voice cutting like a blade. The fight was not merely for control of the room but for the very fate that awaited them all as the tides of war swirled around and within the walls of the embattled stronghold.

The skirmish was fierce. Cornwallis's men, a formidable force of discipline and experience, advanced ruthlessly. In the clash, Harrison was not spared; a soldier's sword found him, his pained outcry a harrowing testament to his unyielding spirit. The sight of his fall and the sound of Eliza's sharp intake of breath were the sparks that set James alight with a protective rage, driving him to fight with a wild, untamed ferocity.

Meanwhile, a soldier's blade, swift and merciless, found its way through James's defenses, biting deep into the flesh of his sword arm. A hot flash of pain seared through him; the shock almost bringing him to his knees. Gritting his teeth against the agony, James's grip on his sword wavered, but he did not let it fall. Instead, he used the momentum to pivot away, distancing himself from the cold steel that had drawn his blood.

With his arm hanging limply at his side, James locked eyes with Eliza. In that brief exchange, a wordless pact was formed—a shared, unyielding resolve to survive. First, they had to escape the confines of Cornwallis's office, a room quickly becoming a cage. With a sudden burst of adrenaline-fueled strength, Eliza turned toward the imposing figure of the general, and with a force that belied her slender frame, she pushed the large man aside. The general, taken aback by the ferocity of this unexpected assault, stumbled, allowing Eliza and James a precious few seconds. She grabbed James, urging him forward, his injured arm a dead weight between them.

They turned on their heels, Eliza supporting James's injured side, his arm draped over her shoulders as they navigated the treacherous path to freedom. Their determination was a living thing, propelling them forward as they dodged through the corridors of the British stronghold. Eliza's keen instincts guided them to an exit less watched, and together, they broke into the night. They ran, the cold night air biting at their faces, the sounds of pursuit fading into the backdrop of a city under siege. They would not be taken today—not without a fight, not without exhausting every ounce of their courage and cunning. This was their covenant of escape, forged in the heat of battle and sealed with their swift flight toward the uncertain safety of the Sinclair's cellar.

Once ensconced in the Sinclair Tavern's shadowy embrace, the frenetic pulse of survival gave way to the heavy stillness of sanctuary. With a calm that belied the storm within, Eliza carefully peeled James's torn shirt away, revealing a jagged gash across his right shoulder, a grim souvenir from the skirmish. The wound, though not life-threatening, was deep enough to concern her, its edges raw and angry-looking. The muscle was grazed rather than cleaved, a stroke of luck. Blood, now drying and sticky, had seeped into the fabric of his shirt, mapping the trajectory of the weapon's bite.

Eliza's hands were steady as she cleaned the wound with a damp cloth, her touch sure despite the tremor that ran through her. She winced sympathetically with each of James's pained intakes of breath, the sharp sting a harsh contrast to the numbness that the shock of battle had left in its wake. Her ministrations were methodical; each movement meant to soothe and secure the flesh.

As she worked, the cold draft of the cellar seemed to echo with the cries of the wounded they had passed in their flight, the same cries that now seemed to emanate from James's gritted teeth. She silenced them with a layer of clean linen cut from her shirt, pressing it gently but firmly over the wound, staunching the blood flow. Then, with hands that betrayed none of the fear clenching her heart, she began to wrap a bandage tightly around his shoulder, securing the makeshift dressing in place.

With each encircling turn of the bandage, Eliza infused her every motion with resolve to shield James from the grim reaper's clasp. The cellar, their sanctuary from the chaos above, was steeped in silence, save for the rustle of linen and the soft cadence of their breathing. Finishing her task, she secured the binding, her fingers lingering on the knot as if to fortify it with her will.

Eliza then gently cupped James's face, her gaze intense and probing. In a moment of vulnerability, she made a silent plea that the man she had begun to love would emerge from behind the facade of the soldier he had become.

CHAPTER SIXTEEN
SHADOWS AND SIEGES

Beyond Yorktown's battered edges, Thomas's every step was concealed by the relentless thunder of artillery. The once daunting British fortifications were now marred with the toll of the Continental Army's persistent siege. Twilight gave way to the darkness of night, shrouding his cautious progress through the ruins. Drawing closer to the embattled stronghold, he moved past redoubts and improvised breastworks, all braced to withstand the next barrage. The formidable British defenses, a complex network of earthen walls and trenches, stood ready for a fight of last resort.

The moats, which in peacetime had been deterrents, now spelled doom, their murky waters mingling with the blood of relentless skirmishes. With its cruel spikes and splintered wood, the abatis lay scattered like the remains of a vanquished behemoth before the defensive lines. Thomas wound his way through the scarred terrain, a ghost in the tumultuous world of war. The shadows cloaked his movements, allowing him to glide past unnoticed, merging with the whispers of intelligence that mingled with the stench of gunpowder.

With every cautious step drawing him deeper into the encampment, the ground trembled beneath him, echoing the relentless drum of guns.

Hidden in the darkness, he witnessed the Continental Army's siege unfold with meticulous coordination.

The Patriots' trenches snaked through the earth like veins; each new channel dug under the obscurity of the night was a lifeline for the impending assault. Now brimming with soldiers poised for battle, these trenches were being carved ever closer to the British fortifications, a silent but relentless advance.

Shrouded in darkness, the men moved with purpose and efficiency, their spades and picks biting into the soil, fortifying their positions, and creating a network of paths for their comrades to follow.

Above them, the artillery crews labored with a disciplined urgency. Cannons were repositioned, their barrels angled with deadly accuracy. Each thunderous volley that followed was a testament to the army's determination to breach the robust British lines. Orders were barked and relayed with a calm urgency, every command a note in the symphony of siege tactics.

In the flickering of lanterns and the intermittent glow of muzzle flashes, Thomas could see sappers laying down fascines to reinforce the trenches and gabions to protect the gunners. Teams of engineers were constructing siege works—a complex array of approaches, parallels, and saps designed to bring the Patriots closer to the enemy's encampment while providing cover from retaliatory fire.

Thomas knew that the British, for their part, would counter with stubborn tenacity. Behind their battered ramparts, the red-coated soldiers worked feverishly to patch breaches and bolster their defenses. Officers moved among them, their voices firm as they issued commands, endeavoring to maintain order amidst the chaos of encroaching defeat.

Yet, for all the British determination, the siege would take its toll. Thomas could sense their fatigue, the strain of constant vigilance against an enemy that crept ever closer under the cover of darkness. The Continental Army, a force once underestimated but now enhanced with French support, showed its prowess in warfare of attrition and patience, chipping away at the might of the British Empire with every hour that passed.

In the interludes between cannon volleys, he heard the rhythmic clink of pickaxes against stones as soldiers fortified their positions, crafting parapets and gabions that would shield them from musket fire and shrapnel. Gun crews labored in synchrony, swabbing and loading their pieces with a practiced efficiency that spoke of countless repetitions.

This dance of war, with its deadly choreography, played out under the cover of darkness. The Patriots' siegecraft was not just a matter of muscle and earth but a chess game of strategy and countermove. Thomas noted the careful placement of sharpshooters positioned to harass and pick off British soldiers daring to show themselves above their ramparts.

In this landscape marked by the strife of revolution, Thomas's mind was filled with thoughts of Eliza and the possibility that she had sought refuge with her compatriots. But as he watched the soldiers and the siege engines, he saw no sign of her. Then an obvious realization dawned on him—there was one place he had not yet looked: the Sinclair's cellar. Perhaps, in the haste of their escape, she had found her way there, to the hidden alcove beneath the tavern that had served as storage space in less troubled times. With renewed urgency, Thomas retraced his steps. Each echo of cannon fire spurred him onward, his determination growing with the realization that Eliza might be close.

As he moved, he could not help but feel ghosts whispering of a time when war was a tale told by traveling bards, not the reality that painted every surface with its soot and sorrow. Skirting the edge of a gathering of soldiers, he ducked into a narrow passageway, its familiarity a comfort. Here, the walls seemed to lean in protectively, or perhaps the years of neglect bowed their once straight backs. He paused, taking a moment to steel himself against the mounting anxiety. He willed his legs to carry him faster with each step, though his breath came in ragged pulls.

Finally, he emerged onto the street that housed the Sinclair. The tavern's sign, which had cheerfully announced its name to all who passed, was a tattered emblem of defiance. Thomas approached the cellar door, its wood splintered, a testament to the violence that had visited this place. The lock, once shiny and solid, hung useless and broken. Swallowing the fear that knotted his throat, he pushed the door open, the hinges protesting with a melancholy creak.

The cellar was dark, the only light seeping through the cracks above, casting long, slender fingers across the dusty floor. The air was cool and heavy, filled with the scent of earth and the faintest hint of spilled ale from days long past. He descended, each step cautious, as if the very ground might betray him.

Before his eyes could adjust, a firm grip seized his arm, a force born of desperation and fear pulling him further into the depths. His heart leapt to his throat, the possibility of capture or death flashing before him. But then, a familiar voice cut through the darkness, its tone blending relief and reprimand. "James, release him," Eliza commanded.

Thomas's arm was freed, and he stumbled forward, guided by the sound of her voice. As his eyes found hers in the candlelit cellar, the weight of a thousand fears lifted. Eliza was here, alive and unbroken. The relief that washed over him was so potent it was almost a physical force, a gale strong enough to sweep away everything else, if only for a moment.

"Eliza," he breathed, the name a prayer and a promise all at once. Here in the bowels of the Sinclair Tavern, with the very earth trembling from the concussions of war above, they stood in a pocket of stillness— a respite carved out of chaos, a quiet space where hope dared to flicker once more.

CHAPTER SEVENTEEN
REDEMPTION

Thomas's entrance was less than graceful as he stumbled into the cellar. The space around him was bathed in the weak glow of a single candle, its flame casting long shadows and making the dust particles dance. The thick scent of earth and antiquity hung in the air, almost tangible in its heaviness.

James eyed the disheveled figure with an unmasked mixture of curiosity and hostility. "Who is this man?" he demanded.

Eliza's response was measured, her gaze never leaving Thomas. "A Loyalist," she admitted, the word tasting of a past she wished to forget, "but once, a friend." She deliberately left the depths of their former intimacy unspoken, an omission that hung in the silence between them.

The flickering candlelight played across Thomas's features, deepening the furrows of his frown and the shadows of regret in his eyes. James interjected sharply, unconcerned, "What brings a traitor to our doorstep at this hour?"

Thomas, casting the inquiry aside, stole a prolonged glance at Eliza. "My worries were for you. It is a relief to see you unharmed," he murmured, offering James a look that carried the weight of gratitude.

James, tinged with suspicion, retorted, "What concern is it of yours? To us, you're the enemy."

Thomas exhaled a weary acknowledgment. "That's clear to me. Yet, I implore you to heed the insight I've gained."

With an indifferent gesture, Eliza signaled for him to proceed.

Gathering the resolve to unburden his spirit, Thomas began. "Cornwallis himself laid upon me a task," he confessed. "A quest to uncover the genuine motives of Washington, to rend the shroud concealing the insurgents' schemes."

Thomas took a moment, collecting his thoughts, the gravity of his next words pulling at the air around them. "In the heart of Philadelphia, I wore the mask of a spy, seeking whispers and signs, shadows that might unveil the true target," he continued. His hands, rough from war, clenched as he spoke. "But there, in the bustle of the city, where the spirit of independence was as palpable as the cobblestones underfoot, a stark realization dawned upon me. The plans for Yorktown revealed themselves not just as military movements, but as the embodiment of a cause—a cause just and true."

His voice faltered, a man unburdening his soul of its ghosts. "It was a vision of the future, one where ideals mattered more than the soil we stood upon, more than the king we served. A future where men were bonded by the ideals of freedom and not by the chains of fealty."

Thomas's eyes, now glistening with a mixture of pain and hope, met Eliza's. "I walked amongst the rebels, not as a wolf amongst sheep, but as a man among brothers. In that revelation, my misguided loyalties crumbled to dust, like the foundations of the tyranny I once upheld."

Thomas had always been a man of deep passions and sudden shifts; his heart easily swayed by the stirring tides of conviction. This time, the impulse to abandon his former allegiances did not just spring from a fleeting passion, but from a profound awakening. As he stood amidst the rebels, he found an alignment with their ideals that resonated more truthfully with his spirit than any royal decree ever had. His previous life, built upon rigid doctrines and unquestioning loyalty to the Crown, began to appear as a distant facade.

"I saw in their struggles a mirror of my own desires for justice and equality," Thomas continued, his voice gaining strength as he spoke. "Where I once saw disorder and rebellion, I now saw a noble cause, fighting against oppression—a cause worth standing for, even if it meant standing against my past."

Eliza listened, her face a canvas of mixed emotions. Thomas's transformation was radical, yet it was not without precedent. His life had been a series of awakenings and realignments, each step forward propelled by a new understanding of the world and his place within it. Now, at this crossroads, it was not just a personal rebirth but a public declaration of his newfound allegiance to the ideals of freedom and brotherhood.

He paused, allowing the truth of his transformation to settle between them. "Eliza, my journey back was laden not with triumph but with a turmoil that grips me still. Can you forgive a man who has seen the error of his ways, who now seeks to mend a tapestry of convictions torn by war?" His question, vulnerable and raw, awaited her absolution.

James's impatience flared as he stepped forward, his face a hard line. "Forgive him? The man's our enemy!" he spat, his hand resting ominously on the hilt of his sword, the universal gesture of a threat. His voice, thick with contempt, mocked Thomas's claim of revelation. "So, the thunder of British defeat rolls in, and suddenly you're struck by a vision of the future?" The sarcasm in James's tone was palpable. "You do not see a future; you see the inevitable collapse of your side. You beg for redemption because you've nowhere else to turn!" The cellar was filled with the echo of James's challenge, throwing the sincerity of Thomas's conversion into sharp relief.

With a calm urgency, Eliza interjected herself between the two men, her presence an unspoken command for restraint. "A moment, James. Our aim here is not vengeance."

In the quietude that followed, her thoughts whirred and clicked into alignment, conceiving a plan bold enough to sway the tides of their struggle. She beckoned James closer, her voice a hushed murmur for his ears alone. "We have a path before us," she confided. "One that requires stealth, not swords."

Eliza's eyes met James's, a spark of daring igniting in the depths of her steady gaze. "If Thomas has the ear of Cornwallis and the trust of his men, who better to retrieve the Codex?" she suggested, the idea unfurling like the map of a hidden treasure only they could see.

James's voice was a furtive whisper. "Eliza, entrusting a Loyalist with the Codex is a gamble. How can we be certain he will not betray us?"

"We have no choice. The Codex may not survive the siege," she implored in a normal voice, her eyes searching the darkness where Thomas stood—a ghost of both their pasts. Purpose alight in her gaze, Eliza bridged the gap to Thomas, her touch on his shoulder a silent acknowledgment of their once shared camaraderie. "You may have a chance to amend past misdeeds," she intoned with gravity.

Thomas's expression crinkled with a mix of anxiety and resolve. "Tell me what I must do," he implored, desperation creeping into his voice. "I will do anything to set things right. What is it that must be reclaimed?"

"There's a stolen treasure known as the Solum Codex," Eliza disclosed, allowing the name to linger in the air, heavy with significance. "It's a manuscript that holds the blueprint for a far more enlightened society than the framers of the Constitution dared to imagine. It is the lost wisdom that could steer America toward its true destiny—a beacon for an enlightened future."

Thomas's eyes narrowed, reflecting a mixture of curiosity and the hunger for deeper understanding. "A guiding light?" he queried, the words laced with skepticism. "What's in this Codex? How does it hold such power?"

Eliza's nod was solemn, her words painting a picture of possibility. "As far as we know, the Solum Codex is not just a manuscript; it's a testament to a society that once thrived on principles we only dare to dream of. It's the blueprint of a utopia that predates us by centuries, offering insights into a society where our highest ideals are not confined to parchment, but are woven into the very fabric of our being. James Madison begins with drafting the Constitution, which is the first step; the Codex carries the wisdom to complete the journey."

Understanding the Codex's significance, Thomas asked, "If it contains such wisdom, to reclaim it … would it be a beacon for enlightenment?"

Eliza nodded, her eyes darting between Thomas and James. "Thomas, you could be the one to bring it back from the shadows. This is how you help us."

Thomas's eyes were a maelstrom of emotion—tinged with the shadows of past regrets and glimmers of hope for redemption. "But why should it be me?" he rasped, a plea for reason in his voice rather than command.

Eliza's reply was firm, carrying the weight of necessity. "Because Cornwallis trusts you, Thomas. We've already tried twice to retrieve the Codex and lost a comrade in our last attempt. You have an opportunity now, a way through the enemy lines unseen. You are the unexpected ally, our Trojan Horse. Once you're inside, find the Codex. It's the key to more than this war—the key to what comes after."

Eliza reached out, her hand hesitating in the air before resting gently on Thomas's arm. "Returning the Codex … it's a deed that could mend more than a fractured nation. It could heal the scars we bear, the ones we've inflicted upon each other," she said, her touch a silent plea for forgiveness and a bridge to a future they might still share.

Thomas's stance softened, the weight of his decision visible in the set of his shoulders, the slight nod of his head. "For redemption," he murmured, his voice steadier now. "For the future we all deserve."

Their plan, steeped in danger and uncertainty, was their only path forward. In the quiet solidarity of that cellar, they found an unspoken agreement, a truce sealed by the fragile hope that this man, Thomas, could indeed be the key to their deliverance.

James, his initial protest dying on his lips, nodded, the tactical advantage clear. They both turned to Thomas, their gazes an unspoken challenge. This was his chance for absolution, his deeds to be the measure of his worth. The path to redemption lay before him, lit by the very flame he once sought to extinguish.

CHAPTER EIGHTEEN
TROJAN HORSE

Using the darkness as his cloak, Thomas slipped through the shadows, the Sinclair's basement now a distant memory behind him. His steps were measured, his breaths controlled—a calm before a storm. In the canvas of his mind, the tale of Troy played out; he could almost hear the creaks of the wooden horse, the silent prayers of warriors hidden within its cavernous belly.

His destination loomed ahead, shrouded in the secrecy that only midnight could bring. General Cornwallis's headquarters—his own personal Troy—awaited, and Thomas was but a lone infiltrator, armed with nothing but his wits and the weight of a mission.

Thomas's journey was shadowed by the specter of Achilles' wrath and Odysseus's cunning. The parallels between his task and those of the ancient heroes fueled his resolve. He was no demigod or a son of royalty, yet the heroic spirit of those legends coursed through him as he edged closer to the heart of his mission.

Like the Golden Fleece, the Codex represented more than just a physical object; it symbolized ultimate knowledge, power, and enlightenment, often attainable only by the most worthy or brave individuals. Could he be the one to rescue a manuscript containing the seeds of a perfect society? The delegates of the new American Congress sought its wisdom, a blueprint to shape a nation's destiny. Eliza's eyes had sparkled with the fervor of belief when she spoke of it, and James, a man he just met, seemed ensnared by the possibility of its truth.

Thomas stood still momentarily, a solitary figure cloaked in the dark, General Cornwallis's headquarters silhouette rising ominously before him. Within those stone walls lay the object of his quest—the Codex. But it was not the only revolution stirring in the night.

As the subtle sounds of the nocturnal world filled the air, so did the echoes of his internal tumult. He had chosen the path of a Loyalist, steadfast in the belief that order and allegiance to the Crown were paramount. Now, he stood in defiance, a Patriot not by coercion of the times but by a genuine awakening of spirit. His heart had undergone a quiet revolution, and as he grappled with the remnants of his former convictions, a profound understanding settled upon him.

Thomas knew that his metamorphosis was viewed with skepticism—Eliza, with her piercing insight, and of course James, saw it as opportunism, a convenient shift as the political tides turned. Yet, within him burned a sincerity that was surprising even to himself. His change of heart was not a mere surrender to the prevailing winds, but a conscious choice, an embrace of the ideals that promised a future of liberty and self-determination.

With each silent step toward the heart of enemy intelligence, he affirmed his newfound loyalty to the cause of the Patriots. He was no longer the specter of a man caught between two worlds; he was the embodiment of the change he had once resisted. The once ominous whispers of the night that had foretold danger now seemed to resonate with a promise of valor, echoing the newfound bravery in his heart.

Thomas's purpose was clear as he moved through the darkness. He was more than a spy seizing secrets in the dead of night; he was a man chasing the dawn of a new era. Tonight, he fought for the colonies but for the essence of truth and conviction that now defined him. On this night, Thomas stood at the threshold of a new identity, ready to face his destiny with an earnest heart that turned toward freedom.

As Thomas breached the threshold of the headquarters, a maelstrom of war's chaos engulfed him. The air was thick with urgency; orders were hurled like cannon shots across the rooms, and each command met with the swift patter of boots as soldiers dashed to fulfill their duties. The pungent tang of gunpowder mingled with the acrid stench of blood, a stark reminder of the price already paid in the currency of lives.

Within these walls, the stark reality of siege lay bare—the wounded, the dying, the desperate cries of men facing mortality. Thomas navigated through this labyrinth of human turmoil, his presence barely noted amid the pandemonium. He was, after all, expected, a known figure now allied with their cause, his loyalty no longer in question to those who manned the defenses of this besieged citadel.

The further he ventured into the heart of this makeshift fortress, the more palpable the weight of impending doom became. Yet, the soldiers and officers he passed seemed not to bow under this pressure but were galvanized by it, their eyes alight with the fire of men who fight for the very essence of their beliefs.

At last, he arrived at the general's quarters. The door stood ajar, revealing a scene at odds with the bedlam outside. Here, strategy overruled chaos; the room was a sanctum of concentrated command. Maps were sprawled across tables, littered with markers denoting troop movements and strategic points, the walls echoing with the general's measured tones as he issued commands that would shape the battlefield's fate.

Thomas entered the room, a brief flicker of recognition passing over the faces of those entrenched in martial strategy. The general, a bastion of calm in the tempest of war, offered him a dismissive nod—a signal that his presence was acknowledged but not required.

Thomas stood aside, giving himself a chance to observe, wondering where something as significant as the Codex would be hidden. His eyes swept the room, the faces of men who sought to pull apart the threads of a future nation, and in that moment, Thomas grasped that history was not only shaped by the knowledge of the few but also by those who dared to chase its elusive promises.

CHAPTER NINETEEN
EXPLOSION

The cellar's damp air clung to Eliza's skin as she crouched beside James, the rough stone walls pressing close around them. Above, the Sinclair Tavern's timbers groaned under the weight of the British occupiers, who, oblivious to the enemy lurking below, arranged snipers at the upper floor windows. Each footstep echoed like a drumbeat of impending doom.

"They're inside," Eliza said, her scrutiny chasing the sounds of the footsteps as they marched across the tavern's floorboards.

James's gaze was fixed on the foundation's support beams, his mind churning with desperate plans. "We need to bring down the house," he murmured, his voice a low growl of determination.

Eliza's heart hammered against her ribs. "How?"

"Gunpowder," James said, his eyes meeting hers. "Enough to engulf them in an inferno."

The explosives were nestled securely in the enemy's arms. Eliza's knowledge of the armory's location was a glimmer of hope against formidable odds. Eliza and James emerged from the cellar, the stillness of the night enveloping them like a cloak. The Sinclair, once a symbol of grandeur, now stood as a haunting silhouette against the starlit sky, its grandiosity overshadowed by the grim reality of war. They moved through the shadows, silent as the grave, aware that every moment in the open was a gamble with death.

The neighbor's grounds, once meticulously cared for, were now marred by the encampment of British soldiers. Tents dotted the landscape like malignant growths, and the air was heavy with the scent of woodsmoke and hushed voices.

As they approached the armory, James's eyes searched for the slightest movement, the softest sound of alarm. The building itself was a stout stone structure, unassuming yet formidable, its purpose betrayed only by the faint glint of metal through the windows and the guards who stood watch.

The changing of the guard was a meticulously orchestrated routine—each soldier relieved at precise intervals, a testament to the military discipline that governed their ranks. Self-acquainted with the rhythm of military life, Eliza and James used this predictability to their advantage. They found a shadowed alcove, a small recess in the armory's wall, and pressed themselves into the cold stone.

The minutes stretched out, each second a drumbeat in their ears as they waited for the perfect moment. A nearby clock tower began its hourly chime, the sound muffled but clear, and as the last echo died away, the guards began their transition.

It was then that they moved swiftly and surely. Eliza led, her form barely a whisper against the night, as she approached the heavy door of the armory. The guards, momentarily distracted by their routine, did not notice the two figures slipping across the open space.

The armory door bore a robust lock, the workings within worn yet dependable. James's hands, calloused and steady, danced with the lock. As a spy, he was a master of silent entries.

Eliza, her hands poised for battle rather than finesse, watched James with awe and impatience. She stood sentry, her gaze darting to the shadows, the grip on her weapon firm and unwavering. Tension coiled in James's shoulders as he worked, a silent symphony of clicks marking the progress of his task. With her warrior's heart, Eliza understood the silent battle being waged at the keyhole. Her eyes remained fixed on the surroundings, ready to spring into action should their secretive operation be discovered.

The picks James wielded were an extension of his will, manipulated with a deft touch that belied the urgency of their mission. His focus was absolute; the only evidence of strain was the slight tightening of his jaw as he felt for the telltale release of the lock's mechanism.

As the lock yielded to his persistent efforts, a triumphant yet muted click echoed softly between them. James eased the door open with a final, confirming nudge, granting them access to the trove that could take down the Sinclair along with at least a dozen British soldiers.

Inside, the scent of gunpowder stung their nostrils. James reached for the keg, his arm screaming in protest from the wound festering beneath his sleeve. He staggered, the weight nearly overwhelming, but Eliza was by his side, her slender frame belying the strength that surged within.

As luck, or perhaps fate, would have it, the ground near the armory's entrance shuddered with the impact of cannon fire. It was a mere stone's throw away, a providential distraction that sent the guards scrambling from their post to assess the sudden threat. The armory, for those vital seconds, lay unprotected.

Seizing the opportunity with urgent strides, James and Eliza grasped the heavy keg. Their movements were synchronized—a silent pact of resolve etched on their faces as they navigated the maze-like network of alleys and streets. With the chaos of battle erupting around them, their path to the cellar was clear.

In the shadowed confines, they worked with feverish haste. James instructed Eliza on arranging the explosive, his voice a hoarse whisper; Eliza's hands shook as she laid the trail around the structure's foundation. The air was thick with the iron tang of blood and the acrid bite of gunpowder. Then, it was time. The fuse was set, and the spark struck. They had only moments to escape the blast they had unleashed.

The explosion did not disappoint. A monstrous roar, a beast unleashed, shook the earth beneath their feet. Once a grand manor, the Sinclair became a hellish inferno, flames licking greedily at the sky as the structure succumbed to the devastation its inhabitants wrought. James surged forward, his right arm dangling at his side and his left hand grasping his sword. Disarray reigned as British soldiers, rattled by the explosion, scrambled in confusion.

James lunged toward the scattering enemies with a battle cry that split the night's heavy silence. Each movement was a battle against his own pain and the disoriented soldiers before him. Their surprised faces blurred into the smoke as James fought, propelled by a single-minded fury. His form was a specter in the melee, each movement deliberate and deadly. Eliza looked on, awe mingling with horror, as James became a whirlwind of vengeance. For those who emerged, wounded and disoriented, from the devastation—their uniforms torn and faces smeared with soot—he was an unstoppable force. His sword sang through the air, and James dispatched the soldiers with grim precision. It was not with cruelty but with a swift efficiency that he ended their struggles, his blade finding its mark again and again in the soft underbelly of their defenses.

The Sinclair was now smoldering rubble, and the once proud force that had occupied it lay vanquished, their plans undone by fire and steel.

As the first light of dawn cast her shadow long and monstrous across the broken ground, Eliza watched James move amongst the fallen enemies. His face was smeared with soot, and his eyes blazed with a fierce light. He was the avenging angel of the battlefield, the deliverer of retribution.

When the last of the enemy was dispatched, he returned to Eliza's side, his breath coming in heavy gasps, the sword slipping from his fingers to thud against the earth. He collapsed beside her, his body finally acknowledging its exhaustion.

"The Sinclair has fallen," he whispered, his voice hoarse with smoke and fatigue.

Eliza reached out, her fingers brushing against his. "And we have risen," she replied, the pride in her voice tinged with sorrow for the cost of their victory.

As the sun rose, painting the sky with pink and gold, Eliza and James sat in silence, the weight of their actions—and the freedom they fought for—settling upon them like the first fall of snow.

CHAPTER TWENTY
A NEW MISSION

The war chamber, a cradle of desperation and dwindling hope, was abuzz with the grave counsel of Cornwallis's officers. Thomas stood in the shadows, a silent witness to the dire forecasts laid bare before the general. "We are ensnared, my lord," one officer lamented. "The French fleet under de Grasse commands the Bay, and with the American and French armies at our door, Yorktown is on the brink."

Another chimed in, his voice strained, "Reinforcements are our only lifeline. Without them, surrender is not a question of if, but when."

The grim chorus of assent rose among the gathered men, each one acutely aware of the stranglehold tightening around the British. His face a mask of stoic resolve, Cornwallis absorbed their counsel like a man bracing against an inevitable storm. His decision was swift, and the command resolute. "We must send word to General Clinton in New York. We need reinforcements, or Yorktown, and all our efforts here will be lost."

In that pivotal moment, under the heavy gaze of a cornered leader, Thomas felt the general's piercing stare upon him. With a subtle nod, Cornwallis beckoned him forward. The murmurs hushed as Thomas approached, the eyes of the room's seasoned warriors appraising him.

"Thomas"—the general's voice cut through the tension—"you have served with courage and cunning. My task is of the utmost gravity and requires a swift passage to New York."

Thomas stood erect, the gravity of the situation cementing his resolve. "I am ready to serve, sir," he replied, the weight of the responsibility already settling on his shoulders.

Beneath the surface of his composed reply, Thomas's mind raced with the implications of his secret defection. His approach to Cornwallis had been a calculated ruse, a deceptive step in a dance of espionage. He'd turned his coat, aligning with the Patriots, driven by convictions that now pulsed stronger than the blood of his lineage. The Codex, a tool of immense strategic value, had been his objective to claim for the Continental cause. But fate had a curious way of casting its dice, offering him a mission that could seal the British's fate at Yorktown.

With each heartbeat, Thomas entertained visions of triumph, not for the Crown but for the nascent republic he had covertly come to embrace. Could he, once a staunch Loyalist, now be an instrument in the Patriots' victory? The irony was not lost on him, nor was the opportunity it presented. To circumvent the delivery of the message to New York could indeed be the act that tipped the scales, a thought that both daunted and exhilarated him.

What would his father say, he wondered, if he knew his son had a hand in securing victory for the Patriots? He would embrace him as a hero, no longer a disappointment. Yet, there was the tantalizing chance of redemption, not just in his father's eyes but in the annals of a new nation and with Eliza—her image flickered in his mind, her spirit as defiant as the cause she held dear. Winning back her regard was a prize no less significant than the freedom of the colonies.

Cornwallis, with a commander's clarity, detailed the urgency of the dispatch. "The reinforcements are our last hope to break the siege. Without them, our position here is untenable," he asserted, his gaze sweeping over maps littered with enemy forces' movements.

Thomas nodded with feigned solemnity, his heart buoyed by his clandestine allegiance toward the Patriot cause. "It will be my honor to serve the Crown in this crucial hour," he declared, his voice steady, betraying none of the internal conflict.

After a respectful pause, he mustered the courage for his next gambit. "Sir, might I request a private audience?" he asked, his expression earnest.

Cornwallis, taken aback by such an unusual plea at a moment brimming with urgency, furrowed his brow but acquiesced. "Very well," he said, leading Thomas into the seclusion of a side chamber, away from the prying ears of the war room.

Once enclosed by the room's silent walls, Thomas's pulse quickened as he prepared to weave a clever tale of the Solum Codex. "General, during my time in Philadelphia, I heard whispers of a secret manuscript called the Solum Codex. It's said to hold ancient wisdom, the kind that inspired the ideals of a utopian society and—"

He hesitated, gauging Cornwallis's reaction before continuing. "—and it is believed to have influenced the very men drafting the American Constitution. Rumor has it that it has come into your possession. If such a treasure exists, would it not be safer away from the encroaching enemy?"

Cornwallis regarded Thomas with a new intensity, the implications of the Codex's existence—and its potential to shape the ideologies of a nation—evident in his eyes. "Indeed, Thomas, your information is correct. Such a document could sway the hearts and minds of men," he admitted, a rare flicker of concern crossing his features.

"Then, allow me to safeguard the Codex, General. Let me ensure it reaches the safekeeping of our leadership in New York."

Cornwallis, after a moment of silent deliberation, gave a curt nod. "Very well. The Codex and the plea shall both be entrusted to you. But heed this, Thomas—the journey is fraught with peril, and the Codex is a magnet for danger."

General Cornwallis lifted a cloth-bound bundle cradled within a vault. The Codex was enshrouded in mystery as much as by the protective fabric that encased it, bound tightly by a sturdy leather belt. Thomas yearned to see the inscriptions that were said to hold immense power, but they remained concealed from his view, a whisper of history's enigma wrapped in silence. He knew, even unseen, that the very essence of the Solum Codex was now tantalizingly within reach.

His heart raced with exhilaration at the thought of what he held. The Codex, a legend made manifest, was the key to more than just military might; it held secrets that could shape the birth of a nation. And yet, Thomas knew it was a key he would never turn. His real mission lay hidden, just like the true allegiance that pulsed quietly in his veins.

General Cornwallis's next words arrested him as he clasped the Codex, ready to step into the mantle of his double duty. "Thomas, this task is of such magnitude that you shall not undertake it alone."

Thomas's thoughts, so recently adrift in the possibilities of his clandestine endeavor, snapped sharply into focus. He turned to see the imposing figure of Lieutenant General Wilhelm von Knyphausen, an emblem of Hessian discipline and martial prowess, emerging from the shadows.

"You will accompany Thomas to New York," Cornwallis commanded, his tone leaving no room for dissent.

Von Knyphausen's gaze met Thomas's. There was no question of the Hessian's capabilities or his dedication to the mission. Realizing the added complexity this companion would bring to his secret defection, Thomas felt a coil of apprehension tighten within him.

Yet, as he stood there, the weight of the Codex in his hands, Thomas understood that the presence of von Knyphausen was a challenge he must navigate with the same cunning that had brought him this far. The stakes were higher, and the play more perilous, but the rewards of success whispered promises of a future nation free from tyranny.

With the Codex secured and his companion at his side, Thomas set forth from the war chamber, the echo of their boots in the hall a somber drumbeat to the rhythm of his dual purposes. The Codex was now his to protect—but not to deliver to the hands that now trusted him. And von Knyphausen, the vigilant guardian of their mission, would be the unwitting shield to his subterfuge.

As the door closed behind them, sealing away the secrecy of the chamber, Thomas felt the finality of the path he had chosen. A path that would lead him away from the orders he had just been given toward a destiny aligned with the values he held deep in his heart—a destiny for which Eliza, his father, and history itself might remember him as the hero he yearned to become.

CHAPTER TWENTY-ONE
THE HESSIAN

James's eyes narrowed as he watched Thomas stride from British headquarters, a laden satchel slung over his shoulder. The weight of its contents seemed to pull at the cloth, suggesting the gravity of what it contained. Had Thomas been successful? Could that be the Solum Codex? James wondered, his pulse quickening.

Slipping like a shadow, James followed, carefully maintaining distance as Thomas made his way to the stables. The dim light of the early dawn cast long shadows over the grounds, and James used them to his advantage. The stables would be his chance to confront Thomas, learn what occurred at headquarters, and if he indeed secured the Codex. He waited as Thomas busied himself with the tack, fitting the saddle onto his steed with practiced ease.

James took a silent step forward, his hand resting on the hilt of his hidden dagger. He was about to reveal himself when the echo of heavy boots on the stable floor froze him mid-motion.

A man's voice, thick with a German accent, sliced through the quiet. "You are prepared, I see," the figure announced, his silhouette broad and imposing in the doorway.

Thomas straightened, his reply carrying a tone of guarded respect. "Lieutenant General von Knyphausen, I did not hear you approach."

James retreated further into the shadows, recognizing the name. Von Knyphausen, a seasoned Hessian soldier, was not one to be trifled with. The Hessians, renowned for their military discipline, were formidable adversaries. As mercenaries for the Crown, they had become a symbol of the lengths to which King George III would go to maintain his grip on the colonies—a point of contention that had stoked the fires of revolution.

The Hessian's arrival signified the gravity of Thomas's assignment. As von Knyphausen imparted his directives, his words echoed the mercenaries' notorious dedication, "We leave at dusk. The general insists upon haste and secrecy." His voice brimming with the assurance of one born to command.

Thomas's response was a nod. His focus was on the saddle's buckles, and his movements were precise and practiced. "Of course, sir. We will not delay," he assured.

Von Knyphausen's sharp and calculating eyes were fixed on Thomas. "Meet me at the old mill by the river crossing. It's secluded enough to avoid the eyes of the Continental Army, and from there, we can find a safe passage north toward New York." His instructions were clear; the plan was to avoid the main thoroughfares patrolled by enemy forces, seeking the secrecy that their mission necessitated.

James watched the interaction with bated breath, the dynamics of power and allegiance playing out before him. Despite their mercenary status, the Hessians were more than just pawns to be easily swayed or intimidated. Their role at pivotal battles, such as Trenton, demonstrated the resilience and danger they posed to the Continental Army.

James watched the shadowy figures of Thomas and the Hessian disappear into the fog. Why was the Hessian accompanying Thomas, and where were they going? Could Thomas's recent show of rebellion against the Crown be merely a ruse? A Loyalist at heart, using the Hessian to smuggle the Codex to the British, securing his own pardon in the chaos of war? Or perhaps the Hessian, a mercenary known for his loyalty to the highest bidder, had his own designs on the Codex's power?

James returned with haste to the modest refuge where Eliza awaited, the urgency of his news etching lines of concern into his face. Stepping over the threshold, James was enveloped by an atmosphere thick with the scent of dried herbs and the whisper of unseen forces. The walls were adorned with talismans, and the glint of candles flickered through crystals. "What place is this?" he murmured, his voice a blend of wonder and underlying dread.

Eliza emerged from the shadows, her presence a calming force. "This is the home of my dear friend Agatha," she said, her hand on his arm guiding him. "She has offered us sanctuary." She spoke with a reverence that told of a deep trust, explaining that this woman, shrouded in mystery and whispered about in the streets, was an ally of rare power and insight.

"Agatha sees through the veil that cloaks this war," Eliza continued, her words steady yet laden with intensity. "She's no witch, though the unseeing eyes of fear might label her as such. Instead, she's a guardian of knowledge, a keeper of the old ways. Trust in her, as I do, for our fates are intertwined now, woven by threads she understands far better than we."

"Foreseeing our fates as one—can such a thing be true?" His skepticism was a thin veneer over his burgeoning wonder at the possibility. He ruminated on her words, his analytical mind wading through the mist of mysticism she presented.

"She speaks of destiny's hand in our meeting." Her voice was soft, yet it cut through the room's hush with a clarity that spoke of her need to make him understand.

As he leaned in, the play of light and shadow danced across his face, sculpting his concern into something almost tangible. "Intriguing as this is, something more immediate presses upon us."

Eliza's response was immediate, her tone a blend of patience and anticipation. "Go on, then. Speak your mind."

In the dimness, their hands met, his grip a silent harbinger of the gravity of his next words. "Eliza," he started, the whisper not quite concealing the tremor of alarm, "there is a matter I've stumbled upon, one that casts a shadow upon your friend, the discontented Loyalist."

As he recounted his encounter with Thomas and the Hessian, locked in covert communion, his words were rushed, the image of

Thomas gripping a mysterious artifact—its significance as clear as its details were obscured—burned into his mind. They were bound for a place concealed from him, veiled in the mists of the unknown. The fracture in his faith in Thomas had widened into a chasm, with the dread that the Codex, their hope of triumph, might be slipping irretrievably into the wrong hands. James's eyes opened, seeking in Eliza's face some reflection of his own alarm, some sign of a shared resolution to face the uncertainty that lay ahead.

Eliza listened, her mind racing, and then, with resolve, she proposed seeking guidance from the cards. She spoke of Agatha's gift, how her visions had once woven through the threads of their own past, and how it could possibly shed light on the enigma of Thomas's actions.

As if on cue, a soft creak announced Agatha's arrival. Her silver hair, long and untamed, cascaded over her shoulders, catching glints of candlelight that danced across her deep-set, knowing eyes. She wore a cloak the color of midnight, embroidered with symbols that whispered of old lore and older magic.

James watched, transfixed, as she moved with a presence that commanded respect and an air of timeless wisdom. "James," Eliza said, turning toward him with an encouraging nod, "this is Agatha. Her vision has never led me astray."

Agatha fixed her gaze upon James, as if she could see through to the marrow of his soul. "Welcome to my home," she said, her voice rich and textured. "The cards await your unspoken questions." And the room fell into a hush of anticipation as Agatha began her sacred ritual, reaching for the worn deck that lay upon the table draped in layers of time-softened cloth.

In the muted gloom, the tarot was summoned. Agatha's hands moved with an ancient grace, cards cascading onto the table, their images rich with hidden meaning. The dim light played upon the surfaces, revealing a tale in the tapestry of symbols—the Codex's journey was not at an end but had taken a veiled path, shepherded by one whose loyalty was questioned.

Eliza's eyes met James's, and a silent communication passed between them. She, too, felt the tremor of uncertainty, even as she stood by the choice to delve into the mystic for answers. Agatha's reading could offer a sliver of light in the dark, a chance to glimpse Thomas's motives, to understand if he truly carried the Codex toward salvation or its undoing.

In the humble sanctuary of Agatha's quarters, where every object seemed to whisper secrets of the past, James sat across from the old seer, the tarot cards laid out like a mysterious map between them. The air was thick with the scent of burning sage and the faintest hint of foreboding. Agatha's eyes, reflecting the flicker of candlelight, invited questions from the depths of James's troubled thoughts.

"Does Thomas possess the Codex?" James's voice was steady, but his hands betrayed him, trembling ever so slightly.

Agatha's fingers paused above the deck, a tremor of uncertainty in the air. She flipped a card: the Magician, its image shrouded in shadows. "The master of tools and knowledge," she murmured, her voice tinged with doubt. "The Codex may be within Thomas's grasp, yet the veil is thick here; forces beyond our sight obscure his hold upon it."

James's gaze sharpened. "And their destination? Where does this obscured path lead them?" His voice barely rose above a whisper, filling the room with intensity.

The Star card glimmered under the candle's glow. "To a haven of hope and enlightenment," Agatha responded, her words floating like a melody. "Yet even this is shrouded; clarity on where the Codex's truth will emerge remains beyond my reach."

The question of the Hessian general's role thundered forth from James, echoing off the walls. Agatha turned The Lovers, its image inverted. "A partnership of shadows and necessity," she intoned. "Their bond is concealed within a web of strategy, the threads of their allegiance woven tight and hidden from the light."

"And their mission? What is their intent with the Codex?" James leaned in closer, as if proximity to the oracle could grant him clarity.

The Tower stood tall on the turned card, yet a smoky mist obscured its base. "They seek to shake the foundations of what is known," Agatha declared, her fingertip circling the fog at the card's bottom. "But the exact nature of the upheaval is clouded, hidden behind a mist that even the cards cannot penetrate."

The final haunting inquiry lingered between them. "Is Thomas to be trusted?" James's voice was a thread woven with hope and fear.

Agatha revealed The Knight of Cups, but this time, the knight's chalice was covered by a shadowy veil. "Thomas rides with purpose, guided by a heart that knows old allegiances," she said, her eyes reflecting the card's obscured image. "Yet, trust is a stream that flows into the mist—its path uncertain and its waters deep and dark."

With each card and its veiled revelation, the fabric of their fate seemed interlaced with more questions than answers. Agatha's insight was a lantern in the fog, casting light but also long, undecipherable shadows. With a spirit now steeled by the enigmatic guidance, James felt the stirrings of a determined resolve. The fate of the Codex, Thomas's trustworthiness, and the true nature of their mission remained enigmas, shrouded by the same shadows that veiled the cards.

James clenched his hand into a fist at his side, the cards before him a jumble of ancient symbols mocking his yearning for clarity. "We're chasing phantoms at every turn," he growled, the frustration boiling over in his voice echoing off the dimly lit walls of Agatha's abode.

With a touch as gentle as the breeze whispering through the open window, Eliza laid her hand on his arm. "Patience, James. The mists of fate are not so easily dispersed," she soothed. Yet her words were like drops of rain falling into an ocean of his impatience.

He shook his head, the resolve in his eyes hardening like flint. "Time waits for none, Eliza. While we seek hidden meanings in these

cryptic tableaux, Thomas and the Hessian draw farther from our grasp."
His gaze flickered to the door, then back to the table. "I must go. Now.
Codex or no."

"Do not blame the cards," Eliza said, her voice steady. "Blame the
questions you pose. Perhaps it's not answers we lack but the right
questions."

In the stillness that followed his query, James found his turmoil
yielding to an unspoken certainty. "Are we fated to uncover the Solum
Codex?" he ventured, his voice now imbued with an expectant tenor.

Agatha's fingers traced the edges of the ancient tarot deck before
selecting and presenting The Chariot card. "The Chariot," she began,
her voice steady, "represents a conquest, a journey propelled by will and
desire. It speaks of a seeker who will face adversity with courage."

James leaned in, studying the card. "And this seeker, could it be
one of us?" he asked, hope and skepticism mingling in his voice.

"Perhaps," Agatha replied, her eyes not leaving the card. "The
Chariot is driven by determination but requires mastery over opposing
forces. It tells me that you, too, must find balance in your pursuit."

"But does it show who holds the Codex?" Eliza interjected, seeking
precision in the sea of ambiguity.

Agatha's eyes held Eliza's gaze, reflecting the candle's flicker.
"The cards offer guidance, but they do not dictate the specifics. The
Chariot's appearance could signify that the Codex is within reach. The
question is, are you both ready to face what is required to retrieve it?"

James mulled over Agatha's words, feeling the weight of their truth. "The Chariot … is about movement and a journey. It's forceful, directed," he murmured, more to himself than the others. "If Thomas and the Hessian are a step ahead, I must follow swiftly. It's a direct course of action—straight as the charioteer would drive."

Eliza, contemplative, paced a small circle before responding. "And The Chariot is also protection," she added, her voice gaining strength as she spoke. "It shields its bearer. I must be the shield here, in Yorktown, with its many eyes and ears. While you follow their trail, I will delve into the heart of this place. It holds its secrets close, but I have ways of coaxing them to light."

The two stood in the flickering candlelight, the gravity of their decision sinking in. It was a choice that split their paths but bound them to a common goal. With the wisdom of the tarot as their guide and the night as their ally, they committed to their separate quests.

CHAPTER TWENTY-TWO
ESCAPING YORKTOWN

Dusk had settled like a soft shroud over Yorktown, accompanied by a tense silence that whispered of impending turmoil. Thomas glanced at his companion, the man known amongst the ranks as Lieutenant General Wilhelm von Knyphausen, now clad in the plain garb of a Colonial. "We should address each other by our birth names, Thomas," Wilhelm insisted, his voice low, the German accent less pronounced than it was when he gave orders. "It draws less attention."

They set off as dusk bled into night, the shadows lengthening to cloak their departure in urgency and secrecy. Sensing the tension in their riders' taut muscles, their horses picked up the pace, hooves silent on the soft earth. Around them, the sprawling encampments of Colonial and French troops bustled with the low hum of impending triumph, the soldiers' voices a confident murmur that mingled with the clatter of tinware and the occasional bark of orders.

Thomas and Wilhelm, now in civilian guise, weaved through the labyrinth of war's temporary architecture. They maneuvered around the flickering campfires that cast a shifting mosaic of light and dark, an illumination that could betray them to a watchful sentinel's eye at any moment. They were but two specters against a backdrop, alive with the vibrant pulse of an army on the cusp of victory, a dangerous contrast to their silent, spectral flight.

The stakes were as high as the gallows that awaited spies and deserters, and every rustling leaf or snapped twig underfoot threatened to be their undoing. The air was thick with the scent of woodsmoke and the heavy tang of gunpowder, a constant reminder of the thin veneer of peace that cloaked the battlefield.

With each step, the two men risked a confrontation with patrols or a chance encounter with a foraging party. Every moment they remained within reach of the allied encampment was a moment too long, yet haste was as much their enemy as discovery. To gallop would draw the eye, but to tarry was to invite disaster.

Their path was one of careful calculation, a thread woven through a tapestry of danger, where each choice could lead to freedom or folly. As they passed by the edge of a clearing, a sudden shout rang, a call to arms that sent a surge of adrenaline coursing through their veins. The camp was roused, and for a heart-stopping moment, they thought their cover was blown.

But the alarm was for another—a deserter caught in the act, dragged into the flickering light to face his fate. The commotion provided them with the distraction needed to slip further into the darkness, away from the glow of the camp and its perils.

This was the gauntlet they had to run: a nocturne of peril, played out in the space between the armies, where every shadow could be sanctuary or snare, and every light a herald of doom. The silent prayer on their lips was simple—let the darkness be their ally this last time.

Following the serpentine York River, they avoided the main thoroughfares patrolled by sentries. They crossed onto the northern neck, where the sparse population offered them anonymity, but every snapped twig or rustle in the underbrush had them reaching for the weapons concealed beneath their cloaks.

The Potomac River loomed ahead, a broad, shimmering expanse in the moonlight. They forded at a narrow, far from the bustling port of Alexandria. Wilhelm was a figure of concentration, his eyes ever scanning the banks behind them. "We cannot delay," he muttered.

In the midst of this nocturnal march, Thomas, moved by a blend of respect and intrigue, cast a sidelong glance at the enigmatic figure riding beside him. "Wilhelm," he ventured, his words cutting through the cool air, "the Hessians' reputation precedes them, fierce and unfaltering. What tale brought you to rank amongst King George's coveted mercenaries?"

Wilhelm's silhouette was stark against the moon's pale glow, his profile as sharp as the sword at his side. "I am a Hessian, true," he began, his voice a low thrum that matched the cadence of their travel. "In my homeland, the art of war is a craft honed from youth—sold to those who value our mettle. King George, in his hunger for dominion over these rebellious lands, has lined the coffers of our princes to secure our blades." A pause, heavy and thoughtful, followed his words.

The air held a hint of frost as Wilhelm's admission lingered between them. He regarded Thomas, his question laced with a genuine curiosity that transcended the boundaries of war. "And you, Thomas, what winds of fate have blown you into the arms of the Loyalists? I imagine such allegiance has brought turmoil upon your home life."

As the night deepened around them, Thomas felt the familiar tug of conflict within—a war of loyalty and regret that no battlefield could match. He cast a furtive glance at Wilhelm, whose own confessions had paved the way for honesty, albeit a measured one. "I was born to Virginia soil," Thomas began, his voice a whisper among the whispers of the forest. "But when the fires of revolution sparked, I foresaw a British victory as inevitable. I sensed an opportunity in the empire's might—that of wealth and status for those who stood with the Crown."

Thomas shifted in his saddle, the leather creaking under him as he sought an elusive comfort that his decisions had long denied him. The faintest shadow of anguish flitted across his face, a testament to the rifts his allegiance had rent in his life. "My own father could not countenance my choice, branding me a traitor to his cause," he said, the words steady but laced with an undercurrent of loss. "And my sweetheart—Eliza, with her fervent dreams of liberty, has cast me aside as though our love was nothing but ashes in the revolutionary fervor."

For a moment, vulnerability threatened to breach the walls of his stoic facade, but he swiftly fortified his expression into one of resolve as his eyes met the distant hills. "The choice was mine, to align with the

Crown for a promise of affluence." Thomas's confession was almost a whisper, betraying the inner conflict that tormented him in the stillness of the night.

Thomas rode silently, his expression as unreadable as the darkened sky overhead. He had once aligned himself with the Crown, believing it to be the side of inevitable victory that would grant him wealth and status. But a recent revelation had sparked a crisis of conscience, a realization that his true allegiance lay with the ideals of the Patriots—the cause he had abandoned.

Now his mission had shifted. He was no longer the Loyalist envoy tasked with delivering the Solum Codex to General Clinton; instead, he was a man desperate to correct his past misdeeds. The Codex, a symbol of his redemption, needed to reach Eliza and James. Surely, they were already on edge, uncertain of his fate, perhaps even mourning him as lost.

The night air was cool against his skin, starkly contrasting with the feverish plotting that inflamed his mind. He needed a plan to extricate himself from Wilhelm's company—permanently, if necessary. Each mile north they rode together tightened the noose of danger around Thomas's neck.

He knew that his next actions could alter the course of the war and, more immediately, determine his own survival. The thought of killing Wilhelm was as cold and sharp as the blade hidden in his boot. Yet, if it meant safeguarding the future of a nation striving to be born, was it not a price worth paying?

Gathering the reins of his resolve, Thomas's outward facade remained resolute. "But make no mistake, Wilhelm, my allegiance to the Crown is unwavering. The path of loyalty is often fraught with sacrifice, and I shall walk it to the end." His words, though firm, belied the subtlest tremor of a man still wrestling with the ghosts of what could have been.

The night was a cloak of quiet around them as they rode, broken only by the occasional snort or hoofbeat of their steeds. Thomas's grip on the reins was firm, his mind preoccupied with the mission at hand, though the true nature of the satchel's contents eluded him. "Wilhelm," he finally said, the question evident in his tone, "I've been entrusted with this satchel, told of its importance, and yet its secrets remain veiled from me. They say it's crucial to the Crown's cause, but how?"

That's when Wilhelm turned to him, the shadows of the night playing across his face, giving him a ghoulish countenance that belied the smirk forming on his lips. "My friend," he began, his voice carrying a hint of derision that was almost palpable, "that manuscript you safeguard so dutifully is the Solum Codex, a tome of unparalleled wisdom, the distilled essence of a civilization that chose enlightenment over conquest."

Wilhelm's smirk grew as he observed Thomas's dawning comprehension. "It is, in fact, the very antithesis of what men like us stand for," he continued with a sardonic tone. "The Congress, in their infinite wisdom, failed to safeguard the Codex. Now, it shall find sanctuary with the Crown, far from the idealistic eyes of the Americans."

He leaned closer to Thomas, his voice dropping to a conspiratorial whisper. "Imagine, if you will, the kind of world that could be constructed with such profound knowledge. A society built on the pillars of peace and reason, not the chaos of war and ambition. An existence so refined, it would hardly have a need for the likes of us—battle-hardened soldiers bred for conflict."

Wilhelm leaned back, the smirk still playing on his face as if amused by the paradox of their existence. "Yes, Thomas, in the safety of the Crown's stronghold, the Solum Codex will remain hidden. A world shaped by its secrets would be a utopia indeed, but utopias have no shadows, and men like us prefer to dwell in darkness."

CHAPTER TWENTY-THREE
FAREWELL

As the oppressive siege cast its long shadow over Yorktown, the air hung heavy with the mingled scents of gunpowder and anticipation. Eliza, her cloak drawn tight against the encroaching chill of the impending night, contemplated the enigmatic nature of their plight. Having double-checked each strap and buckle on his steed, James now faced her with a visage carved from the same determination that had fortified their cause from the outset.

"The siege will not wait, and neither can we." James spoke with a firmness that revealed his inner turmoil. "The cover of night is our ally."

Eliza's breath hung before her, a fleeting wisp in the cool air. "Agatha's words were veiled, shrouded," she murmured. "Do you suppose Thomas actually possesses the Codex?"

Looking beyond, James's gaze followed the path that wound northward, a serpent disappearing into the twilight. "It's a possibility that gnaws at me. But why now? Why would Thomas and the Hessian be sent forth under such dire circumstances?"

"Perhaps they seek to tip the scales back in their favor," Eliza said, the strategist within her mapping out the unseen battlefields. "Reinforcements, messages … anything could be at play."

James furrowed his brow, troubled by a nagging thought. "But why Thomas? If the Codex is as vital as we believe, why entrust it to him?" His grasp tightened on the reins, a tangible expression of his unease.

Eliza's eyes held a depth as she spoke. "Thomas, like you, has a particular set of skills. He's not just a soldier; he's adept at moving unseen and gathering intelligence. His capabilities in espionage could be what Cornwallis is banking on."

James caught a certain tone in her voice, hinting at something personal. "You speak of him with a certain … familiarity. Is there something between you two I should know?"

All Eliza could do was exhale a sigh and lower her eyes.

"Were you two a couple?" James's voice held an edge, the words rough like stone.

"We were," Eliza confessed. "But it ended when he chose to become a Loyalist," she continued, disappointment lingering in her tone. "And that was a path I could not walk beside him on. His allegiance to the Crown betrayed the cause for our independence."

"I see," said James with a raised brow.

"I chose a future I believed in," Eliza added, her commitment to their fight shining through her words. "So, our ways parted, and my heart closed the door on what was." Her hand reached for his, a symbol of her present and future. "It's truly over with Thomas."

James processed her words, the betrayal stinging less than he'd expected. He realized that their shared past was just that—past. What mattered now was the bond he and Eliza had forged, unbreakable even by the ghosts of yesteryear.

"You must follow them," Eliza reiterated, pulling him back to the present. "Determine whether they bear the Codex or merely a ruse." Her past with Thomas was a closed chapter, but the mystery he now carried could decide the fate of nations.

James felt the weight of their impending separation, a leaden cloak upon his shoulders. "By the stars, I will pursue them through the night. But Thomas … he remains a mystery cloaked in the guise of an ally."

Eliza's fingers brushed against his, a fleeting touch that spoke of unity and strength. "And it's a mystery you're fated to unravel," she said, her voice a whisper against the backdrop of war. "Thomas has always been a chameleon, his colors shifting with the wind. Be wary of him."

James's smile was tinged with concern. "I've walked through this war with caution as my shadow. But you, Eliza, in this maelstrom, how will you ensure your safety?"

Her stance was resolute, her determination unwavering. "I've laid plans of my own," Eliza proclaimed. "Many within this town remain loyal to our cause, shadowed figures ready to reveal what they know. I intend to learn if the Codex remains with Cornwallis. Perhaps what Thomas carries is nothing but a clever deceit—a decoy to mislead, while the true Codex remains hidden here in Yorktown."

"If the city falls before I return"—James's voice was a hushed murmur—"Cornwallis may well consign all his secrets to the flames to keep them from Patriot hands. That includes the Codex."

"We have little time, then." Eliza's voice carried the strength of iron yet the softness of compassion. "Discover their objective, and Godspeed your return."

As the world held its breath, James drew Eliza into his arms. There, in the quiet before the storm, their kiss was a lingering defiance of the chaos that raged beyond the fragile bubble of their union. James savored the warmth of Eliza's lips, a poignant contrast to the cold bite of the air.

In the stillness that followed their parting, the distant rumble of cannon fire jolted James back to grim reality. Though Eliza's warmth had left his side, the memory of her fierce and tender kiss lingered on his lips, infusing him with a purpose that transcended the fight for liberty—it was a fight for her heart. As the shadows enveloped him, Eliza's resolve, her unwavering spirit, clung to his thoughts, a beacon in the encroaching night.

James moved with stealth, and every step he took was a silent oath, his bond with Eliza an anchor in the tempest of war. The distance might stretch between them, but their connection was ready to spring forward at the moment of their reunion.

His training kept him a specter in the darkness, his presence unknown to his quarry or the enemy. The Hessians' reputation for ruthlessness preceded them, and Thomas's ever-changing loyalties threatened to unravel the threads of trust they had woven. The temptation to alert the sentries to Thomas and the Hessian's presence tugged at James, yet he resisted. To reveal them now would be to play his hand prematurely, potentially losing the Codex to the winds of chaos. James knew the art of war was fought not just with swords, but also with the patience of a predator in wait.

Eliza's image, steadfast and determined, bolstered his resolve. She was more than a distant figure; she was the compass guiding him through the labyrinth of deceit and intrigue.

The mystery of Thomas's intentions at this hour, with the siege tightening like a noose, was a puzzle that beckoned. James was resolute in his pursuit—whatever secrets Thomas held, whatever allegiance his heart now claimed, James would strive to uncover it all. The path ahead was fraught with shadows and uncertainty, but his mission was as clear as the dawn that would soon break over the horizon. If Thomas possessed the Codex, he would secure it and return to Eliza's side, their love a defiant flame against the consuming darkness of the siege.

CHAPTER TWENTY-FOUR
THOMAS MAKES A MOVE

The night deepened as Thomas and Wilhelm, guided only by the celestial map above them, continued their journey northward through the Maryland countryside. The familiar constellations and the gentle burble of the Sassafras and Chester Rivers were their companions as they steered clear of the more frequented roads, seeking the obscurity that the shadows provided.

Weighed down by weariness, Thomas and Wilhelm sought refuge within a dense thicket. These woods stood watchful and steadfast, offering them a place to rest, hidden from the world's turmoil. In Delaware, a haven of relative calm amidst the conflict, they allowed themselves a moment's reprieve.

With a mind for strategy as sharp as his sword, Wilhelm carefully selected their resting place. The natural dome created by the overhanging branches provided more than shelter from the elements; it served as a cloak against discovery. Such a location was chosen not for comfort and concealment, for the skies were often scoured in these revolutionary times for telltale signs of human presence. A wisp of smoke and a campfire's glint could betray them to enemy scouts. Thus, under a canopy woven by nature's hand, they found obscurity, ensuring that no searching gaze from afar would find them through the veil of leaves and shadows.

In the tranquility of the thicket, with night's velvet drapery unfolding across the sky, Thomas ran a hand over the satchel's worn leather. Each crease and fold seemed to pulse with the weight of histories unwritten and futures yet to unfold. The wax seal, embossed with an intricate coat of arms, was more than a mere symbol of confidentiality—it was the guardian of potential, a keeper of the revolutionary ideals that could forge a nation unlike any other.

He pondered the Codex's rumored contents, imagining the architects of America's destiny pouring over its pages, seeking inspiration for the foundations of a society built on the pillars of freedom and equality. The very thought that within this satchel lay a document that could rival the influence of the Magna Carta or the philosophies of Locke and Rousseau stirred within him a mixture of awe and trepidation.

Thomas mused about what sort of world it would be, where every individual's worth was recognized, where the chains of servitude and the shadows of inequality were dissolved under the light of reason and compassion. The Codex promised a land governed by the people's will, not the whims of the throne—a land where justice was not a privilege but a birthright.

Yet, the very existence of the Codex was shrouded in whispers and shadows. If such a blueprint for society did exist, why had it not been declared to all? Why did it travel secretly, like a fugitive, from hand to hidden hand?

His thoughts were like leaves caught in a tempest, swirling with the possibilities of what changes the Codex could bring to a war-torn land craving direction and hope. Could he, Thomas, hold the key to a new dawn for America?

As Thomas pondered the weight of the Solum Codex, his mind grappled with the guilt of his past choices as a Loyalist, casting long shadows over the man he had become. Yet, amid the turmoil of his thoughts, a glimmer of redemption began to take shape. Here, nestled within the leather-bound potential of the Codex, lay his path to absolution. Returning this manuscript to the Continental Congress was more than a symbolic act—it was his chance to right his wrongs, to realign with the ideals and people he had forsaken. With each step back toward the Patriots, Thomas felt the shackles of his betrayal begin to loosen, replaced by a burgeoning sense of purpose. With its profound insights, the Codex could pave the way for an era of American prosperity and unity. In his heart, Thomas knew that delivering the Codex to its rightful custodians might not erase his past transgressions, but it could certainly shape a brighter future for his homeland.

With the weight of history pressing upon him, he sought the counsel of his unlikely comrade. "Wilhelm," he began, his voice barely above the crackling of the fire, "they say this satchel holds a future for a nation. What truths lie within these pages? What visions of a world reborn?" The question hung in the air, mingling with the smoke and the scent of the earth, awaiting the revelation that would come with the Hessian's reply.

With a fire in his eyes reflecting the campfire before them, Wilhelm leaned back against a fallen log. "Ah, the Codex," he mused, a smirk playing upon his lips. "It is indeed a remarkable artifact. More than a collection of words, it holds ideals that could sway the hearts and minds of men—ideals of equality, governance, a society where power is checked, and liberty is boundless."

Thomas listened, captivated, as the Hessian spun tales of the Codex's wisdom—its bold propositions for wealth distribution, public education, freedom of worship, and economic models that would foster both individual ambition and communal good. It was a manuscript that dared to envision a world where civic duty was not just expected but embraced with zeal, where the philosophical debates of the Enlightenment took tangible form.

"The Codex," Wilhelm continued, "outlines principles that could sculpt a nation unlike any other—a true utopia."

Thomas, his brow furrowed, pondered the implications. "But how," he inquired, "do you come to possess such intimate knowledge of this document?"

Wilhelm's gaze met his, steady and unblinking. "Because, my dear Thomas, I am the one who stole it."

A chill ran down Thomas's spine as he absorbed the gravity of the general's confession. The satchel's contents were not just a strategic advantage, but a stolen dream, a hijacked blueprint for a society that might have been. This revelation blurred the lines between friend and foe, and Thomas found himself at the crossroads of history, holding the key to America's unwritten future.

As Wilhelm's words hung in the air, Thomas felt the weight of his legacy press upon him. The revelation that the general was the architect of the Codex's theft sent a torrent of emotions coursing through him. The satchel he carried—a token of potential upheaval—suddenly felt heavier, pulsing with the power to reshape a nation gasping for breath amidst the chaos of war.

The man who stood before Thomas, once an ally in arms, now personified the essence of betrayal. Thomas's mind raced with the implications of what returning the Codex could mean for the burgeoning nation yearning for direction, for the dream of what America could become. The ideals of liberty and justice within the Codex's pages were not mere words; they were the very soul of a country yet to be fully realized.

With his unwavering stare, Wilhelm represented a past Thomas had come to regret. The choice before him was stark and irrevocable: to continue as a pawn in a game of empires or to seize this moment of destiny. Could he dare to betray the betrayer, to snatch from the jaws of the enemy a future where freedom reigned?

The options before him were fraught with peril—eluding the Hessian, a seasoned military mind, would be a daunting task, and the thought of taking his life was a dark tempest that threatened to engulf Thomas's soul. Yet, the Codex called to him, promising redemption.

In the quiet of the night, with the whispers of the wind as his counsel, Thomas realized the Codex's return to the Americans was a penance, a way to salvage what remained of his honor. It was his chance to stand on the right side of history—to be remembered not as a traitor but as a man who, in the eleventh hour, chose to try to change the course of a nation. With a resolve hardened by the prospect of redemption, Thomas began plotting his next move, knowing full well that the road to Philadelphia would be as treacherous as the war surrounding him.

CHAPTER TWENTY-FIVE
SURRENDER AT YORKTOWN

As Eliza's mind wove through her next steps, the pressing question of the Codex's whereabouts held her in a silent thrall. Did it indeed journey away with Thomas, or did it linger close, cloaked in the shadow of Cornwallis's defeat? Her mind, a tempest of strategy and emotion, turned toward James. Was his pursuit of Thomas and the Hessian fruitful? Had he unraveled the mystery of the true manuscript, or had they all been ensnared in a cleverly spun web of deceit? The significance of the Codex was no secret.

Yet, beneath the tumult of war and intrigue, Eliza's heart waged a battle of its own. With his fierce passion and newfound love, James ignited a wildfire of exciting and intense emotions in her.

However, the ghost of her affection for Thomas lingered, a specter that refused to be silenced. No matter how she tried, she could not extinguish the embers of what once was. Thomas, now an emblem of her past, a man she had once loved with a tenderness that time could not erode, had chosen a path that severed their destinies.

This internal maelstrom of loyalty and love, old and new, swirled within Eliza as she stood resolute amidst the chaos. It was a convergence of the personal and the political, each battle as fierce as the other, each choice a step toward a future uncertain.

In the fading twilight, as the clamor of war gave way to the promise of peace, Eliza stood among the streets of Yorktown, transfixed by the scene that unraveled before her. The air was heavy, laden with the remnants of gunpowder and the resounding triumph, vibrating with the day's fervent energy. The siege of Yorktown was reaching its inevitable conclusion, signaling an end to the battle and a historical pivot toward a future shaped by the victors.

Though distant from the city's core, where the tangible triumphs of the Continental Army were unfolding, Eliza's mind painted vivid scenes of celebration. She envisaged the soldiers, emboldened on the precipice of a monumental victory, their spirits alight with the fervor of freedom. In her mind's eye, she saw them not just as warriors but harbingers of a new age, their once weary voices now harmonizing with the solemn anthems of liberty that she imagined would score their march toward a nation's inception.

Meanwhile, a stark silence had befallen the British ranks. Their once daunting force was now cornered and reduced. Eliza saw in the countenances of the British soldiers a canvas of fear, resignation, and incredulity. Once perceived as unassailable, the formidable British Empire had been subdued by an unwavering adversary, and the fog of their uncertain future was as oppressive as the siege itself. While some accepted their fate with stoic reserve, others sought comfort in hushed, anxious murmurs.

Eliza's empathy extended toward those ensnared in defeat's harsh grasp. War, with its impartial toll on victor and vanquished, had bestowed upon her an insight beyond her years. She recognized that the Patriots' celebrations, though warranted, represented only a fraction of the human narrative playing out before her eyes.

Eliza navigated the dense crowd with a sense of urgency, her eyes soon finding the familiar red of Michael's uniform amidst the sea of somber faces. He was a beacon of the past, a friend of hers and Thomas, and a reminder of times before the fissures of war had torn their world asunder. As Eliza and Michael drew closer to the field where the fate of empires would be sealed, she leaned in and asked, "Where's your illustrious general?" Her voice was a mix of curiosity and concern as she searched the line of British troops for their leader.

Michael's gaze met hers, laden with an understanding born of shared history and the bitter taste of defeat. "Cornwallis could not be here," he revealed, the words falling like a heavy shroud over his shoulders. "He's holed up, feigning sickness. O'Hara has been cast to shoulder the yoke of surrender."

Together, they arrived at the surrender field, an austere plain that seemed to stretch endlessly under the gray sky. In its midst, a lone wooden table stood, its surface laid bare save for the peace documents, which were nothing less than the quill strokes of history. The perimeter of the field was ringed with a silent cadre of American and French soldiers, their expressions carved from the solemnity of the occasion.

Michael pointed toward the British deputy, his hand drawing a silent arc through the air as Brigadier General O'Hara stepped forward with Cornwallis's sword, extending it toward Rochambeau. But with a deferential nod, the French commander gestured to Washington. "See, the honor falls to him," Michael whispered.

Yet Washington, a stately figure of quiet strength, refused the gesture with a dignity that held the field in rapt silence. "He declines." Michael's voice softly commented on the tableau unfolding before them. "Instead, he beckons General Lincoln—there is a circle closing from the Patriot's devastating defeat at Charles Town."

The exchange of the sword was not made with pomp or grandeur but with a poignant simplicity that belied the enormity of its significance. As the British laid down their arms, the act sent ripples through the ranks, a choreography of surrender that resonated with the quiet dignity of men making peace with their fate.

Eliza knew she would always remember the scene: the table, solitary and unassuming; the field, a canvas of closure; and the soldiers, now architects of a future built upon the foundations of reconciliation and hope.

With the ceremony complete, the British soldiers faced their uncertain future as prisoners of war. Officers, granted parole, wore their freedom tentatively while the rank and file were corralled into makeshift camps. The fate of each man was as yet unwritten, mirroring the fragile infancy of the nation they had fought against.

As Eliza watched the regimented retreat of the British forces, a growing curiosity about Cornwallis's whereabouts tugged at her. With the surreptitious ease of a shadow, she withdrew from the crowd and wove her way back toward the town, her steps quick and quiet against the drum's solemn echo. The battlefield lay still, and she moved through it like a ghost, unnoticed amidst the chaos of defeat and victory.

Reaching the British headquarters, a somber edifice now housing the remnants of a once formidable force, Eliza slipped inside. No longer echoing with orders and strategy, the dim hallways whispered the quiet resignation of an empire's waning. Guided by a mixture of intuition and a keen ear for the hushed tones of urgency, she navigated the now familiar maze of rooms until she came upon Cornwallis's chamber.

The slightly ajar door afforded Eliza a narrow view of the room within, the air thick with impending departure. There, amidst the retreat, stood General Cornwallis, his figure casting a long shadow in the candlelit chamber. His movements were swift yet precise as he navigated through the chaos of maps, documents, and personal effects scattered about. His face, usually an unreadable mask of command, now showed a sense of urgency that bordered on desperation.

Hidden in the shadows, Eliza watched intently as Cornwallis paused before an open, wooden chest. His steady and deliberate hands reached inside and extracted an item wrapped in a piece of dark cloth. The general unwrapped the object with an almost palpable reverence, revealing a tome of considerable age. Its leather-bound cover was etched with symbols that shimmered in the flickering light, symbols that spoke of ancient knowledge and power.

With a careful glance over his shoulder, as if sensing the presence of unseen eyes, Cornwallis placed the book into his satchel. Whether this was the elusive Solum Codex or merely a clever ruse designed to mislead was unclear. Eliza considered that Thomas and the Hessian might have been entrusted with the real artifact, and what was before her eyes now was a decoy. Yet, as Eliza observed the general's actions, her instincts whispered that this was the actual Codex. The care with which he handled the book, the urgency of his movements—all pointed to the significance of the volume now concealed within his satchel.

Eliza's heart quickened. A clandestine network of Colonial spies and scholars had entrusted her with the mission of retrieving the Codex, or at least ensuring it did not fall into the hands of those who would use its power for tyranny.

As Cornwallis turned his attention back to the room, issuing orders to his aides with a voice that brooked no argument, Eliza knew she had to act fast. With the British forces in retreat and the American rebels closing in, the chaos of war provided the perfect cover for her mission. Yet, the risks were immense. Being caught could mean not only her death but also the loss of a chance to secure a potential advantage for the cause of liberty.

Eliza retreated from her vantage point, her mind racing with plans and possibilities. She needed to devise a strategy to intercept Cornwallis before he could transport the Codex to safety. What she did next could alter the war's fate, perhaps the country's future.

She watched as the general, stripped of his authority and command, was reduced to mere flesh and blood, ensnared by the unraveling threads of his own making. The vulnerability of his hurried concealment stripped away the facade of the soldier, revealing a raw, human core.

Eliza withdrew as silently as she had arrived. The image of Cornwallis—a man defeated and bent on preservation—seared into her memory. The weight of the Codex's future, intertwined with the destinies of men and nations, hung heavy in the air as she retraced her steps, leaving behind the dim corridors for the uncertain light of a new era dawning outside.

Eliza emerged from the gloom of the British headquarters into the fresh air of a world on the cusp of change. Her mind pieced together the fragments of a puzzle that now seemed to hinge upon the decisions of one weary general. James, steadfast in his duty, was pursuing Thomas and the Hessian, convinced they held the key—the Solum Codex. Yet, in the quiet of her own contemplation, Eliza's instinct screamed a different truth: the real Codex was still within Cornwallis's grasp, and he was being granted safe passage to New York.

With the conviction of her newfound knowledge, she had to act. The implications of the Codex remaining in Cornwallis's hands were too great, its secrets too powerful to be whisked away under the guise of an honorable defeat. Her resolve hardened; she must reach General

Washington. It was a race against the very currents of history, a chance to intercept a narrative that could define the future of a nation.

Eliza hastened her pace, weaving through the scattered celebrations and somber reflections that filled the streets of Yorktown. Her message was crucial, and time was the merciless gatekeeper she needed to outpace. With each step, she moved toward not just Washington, but toward a confrontation with fate itself.

CHAPTER TWENTY-SIX
JERSEY DECOY

As the evening's embrace spread across the Jersey woods, James wove silently between the trees, a shadow among deeper shadows. He advanced with intentional quiet, as stealth was paramount. His targets were clear: Thomas, a man whose heart had once been tightly knotted with Eliza's, now seemingly a turncoat twice over. He had cast aside his Loyalist ties, citing allegiance to the Patriot cause—a shift James suspected was as strategic as it was sincere, sensing that Thomas foresaw the enemy's loss and sought to align himself with the emerging victors. The second motivation, James discerned, was more personal: Thomas yearned for reconciliation with Eliza, a woman whose affections James himself now coveted.

Therefore, Thomas's declarations of loyalty were mired in ambiguity; to James, they represented a dual gambit to secure his future, in love and war. From what he was told, Thomas had once pledged his heart to Eliza; their passion ignited briefly like a match's flare before being extinguished by ideological divides. Now, as the war's tides ebbed and flowed, it was not hard to realize his desire to reforge old bonds in the fire of revolution, to heal old wounds, and to carve a place for himself in a new, uncertain world.

With the nighttime serving as his cloak, James moved toward the location his shared intelligence had alluded to—a decoy camp of the Continental Army's making. He had heard plans of the ploy; a grand deception played on the British, a staged battleground meant to misdirect and mislead. As the outline of tents began to form against the moonlit sky, the truth of these tales materialized before him.

Drawing closer to the supposed campsite, James could see the intricacies of the ruse. The Continental Army had devised an elaborate façade that was shaped like a military encampment poised for battle. Rows of tents stood empty yet gave the convincing appearance of housing an army in wait. Smoldering fires attended by a few hidden Patriots suggested a legion's worth of soldiers going about their evening routines, with the glow of flames dancing like a bustling military life.

Among the deserted quarters were all the makings of war: idle muskets propped against trees, cookpots suspended over fires brewing phantom meals, and patriotic banners catching the soft whispers of the wind. The camp bore the marks of readiness, the artifice of activity.

The illusion was ingeniously crafted, realistic enough to deceive any distant onlooker. Canvas backdrops and strategically driven wagons masked the absence of soldiers and gave the illusion of a camp teeming with Patriots. Even the ambient sounds had been cunningly mimicked— crafted to resonate through the woodland and emulate the fervent pace of an army preparing to strike.

This spectacle of deception was a bold proclamation of an assault on New York, a theatrical ploy so convincingly mounted it was destined to mislead the British into an ill-advised course. Amid this scenario of guile and misdirection, James had located Thomas and Wilhelm. The ruse of warfare around him provided the perfect setting for his covert affairs—a personal confrontation masked by the greater stratagem at play.

Hidden within the brush, James's eyes flickered with the flames of the campfire, studying the men he considered adversaries. Thomas spoke in hushed tones, passing a worn satchel back to Wilhelm with the care of one handling a newborn. It was the very satchel James had seen in the chaotic retreat of Yorktown, the one he was certain contained the Codex.

But could he trust Thomas? The man was a cipher, wrapped in a mystery, cloaked in revolution. James needed the Codex, and his patience for games and trickery had worn as thin as the waning crescent moon overhead. The decision crystallized in his mind like frost upon the autumn leaves: he would claim the prize tonight.

James measured his breaths, letting the cool air of the evening temper his resolve as he crept closer to the campfire's edge. The Hessian's silhouette was a stark line against the low-burning flames, an outline of a warrior at rest but never truly at ease. James knew the kind of man Wilhelm was, a soldier molded by the rigor of relentless combat.

To best such a man would require not just brute force but cunning and timing more precise than the workings of a fine watch.

He positioned himself with care, his eyes fixed on Wilhelm, watching for any sign of vulnerability. Then, with the silence of an owl's flight, he advanced, a ghostly figure poised to take what was lost. As he closed the distance, James recalled the countless drills, the silent count to three, the feint to the left that would draw the Hessian's gaze just a fraction—but a fraction was a chasm in the dance of death.

Veiled by the night's embrace, James closed in on the enemy encampment with predatory silence, his every step a calculated whisper against the earth. The campfire's glow, a beacon of deception to those it meant to deceive, now guided his approach to Wilhelm and Thomas. The air was tense with the electricity of unspoken thoughts, the crackling of the fire a subtle soundtrack to the unfolding drama.

As the silhouettes of the two men came into focus, James could see Wilhelm's broad back, an unyielding fortress, and Thomas, whose face was turned away. With a surge of adrenaline fueling his resolve, James sprang forward, his dagger poised to strike. The assault was meant to be a specter's touch—there and then gone—but Wilhelm, the Hessian, was a veteran of shadows and strife.

The seasoned soldier pivoted with a dancer's grace; his instincts sharpened on the whetstone of war. His hand flew to his own blade, drawing it with a swift, practiced motion that belied the serenity of the evening.

"Wilhelm!" Thomas's voice cut through the night, a blend of surprise and horror as he turned to witness the struggle. "What in God's name?" His words were drowned by the clash of steel, the ring of metal biting metal, the low grunts of effort and survival. The seasoned warrior pressed his advantage, forcing James back with a brutal series of strikes, a battlefield's ruthless poetry.

James's foot snagged on an unseen root, sending a spike of panic through him as he stumbled. Wilhelm, ever the predator, sensed his prey's momentary weakness and pounced, the cold kiss of his blade threatening James's exposed neck. James's thoughts careened—of Eliza, the Codex, the many turns of fate that had led him here. There was no time for a warning, no moment for a plea.

Then, a shot cleaved through the night, abrupt and deafening. Wilhelm's eyes widened, not with aggression but with the stark surprise of betrayed. The Hessian's grasp faltered, and he staggered back, his final chapter written in the bloom of red that marred his coat. Blood— not his own—spattered across James's face, a hot, visceral shock.

James remained frozen, the echo of the gunshot rolling through the woods. Thomas lowered his smoking pistol, his face a stark mask of resolve. No words of warning had come, only the definitive act of a man deciding their shared fate with the squeeze of a trigger. After a moment, James's gaze locked with Thomas's, a tumult of realizations passing between them. His life, once held on the knife's edge, had been saved by the very man he had doubted. Wilhelm's figure lay like a great oak felled by a woodsman's axe. Thomas, gun in hand, looked first to Wilhelm, his expression unreadable, then to James. "Are you hurt?"

A wave of relief washed over James. "I … I am fine," he replied, still reeling from the brush with death.

Thomas holstered his weapon and approached with careful steps. "What in the heavens led you here? I did not expect your shadow to follow us from Yorktown," he admitted, a hint of astonishment threading his words.

The stillness of the night enveloped them once more as the echo of the gunshot dissipated into the depths of the forest. Wilhelm's lifeless body lay heavy on the ground, a stark reminder of the night's deadly events. As James caught Thomas's gaze, the weight of what had transpired passed silently between them. Clutching his wounded arm, James managed a strained whisper, "We must move him before we are found." His voice bore the mark of both urgency and pain, urging quick action despite his injury.

Without a word, Thomas nodded, and together, they hefted the Hessian's body into the underbrush, cloaking it with shadows and leaves. The urgency of the task bound them, two former adversaries now allied in concealing the evidence of their encounter. Once done, they returned to the satchel. The royal seal of the crown, stamped into wax on the Codex's wrappings, glared at them in the firelight—a bold declaration of the document's significance. Breaking it was both an act of defiance and a commitment to a path from which there could be no return.

Thomas and James looked at each other long and tensely, aware that their next steps would irrevocably alter their lives. They could not risk revealing the Codex in the open, with dawn approaching and the chance of enemy patrols. "We must find shelter," Thomas said, his voice low but urgent.

"Somewhere safe to confirm what we have," James agreed, and they gathered their few belongings and the precious satchel, moving like wraiths through the trees.

CHAPTER TWENTY-SEVEN
ELIZA MEETS THE GENERAL

Eliza quickened her pace as she neared the command post of General George Washington, the Commander-in-Chief of the Continental Army. Each step through the Virginia autumn brought her closer to the heart of revolutionary fervor, where victory was etching itself into history amid a blend of American exultation and British silence.

She maneuvered through the clusters of soldiers, pulling down her bonnet to shield her face. There, amid the triumphant chaos, stood an expansive tent that pulsed with the newfound heartbeat of a nation. Eliza's hurried steps carried her forward, but a stern-faced sentinel blocked her advance. "It is imperative I speak with General Washington at once," she demanded, the urgency clear in her voice, though her palms sweated with anxiety.

The guard, unyielding, scarcely glanced her way. "General Washington is engaged with matters of the surrender. He shall not be disturbed," he stated flatly, his hand raised in a halting gesture.

But Eliza, fueled by desperation, would not be so easily dismissed. "Sir, this concerns the security of the very cause we have bled for—the Solum Codex is at stake," she pressed, her voice rising in a crescendo of conviction.

At the mention of the Codex, a flicker of alarm crossed the sentinel's features, eyes darting with sudden concern. Hardly had a second passed when an officer, drawn by the commotion, approached rapidly, his face etched with urgency. "Enough of this talk," he barked sharply, casting a wary look. "Move along, miss. These are delicate matters not meant for idle chatter."

"Please, sir, this is a matter of the utmost importance." Eliza's insistence caused a flicker of hesitation in the sentinel's gaze.

"Ma'am, all concerns will be addressed in due course—"

"No, you do not understand. I have seen it with my own eyes. General Cornwallis … he has the Solum Codex. If he is allowed to escape, we may never recover it." Her plea hung between them, desperate and raw. From inside the tent, the clamor of strategizing voices, the rustle of maps, and the clinking of weaponry against the tabletops leaked into the cool air. Eliza's words managed to cut through the din, reaching the ears of an aide who peered out from the tent's fold.

"Admit her," resonated an authoritative tone from within the canvas walls.

As Eliza stepped through the tent's opening, the cool interior starkly contrasted with the midday sun. She found herself gazing upon the man who led her fellow compatriots to victory. General Washington stood tall, his presence a stoic pillar amidst the sea of military fervor. His blue and buff uniform spoke of his rank with simple but commanding elegance; his eyes, the color of the Virginia sky, met hers with a potent mix of curiosity and stern appraisal.

In the periphery of this historic tableau were three officers, each bearing the mark of service and the burden of decisions that had shaped the battlefield. To Washington's right stood a man with a scar trailing his cheek, a testament to the close calls of war. His gaze upon Eliza was narrow and calculating, as though he were sizing up an opponent rather than a compatriot.

Beside him was a younger officer, his uniform pristine, as if the war had scarcely grazed him. Yet, his eyes were jaded and suspicious and fixed on Eliza as if she could unravel the tapestry of their hard-fought gains.

The third, leaning on a makeshift desk, was a grizzled veteran whose medals clinked softly as he shifted to observe the newcomer. His look was one of wary consideration, weighing her sudden appearance against the backdrop of war's constant surprises.

Collectively, their stares formed an almost tangible barrier of distrust that Eliza now had to penetrate with nothing but the truth she carried. "General," Eliza began, her voice steadier than she felt. "Please pardon this abrupt interruption. I am Eliza Sinclair, of Yorktown. The Solum Codex—its knowledge foundational to our republic's very philosophy—has been stolen. Cornwallis has it and plans to carry it from Yorktown."

The general's brow furrowed, the lines on his face deepening like the grooves of an ancient oak, "The Solum Codex," he mused. "A compendium of principles that could shape the bedrock of nations."

Eliza nodded earnestly, her words tumbling in a rush. "Yes, General, and I witnessed—"

But Washington raised a hand, stilling the room. "Your words weigh heavily, miss," he acknowledged. "Yet our focus must remain. The terms of surrender grant safe passage to officers and their possessions. Even if the Codex is among them, retrieving it is not within our scope."

"But the Codex was taken from the Patriots, not a personal belonging of theirs by right. It belongs to the very soul of our burgeoning nation," Eliza implored.

Washington met her gaze with the steadiness of one who had faced tempests without flinching. "I understand the gravity of what you bring before me," he acknowledged, "but we must now focus on securing the present rather than reclaiming what has slipped from our grasp."

Eliza's disbelief at Washington's stance was palpable. His attention had already shifted, his strategist's mind weaving through the labyrinth of nation-building.

"Tell me," Washington asked, his attention returning. "How does someone like you come to know of such a clandestine matter?"

Drawing a deep breath, Eliza recounted her connection to James Ardmore and his noble quest for the Codex. She spoke of the fateful night when Harrison Johnson, having stumbled into her establishment, divulged the document's perilous journey to James Ardmore. Her voice broke, recounting Harrison's demise as he struggled to wrest the Codex from Cornwallis's grip.

A shadow of surprise crossed Washington's features upon hearing James Ardmore's name, a momentary softening in the firm lines of his face. "Ardmore? His reputation precedes him," he acknowledged. "Is he engaged in this matter nearby?"

Eliza's reply came with a somber shake of her head. "He is not, General," she stated. "James has followed the trail of two men suspected of possessing the Codex to New York."

Washington's voice carried a note of skepticism. "But you previously claimed Cornwallis held the Codex."

Eliza stood resolute, though her voice betrayed her inner turmoil. "The certainty of its whereabouts eludes us, sir," she confessed, "but I believe Cornwallis harbors it still as a final grasp at control."

Washington pondered her conviction, his eyes narrowing thoughtfully. "Miss Sinclair," he began, "the scenario you propose— that Cornwallis does not possess the Codex—might indeed carry significant implications, perhaps even more so than if he retained it."

"But what if he does have it? We must be sure," Eliza insisted.

The tent grew silent as they all turned to consider the broader impact of Eliza's proclamation. "Stay vigilant and inform us of any new developments," Washington commanded, his attention shifting back to the urgent matters sprawled before him on strategic maps and documents.

With a sigh, she took her leave. Exiting the tent, she stepped from the bustle of the siege headquarters, her presence swiftly fading. As she made her way through the throngs of celebratory soldiers and down to the town, her thoughts turned to the path that lay ahead. With the Codex's fate uncertain and her means to pursue it exhausted, Eliza found herself alone, with nothing but the relentless pursuit of a truth that seemed just beyond reach.

CHAPTER TWENTY-EIGHT
THE REVEAL

In the shadowy calm before dawn, Thomas and James sought solace in the hollow of an age-worn oak. As the first whisper of light teased the edge of night, they faced their immediate concern—that the body of the Hessian would remain concealed within the forest's embrace.

The gravity of their actions was not lost on them; the slain soldier's discovery would unleash a storm of retribution.

They turned their attention to the sealed package that lay ominously between them. This was the catalyst of their ordeal, the harbinger of both their fates. Taking a deep, steadying breath, they moved to break the seal. The wax's sharp snap sounded like the world fracturing under the weight of their decision. Peeling back the layers of cloth that swathed the contents, they looked for the Solum Codex, a document rumored to hold power enough to shift the tides of empires.

As the final cloth layer parted, what lay beneath was the unmistakable cross of a common Church of England Bible. Quickly, James pulled back the cover and thumbed through the gilded-edged pages. In that muted light, it dawned on them—Cornwallis had anticipated a spy like James, especially after two attempts to plunder the tome from his office. This was merely an ordinary Bible and a ploy set by a general.

Thomas murmured, "It's a decoy," his disappointment clear in his tone.

James closed the book with a weary sigh. "That means the real Codex remains in Yorktown, under Cornwallis's watchful eye." The sting of their fruitless quest settled upon them like the dust from the Bible's pages.

Their gazes met; the high-stakes game of espionage had turned, leaving them empty-handed. The wisdom they had sought in the Codex remained locked away. With the morning light creeping upon them, they prepared to venture back to Yorktown, carrying with them the burden of their unfulfilled mission and the lingering question of what move Cornwallis would make next.

*

As their horses' hooves drummed a steady tattoo on the road back to Yorktown, Thomas found his thoughts drifting to the days before the war. "It was different then," he mused aloud in response to James's inquiry. "Life was simpler, happier. Eliza and I … we were going to marry," he said with a reminiscent smile. "We imagined a future where every day ended with the warmth of the Sinclair Tavern's hearth and the company of our friends."

James cast a sidelong glance at Thomas, sensing the undercurrent of regret. "But you chose the Crown over her," he observed, his voice edged with a note of accusation.

Thomas winced as if the words were a physical blow. "Yes," he admitted, his voice tinged with sorrow. "I chose order over love, allegiance over happiness. I now realize my mistake."

James's grip tightened on the reins, his jaw set. "And now you think you can just return and claim her? After all this time, after choosing the Crown over her heart?"

Thomas turned to him, a desperate plea in his eyes. "It is never too late for redemption. I hope to reclaim her heart and show her my love is true."

James let out a harsh laugh. "Redemption? Do you think you can undo years of betrayal? Eliza is her own woman, and she has chosen a cause greater than any crown—freedom. And she has chosen me."

Before Thomas could reply, the sudden crack of a twig underfoot cut through their heated exchange. The two men stiffened, and the horses snorted, sensing danger. From the thickening shadows of the dusk, figures emerged, their intentions clear. "Stand and deliver!" came the harsh command.

In an instant, personal grievances gave way to a more pressing battle for survival. Swords were drawn in swift, fluid motions, reflecting the scant light as Thomas and James prepared to defend themselves against the bandits. Their conversation was silenced as the peaceful path transformed into an arena of conflict. The demand for coin or life hung in the air, a foul promise from the silhouettes that emerged with predatory ease. These men, perhaps once Colonial soldiers or Loyalists, were reduced to the desperation of outlaws.

Thomas and James reacted with the cold clarity of warriors. As they dismounted, their movements were fluid—a choreography refined by the urgency of survival. "We have naught for thieves but steel," Thomas pronounced, his stance as unyielding as the oaks surrounding them.

The woods were suddenly alight with swords drawn and glinting like the shards of a shattered mirror in the dim light.

The woods transformed into a frenetic display of clashing swords, their blades flickering like broken shards of mirror in the dimming light. Compelled to defend himself with his weaker left arm, James faced the combat at a stark disadvantage. Yet, with resilient determination, he met the initial onslaught; his left-handed parry diverted a deadly thrust aimed directly at his heart. Employing a skillful maneuver learned from numerous battles, he executed a swift riposte, catching his larger opponent off guard and forcing him to stagger back, struggling to regain his footing.

Beside him, Thomas was an avatar of retribution, his sword cutting a path through the air with lethal grace. One bandit lunged, his knife a glint of death, but Thomas's blade was quicker, sweeping aside the threat and biting deep into the man's side. The bandit fell with a choked scream, his lifeblood seeping into the soil.

The air was filled with the sounds of steel, harsh breaths, and cries of the wounded. James spun, his sword a blur, deflecting a vicious slash and responding with a calculated thrust that sent another adversary reeling, his knife clattering to the ground abandoned.

A young and reckless bandit made for Thomas with wild swings, but the older man's experience showed. With a parry and a twist, Thomas turned the youth's momentum against him, sending him tumbling to the earth, disarmed and dazed.

Yet, as is the way of battle, a knife-wielding bandit, his movements a desperate flurry, found a chink in Thomas's armor. The blade sliced through cloth and skin, drawing a sharp gasp from Thomas as he faltered, pain flaring hot and bright against his ribs.

Seeing his companion wounded, James unleashed a ferocious assault, his sword a vengeful force that none could withstand. The bandits, their confidence shattered, retreated into the dark embrace of the woods, leaving behind their intentions and the blood they had spilled.

Thomas, leaning heavily on his sword, grimaced against the pain. "I must tend to this," he said through clenched teeth. James nodded, supporting Thomas as they made for their horses. "Williamsburg," Thomas gasped. "My family can aid us."

As evening draped the world in its shadowed cloak, Thomas and James bore the scars of the day's skirmish, a testament to their shared resolve in the face of danger, yet within each beat of their hearts pulsed the unspoken tension of a battle yet to come—for Eliza's heart.

Their camaraderie, forged in the heat of combat, was complex, laced with the intricacies of love and regret. As they steered their horses toward Williamsburg, the promise of a sanctuary was tainted by the knowledge that the road would lead them to confront not only the repercussions of war, but also the tender and tumultuous battleground of the heart.

CHAPTER TWENTY-NINE
ELIZA'S DILEMMA

Eliza stood alone, the charred remains of the Sinclair Tavern lying before her. Her entire life had been entwined in this place, every broken beam a chapter now ended. As the reality of her loss settled in, she pondered the uncertain future with James or Thomas and what might yet be.

Eliza's encounter with James, a man embroiled in the heart of the revolution's climax at Yorktown, had been brief yet intense. A bond had formed swiftly between them, a potent connection stretching beyond the mere weeks they had known each other. Their whirlwind romance blossomed amid the urgency of war, with James now charged with a new mission—recapturing the stolen Solum Codex. Eliza felt an inexplicable familiarity, a sense of love that seemed to echo through time, a sentiment that Agatha's tarot reading had mysteriously suggested was rooted in a shared past life.

James was now a shadow in the war's twilight, his spy's cloak trailing the elusive Thomas. And Thomas—he had once stood for all she believed in before his loyalty to the Crown had betrayed her and their shared dreams. Would he return to this new world taking shape, or had his path diverged too far from hers?

With no hearth or home to call her own, Eliza sought Agatha's counsel again. Perhaps she could discern the silhouettes of her romantic destiny in the wisdom of the tarot cards. Should she hold hope for James, with his silent understanding, or Thomas, whose betrayal still stung with the freshness of an open wound?

The embers of twilight flickered as Eliza stepped across the threshold of Agatha's abode, a sanctuary of arcane knowledge and whispered histories. Agatha, a figure woven into the fabric of Eliza's earliest memories, greeted her as she had countless times before—with the warmth of a guardian whose promise had been a constant through the years.

"Eliza, my child," Agatha murmured, her voice a balm to the sting of loss, "this door, as it was in your dear mother's time, remains ever open to you." The walls, lined with shelves of ancient tomes and the soft glow of candles, bore witness to the bond formed in days past when Eliza's mother and Agatha had shared secrets and laughter within these walls.

Agatha's home seemed to sigh with the weight of their reunion. The woven, colorful carpets on the walls and trinkets were infused with the essence of a friendship that transcended time and the turmoil that raged beyond the stone enclosure. Here, amid the flickering shadows, Eliza was no longer a weary fugitive but rather a cherished soul returned to the hearth of her youth.

In the comfort of Agatha's home, the walls echoed with the soft cadence of two friends conversing through the silence of understanding. Eliza's voice was a mere whisper as she unfolded the layers of her heart to Agatha, revealing the depth of her turmoil.

Tears welled in Eliza's eyes, a storm of sorrow and love that refused to fall as she gazed upon the flickering tarot spread before her. "James," she whispered, the name a tremor of hope in the quiet room. "The cards declare him my destiny, Agatha. A soulmate from past lives. Can the stars truly ordain such a thing?" Her voice was a fractured whisper, the desperation clear.

Agatha reached across the table, her fingers grazing Eliza's trembling hands. "My dear, while the stars align, they do not bind," she said, her voice steady yet soft. "James has the strength of silent mountains and the eternal rivers' steadfastness. Yet even the stars can only suggest, not compel."

"And Thomas?" Eliza's voice cracked like a heart under strain as she uttered the name. "He returns to us draped in the colors of our cause, but can I trust this change? Is it a genuine shift of soul or merely another move of convenience?"

Agatha's eyes held sorrow and understanding, lit by the candle's dance. "The heart's melodies can haunt us longer than the mind's logic, Eliza. Thomas stirs a symphony of memories within you, yet can an unfinished symphony find resolution after such dissonance?"

Eliza bowed her head, the unshed tears now cascading in a silent waterfall of release. "But how do I choose? How does one weigh the soul against the heart? Tell me, what do the cards say?"

"The cards"—Agatha sighed, gathering them in her aged hands—"speak of energies and forces, potentials and crossroads. They offer insight, not decisions, for the heart's journey from darkness to light must be undertaken alone. They reveal souls intertwined, yes, but the heart … oh, the heart is the only compass that can navigate its own seas."

Eliza's breath hitched as her internal maelstrom quieted to a poignant stillness. The cards imparted their secrets, but she, Eliza, must interpret their enigmas. As the night's shadows stretched and yielded to the approach of dawn, a new determination began to crystallize within her. "You're saying I must choose the path myself," she stated more than asked.

"Exactly so," Agatha affirmed, her gaze both tender and fierce. "Your destiny is not a prize to be captured by these men; it is a kingdom to be ruled by you, and you alone."

Eliza rose, the first light of dawn casting a celestial glow upon her face. She turned to Agatha, and their embrace was an unspoken pact of sisterhood and solidarity. Stepping across the threshold, Eliza faced the newborn day not as a woman torn between two loves but as a sovereign of her fate. The past with Thomas, the bond with James, and the enigma of the Solum Codex were all chapters in her saga, but she knew now that she held the pen. And with the dawn's golden light as her witness,

she resolved to write her story with the courage of a heart that had found
its own way.

CHAPTER THIRTY
REUNION

James sifted through the remnants with a contemplative air as the dust settled on the scarred desks and discarded emblems of war in Cornwallis's abandoned offices. His fingers grazed over maps marked with the strategies of battles long concluded, each a testament to the ebb and flow of a bygone struggle. James's mind wandered, retracing the path that brought him back to the scarred battlegrounds of Yorktown. His journey with Thomas wove through the tapestry of tumultuous times, carrying them to Williamsburg for the mending of Thomas's ghastly wound. There, James observed the dynamics amidst the echoes of their familial battles. His mother, a beacon of nurturing resolve, swiftly tended to her son's gash without a whisper of hesitation, her hands deft in the arts of sewing and healing. Yet, the air turned heavy with tension as Thomas's father eyed his turncoat son with suspicion. He saw him as a renegade, a traitor, labels that hung in the silence between them.

James attempted to explain to his father about his son's awakening to the Colonial cause. But years of disappointment and betrayal are not swiftly healed. Though with earnest words, James wove the tale of Thomas's valor, of a moment suspended between life and death where their son had been his shield against the encroaching shadows.

In the dim light of the hearth, the room brimmed with the heaviness of a storm about to break. Thomas's father stood as if carved from the same stoic oak that lined the Williamsburg roads; his gaze locked onto his son with an intensity that spoke of a deep and personal betrayal. In this charged silence, James, weary from travel and the weight of the story he carried, began to unravel the threads of Thomas's valor.

"Mr. Reddington," James began, his voice a mere whisper that cut through the tension. "I stand before you not just as a fellow Patriot, but as a living testament to your son's courage."

Thomas's father, his brow knitted with years of stern discipline, shifted his gaze toward James. "Courage?" he echoed, skepticism lacing his tone. "Or treason, sir?"

"It was courage," James insisted, stepping forward into the light, the flickering flames casting dancing shadows across his earnest face. "For in the heat of battle, when a Hessian's blade sought my heart, it was Thomas who barred its deadly kiss."

Thomas's mother, a silent sentinel by the hearth, clutched her hands tightly, knuckles white as the linen she had used to bind her son's wound.

"Your son," James continued, "threw himself upon the blade, fearless of the harm he might suffer, all to save a life—my life."

A pained silence followed, one that stretched and twisted, filling the room with the echo of that fateful encounter. James reached within the folds of his coat, his fingers finding the crumpled, bloodstained letter that Thomas had penned—a missive of repentance meant for the father he had defied.

With a hand that trembled not from fear but from the gravity of the moment, James extended the letter. "Before our arrival, afraid he might pass on, Thomas wrote this … for you. His words. His change of heart."

Thomas's father took the letter, the paper crackling under the strain of his unreadable expression. Eyes moving across the script, a storm of emotions played upon his features—disbelief, pain, and slowly, the softening edges of understanding.

"My son," he whispered, the word a surrender to the truth before him. "You have become more than I."

Thomas, who had stood as a statue might, flinching neither at reproach nor praise, now moved toward his father. "I have been many things," he said, his voice barely above a murmur. "But it took facing death to truly understand life—to understand you, Father."

In the span of a heartbeat, the distance between father and son shrank, bridged by shared revelations and unspoken forgiveness. Embraced in the warmth of the hearth and of newfound understanding, they stood together, not as adversaries but as kin, reconciled.

Thus, within that hallowed chamber of heart and home, the fabric of their relationships was indeed stitched anew. Theirs was not just a tale of loyalty and love but also a poignant reminder of the complex emotions that bind us in our shared humanity, especially as they journeyed through the very essence of revolution.

As James lost himself in the memory of Thomas's familial healing, he failed to notice the silhouette that now framed the doorway. It was Thomas, unnoticed until the creak of a floorboard announced him.

They spoke of Cornwallis's mysterious retreat and the Codex's enigmatic disappearance—a subject that seemed to pull at the corners of the room with intrigue. Thomas's voice reflected on the irony of their current station: "To think, this is the very chamber where once I felt so diminished before the general's might."

James nodded, offering a polite smile.

Thomas's gaze drifted, a far-off look as if he could see the shadows of the past still lingering in the corners. "James, have you sought Eliza's counsel since our return to Yorktown?"

The question hung in the air like a challenge, pulling at James's resolve. "No, I have not," he replied, the weight of his omission heavy in his heart. "But I will." His gaze hardened with determination and a silent promise.

Just as the familiar sting of their rivalry over Eliza's affection prickled anew, she manifested like an answer to an unspoken summons. It was as if the room itself had conjured her, their thoughts and tensions weaving a spell that could only be completed by her presence.

Her figure seemed to bring with it a breath of the gardens outside, her dress carrying the faint scent of blossoms and the freshness of the Yorktown morning. The atmosphere shifted palpably, the air charged with all the things unsaid and feelings unexpressed.

As she stepped into the room, the subtle competition between the two men was momentarily forgotten, overshadowed by the sheer force of her presence. For a heartbeat, they were united again, not as rivals, but as admirers of the grace and spirit that Eliza brought. And in that fleeting moment, they understood that regardless of where her heart ultimately lay, Eliza was the compass by which they both navigated this new and uncertain world.

"Eliza," James began, his voice carrying the warmth of a hundred unspoken conversations. "Your presence brings light to these weary walls."

Thomas stepped forward with an intensity that bordered on fervor. "We have felt the absence of your spirit keenly," he confessed, his gaze lingering just a moment too long, betraying the depth of his sentiment.

The air hummed with the energy of their declarations. Yet Eliza, the master of her own heart, met their ardor with a poise that spoke of her inner resolve. She acknowledged their affections with a grace that neither stoked nor quelled their hopes, her smile a gentle reminder of her enduring autonomy.

"Welcome back, my brave men," Eliza greeted them, her voice a soothing balm to the palpable tension. "Let us not be waylaid. Our mission beckons with urgency, and our unity is its cornerstone."

James, with a respectful bow of his head, acknowledged her words. "Indeed, Eliza, our focus must remain steadfast on the task at hand."

Thomas nodded in agreement, his eyes never straying from her form. "Your guidance remains our North Star, unwavering and true."

In the quiet room, tension still hung in the air, its edges barely contained as Eliza, with composed assurance, brought the focus back to their shared destiny. "Agatha the Seer has imparted to me a truth," she said, her eyes meeting each of theirs, tethering them to the gravity of her revelation. "The path to wisdom is seldom found in the destination but rather in the pilgrimage we undertake." The guiding light of their mission—to retrieve the enigmatic Codex—seemed to rekindle in their hearts with a vigor that surpassed personal longings.

Eliza paused, her silhouette a stark contrast against the twilight seeping through the window, her eyes alight with the forethought of their next endeavor. "But before we find ourselves entwined in the footsteps of Cornwallis, we should first make for Philadelphia," she proposed, her voice tinged with the resolve that so often steered their course. "It is time we unraveled the intentions of those who set us on this path."

Her suggestion settled over the room, a quiet call to action that seemed to align with the very destiny that tugged at their spirits. The journey ahead would not just be a physical trek to the halls of Congress but a venture into the depths of their purpose, a search for answers that the Codex alone could not satisfy.

With a shared nod, they acknowledged the wisdom in her words. And so, to Philadelphia, they would go, their hearts buoyed by the gravity of their charge, each step a stride into the annals of history that awaited their indelible mark.

CHAPTER THIRTY-ONE
PHILADELPHIA

The relentless clop of hooves against the compacted earth had become a familiar rhythm to Eliza, James, and Thomas as the spires of Philadelphia began to etch themselves against the horizon. Weary from the road but fueled by purpose, they absorbed the sight of the burgeoning city—the heart of revolutionary thought and fervor.

In the waning light of day, James broached the subject that had been simmering in his mind throughout the ten-day trek. With the city's outskirts welcoming them, he turned to Eliza and Thomas, a determined glint in his eye. "We should make haste to secure an audience with James Madison upon our arrival," he suggested, his voice carrying above the din of travel. "It was Madison, after all, who understood the stakes when he dispatched Harrison to enlist my services in Yorktown to recover the Codex."

Eliza, ever cautious, considered James's words, her mind weaving through the implications of such a meeting. With his characteristic resolve, Thomas nodded in agreement, Madison's name igniting a spark of anticipation.

Sensing the need to cement his proposal, James began his persuasive oration. "With the formation of governance as fragile as the pages of the Codex we seek, Madison is the one man whose counsel could illuminate our path forward," he said, the shadows of the approaching city playing across his earnest features.

Eliza and Thomas listened intently, their gaze fixed on James as he paced before them, his silhouette outlined against the fading light from his horse. "Madison's vision for our nascent nation is clear: he envisions not just a confederation but a unified republic. His writings are a beacon to those who would forge our future," James continued, his words painting a portrait of Madison as a linchpin in their quest. "If the Codex speaks to the order and liberty of a society," he posited, "then Madison is already laying the groundwork for such ideals. His wisdom is the key to unlocking the deeper truths that may lie hidden within our quest."

As the trio entered the heart of Philadelphia, the gravity of their mission settled upon them with renewed weight. James's impassioned argument lingered in the air, as did the prospect of meeting the man who could hold the answers they so desperately sought. "Beyond his intellect, Madison's connections to the other key thinkers and leaders render him indispensable," James concluded, his eyes meeting those of his companions. "His presence in the debates that shape Congress, and his understanding of the structure of our government, may provide us with the reason for recovering the Codex."

With Philadelphia's cobblestone streets now beneath them and the murmur of the city's evening life beginning to swell, the trio steered their horses toward the heart of enlightenment and intrigue, where

James Madison awaited—and perhaps with him, some enlightenment concerning their quest.

*

As they approached Madison's sprawling Philadelphia estate, the air buzzed with the tension of their arrival. The estate itself was a picture of Colonial elegance, its red brick facade standing proudly against the lush greenery of the surroundings. The trio made their way toward the stables, where they would likely find the man of the hour.

Madison was there, as expected, sleeves rolled up, tending to a spirited bay mare with the kind of attention that spoke of his love for these creatures. Hearing footsteps, he straightened up, turning to face the newcomers with an inquisitive look that softened into recognition upon seeing James.

"Ardmore!" Madison exclaimed, a genuine smile breaking across his face as he wiped his hands on a cloth. "And friends," he added, nodding at Eliza and Thomas with a polite curiosity.

James stepped forward, the urgency of their mission casting a shadow over the pleasantries. In the dimming light of the evening, with the bustle of the estate a soft murmur in the distance, James locked eyes with Madison, a silent plea etched in his gaze. "Sir, may I speak candidly?" James implored, his voice low. "Time is a luxury we do not possess." Madison's brows lifted in a mix of intrigue and apprehension. James stepped closer, a conspiratorial edge to his posture. "Eliza and Thomas"—he gestured to his companions with a respectful nod—"are as much a part of this as I am. They have proven themselves trustworthy and indispensable."

Madison's gaze shifted, appraising the two as if trying to read the pages of their past in their faces. Eliza met his scrutiny with a calm resolve, her eyes unflinching; Thomas stood with the quiet confidence of one who has faced down doubt and emerged the stronger for it.

"We have been through fire to get here, sir," James continued, his voice steady but laced with fervency. "The pieces of this puzzle have been falling into place with a haste that, I confess, has outstripped our understanding. The Codex—it's more than a mere historical artifact. Its relevance to the Constitution and everything we believe in is profound. And, sir, hopefully, with your insight, the full measure of its significance can finally be grasped."

Madison's expression softened, the initial resistance in his eyes giving way to the dawning realization of the sincerity and importance of their plea. He studied them for a long moment, weighing the risks against the palpable urgency that hung between them. At last, he nodded slowly. "I see the earnestness in your stance and the honesty in your eyes. I trust you have not chosen your confidants lightly." A wistful, almost imperceptible smile graced the edges of his lips. "Let us then retire to my study, where history is often in the making, and our present conversation may make history again."

With that, Madison signaled for them to follow, ushering them into his home. As they walked, James shared the essence of their journey.

How each clue unraveled led them closer to understanding the pivotal role the Codex played in the past and how it could shape the future. He spoke of the dangers they'd encountered and the revelations that had come to light.

Madison listened intently, nodding, his brow furrowed in concentration. The significance of the Codex to the drafting of the Constitution was not widely known, shrouded as it was in layers of secrecy and speculation. It was a subject Madison had pondered over many long hours, aware of the power such knowledge could wield.

Finally, James finished his recounting in the seclusion of Madison's private study, surrounded by books and papers that spoke of a dedication to the nation's founding principles.

Madison took a moment before responding, his gaze lost in the distance as if visualizing the magnitude of their discussion. "The Codex," he began slowly, "holds keys not just to the past but to the very ideals we sought to embed within the Constitution. Its significance goes beyond mere words; it embodies the essence of liberty, governance, the separation of church and state, and the balance of power. Understanding its contents could well mean grasping the foundational principles that could guide us in preserving the republic against unforeseen challenges many decades and perhaps centuries into the future."

He turned to face the trio, his eyes alight with a mixture of resolve and caution. "What you seek is not without risk, for within the Codex lies the knowledge that could either fortify or fracture the very foundations we've worked so hard to build."

Thomas leaned in. "What do you mean unforeseen challenges?"

Madison paused, the weight of history pressing upon his words. "Our new nation is a vessel navigating uncharted waters," he intoned gravely. "The principles within the Codex offer a chart by which to steer clear of tyranny's rocks and the whirlpools of anarchy. These are but ink and intention without wisdom to wield them." He locked eyes with each of them in turn. "The challenges I speak of are those born of complacency, of power's corrupting allure, threatening to ensnare our country's soul."

Thomas nodded, understanding dawning like the first light of daybreak. "Then we must secure the Codex," he declared, his voice resolute. "If its wisdom is the compass to maintain our course through the storms of the future, we cannot let it fall into hands that would use it to chart a course back to the shadows of oppression."

CHAPTER THIRTY-TWO
THOMAS JEFFERSON

As the long Philadelphia day waned into twilight, the study of James Madison's estate buzzed with palpable tension. The great Thomas Jefferson, a figure as commanding in thought as he was in stature, entered with an air of composed urgency, his gaze sweeping over James, Eliza, and Thomas. They had been assembled to plunge into the depths of the mysterious Solum Codex, a document rumored to hold profound insights into the shaping of nations.

Madison respectfully dipped his head and acknowledged his colleague: "Mr. Jefferson, your wisdom here is as indispensable as the Codex itself. We stand on the brink, our Constitution in hand, yet we venture into uncharted waters teeming with hidden treacheries."

Jefferson nodded, the lines on his face carving a map of his intellectual journeys. "Mr. Madison, you spoke of a grave subject," Jefferson intoned, the timbre of his voice seeming to give weight to the very air. "Shed light upon these shadows you fear may darken our fledgling republic."

Madison exhaled deeply, the air seemingly weighted with the fate of ages yet to come. "In crafting our great experiment," he began, his voice laden with a sobering gravity, "we've sought to chart a course for a future bright with promise. Yet the Codex intimates dilemmas not yet dreamt by our most astute minds. It warns of the rise of leaders not bound by the integrity that guides us—those who would seek not greatness for our republic but their own glory."

Jefferson's expression darkened, his concern palpable in the tightening of his gaze. "It is precisely this peril that stands at the heart of our endeavor," he acknowledged. "For while we lay the cornerstone of this democracy with clean hands and clear eyes, there may come those who do not share our commitment to the public weal. The allure of dominion, unchecked, has the power to transmute our most cherished institutions into mere facades."

Their discourse set the stage for a pivotal discussion that would delve into the intricate and vulnerable governance mechanisms and the wisdom hidden within the Codex.

Madison paced before the hearth, the firelight casting dynamic shadows on his face. "It is exactly this—our system relies upon the balance of power. But what if one branch overreaches? What if, for instance, religion, which has been the bane of European capitals, creeps insidiously into the governance of the people?" Silence fell, the crackling of the fire punctuating the gravity of his words.

Eliza shifted, her mind racing, while Thomas clasped his hands tightly, feeling the weight of history upon their shoulders. Ever the visionary, Jefferson spoke softly. "Our faith has guided us, yes, but it must not govern us. The union of church and state has birthed centuries of conflict across the ocean. We cannot—will not—allow such seeds to take root here."

Under the glow of candlelight, which flickered against the earnest faces gathered in Madison's study, the gravity of their mission pressed upon the room with an almost tangible weight. Ever the thinker, Madison pondered the implications of the Codex's disappearance. "This Codex could very well dictate the fate of our republic. Its loss to the hands of someone like Cornwallis could be catastrophic."

Thomas, who had known the yoke of Colonial rule and now embraced the cause of liberty with the zeal of a convert, sat upright. "We must reclaim this Codex. If it leads us to the shores of England itself, so be it," he declared, his hand clenched in resolve.

Jefferson nodded in agreement, his mind already charting the course of such an audacious pursuit. "To secure this Codex, we must be as cunning as we are resolute. Madison and I can ensure you have the necessary funds."

Eliza, her intelligence as keen as the edge of a blade, added, "We will need not only funds, but also letters of introduction. We will need allies, perhaps in France or Spain, who disdain the British enough to aid us."

Madison leaned in. "Cornwallis may think the ocean divides us from our goal, but he underestimates the reach of our new nation's determination. You will have the resources; you need only to find the opportunity." The air in the room seemed to hum with newfound purpose as plans were laid and the path forward, fraught with danger and uncertainty, began to be clear.

As the embers in the fireplace dimmed to a soft glow, the intensity of their conversation did not wane. James, Eliza, and Thomas leaned in closer, their faces alight with curiosity and the reflection of the dying flames. "Where," James asked, "did this Codex originate? What is the source of its profound insights?"

Madison hesitated, understanding the magnitude of what he was about to reveal. "The origins of the Codex," he began, "lie shrouded in the mists of a time far preceding the rise and fall of empires we have come to learn from history. It speaks of a place called Lemuria."

Eliza's brows knit together, a question forming. "Lemuria?" she echoed, the name a whisper of legends long forgotten.

Madison confirmed, "Yes, Lemuria is believed to be from a land of ancient lore, a continent lost to time, much like the Atlantis of which Plato spoke, submerged beneath the waves of a great ocean."

Thomas, his mind always ready to embrace the mysterious and the profound, prompted, "Please, tell us more of this land and its people."

"The Lemurians," Madison continued, his voice lowering to match the gravity of the tale, "were said to be beings of a spiritual nature, profoundly connected to the Earth and its elements. Their senses and abilities were unlike anything we know today—clairvoyant, ethereal, transcending the physical constraints we are subject to."

Eliza found herself captivated by the idea. "A society so advanced in spirit and intuition," she mused, "must have held knowledge of incredible depth."

Madison nodded. "Indeed, Lemuria was a utopia in the truest sense. It's been said that without a structured government or codified laws, its people lived in unparalleled harmony, guided by innate morality and ethics. They communicated without words, their minds linked in a collective consciousness that extended to the plants and animals around them."

James, ever the pragmatist, asked skeptically, "What was their downfall? A society so perfect could not simply vanish without cause."

"Their demise," Jefferson began, his voice laced with a somber timbre as he peered into the flickering shadows, "was as much a tragedy of external conquest as it was a testament to their ideals. They had something that threatened the world's power structures—true freedom."

Eliza leaned in, her curiosity piqued. "They were destroyed for their way of life?"

"Exactly," Madison interjected. "Powerful kings saw in Lemuria a risk to their realms. The very notion of a society without rulers, living in blissful anarchy, was antithetical to their dominion. Where there is power, there will always be those who hunger for it."

Jefferson added, with a fire in his eyes, "These monarchs could not allow the thought to spread that people might govern themselves by the nature of their own goodness." His fist clenched as he continued, "The unity of Lemuria was their shield, yet in the end, it became their doom. Armies marched not against a resistance but against a people at peace. Lemuria fell, scorched from memory, its wisdom nearly lost to the avarice of empires."

Madison's gaze fell to the worn map on the table, to an unknown place where Lemuria was once marked and now left blank. "Yet the essence of Lemuria—the spirit of that collective consciousness—survived. It lived on, hidden, protected by those who fled, those who believed in preserving their knowledge for a future they hoped would be ready for it."

Madison's voice was soft but carried the weight of history. "The roots of the Codex we seek," he began, "are as ancient as they are profound, tracing back to a land shrouded in legend—Lemuria."

Eliza whispered, "The Codex… is a remnant of Lemuria?"

"More than that," Madison replied. "It is the distilled essence of their society, holding the potential to illuminate our own path."

Jefferson leaned forward, his hands animated as he spoke. "Indeed, it came into the hands of the French, where it lay hidden, a treasure unknown, as their country teetered on the brink of revolution. Blinded by power, King Louis XVI would have seen it destroyed, fearing its capacity to inspire a new world order."

"So, it was Lafayette," Madison mused, "who recognized its value, who took the mantle to protect such a treasure."

"And ensure its passage to us," Jefferson continued with a knowing smile. "Lafayette knew that if this Codex could survive, it might serve as a cornerstone for our burgeoning nation."

Madison's eyes shone with conviction. "A nation that might, if guided by the wisdom of the past, aspire to the balance and enlightenment of Lemuria."

Moved by the depth of their charge, Eliza said, "We stand to forge not just a new country but a new kind of society."

"Yes," Jefferson affirmed. "And with this Codex, we have a touchstone to the spiritual legacy of a world long vanished."

The room fell silent, and James finally spoke. "Then we must recover it."

As the night deepened around them, their shared determination became palpable, a silent vow to the wisdom of the ancients. They would embark upon this quest together, their resolve unshakeable, the legends of Lemuria fueling their vision for a society that would seek to embrace an enlightened harmony—a nation resilient in the face of time and human imperfection.

CHAPTER THIRTY-THREE
THE HUDSON

The morning air was crisp, with the bite of impending winter as the trio set out from Philadelphia. Their breaths clouded the air before them as they rode, the steely sky promising a test of their resolve. Though the Continental Congress had provided for their journey with ample funds and winter gear, no provision could insulate them against the creeping cold that sought to claim the countryside.

As they made their way along the narrow, snow-dusted trails, the first flakes of a relentless snow began to descend; each flake was a harbinger of the deluge to come. The horses, resilient beasts, plodded onward.

By nightfall, the world was an expanse of white. With the storm intensifying, they found shelter beneath the skeletal boughs of a copse of trees. The tents provided were their only refuge from the merciless gusts that howled like specters through the landscape.

Inside, the tent was a sanctuary of a sort, but one not without its discomforts. Close quarters meant the three of them must huddle together for warmth, sharing body heat and the heavy blankets they were supplied. Eliza, nestled between James and Thomas, found sleep elusive. Though heavy, the fabric of her dress did little to ward off the chill that seemed to seep into her very bones.

The frigid night bore down upon the canvas sanctuary, where Eliza discovered herself entwined in a tableau of war and passion, flanked by the two men who had claimed pieces of her heart. James, her newfound love, whose allegiance to the nascent nation's future was as fervent as the kisses they had shared, lay to her left. His whispers spoke of a world that could be, each word a breath of warmth that tickled her senses and conjured memories of stolen moments.

To her right was Thomas, his body a familiar landscape now made foreign by his betrayal and subsequent return to the cause. He was the past that tugged at her soul but whose earlier desertion left a fissure of doubt. The steadfast timbre of his voice, as he spoke of wisdom and interpretation of ancient lore, was the same that had once vowed eternal affections beneath the starlit sky.

Eliza felt the pull of her own divided loyalties—the safety of past love and the promise of new, each competing for her heart's territory. Their breaths mingled in the cold air, creating a rhythm that seemed to pulse with the questions of her own heart: Whom did she truly love? But even more importantly, who could she truly trust?

Eliza's mind wandered to the future, post-war, post-revolution, where choices would have to be made. The uncertainty in her heart mirrored the uncertain journey ahead. The men beside her, one her past, the other her future, both spies in their own right, had made their own gambles—but it was Eliza who felt like she was the one rolling the dice.

In the cocoon of their makeshift refuge, the storm outside seemed distant, a mere echo of the tempest that raged within Eliza. Her feelings, a tangled web, lay as intricate and complex as the path to independence they all sought. Sleep came in fleeting moments, a respite from the emotional maelstrom that held her thoughts captive.

As dawn approached, its tentative light casting shadows that danced upon the tent walls, Eliza's heart waged its silent war. By the time the snow ceased and they emerged from their shelter, she knew the world they stepped into would demand decisions. The true test of their mission would be not only their nation's birth but also which love she would nurture in the newfound light of day.

*

Having traversed a labyrinth of icy woodlands, Eliza, James, and Thomas found themselves at the hushed shore of New Jersey. A mighty river stretched before them, a serene but daunting gatekeeper to their surreptitious mission into the lion's den.

Under the pallid shroud of morning, absent the sun's warmth, the challenge of crossing loomed large. The expanse of the river, both wide and menacing, posed a significant obstacle. Yet, with the British forces in disarray following their defeat at Yorktown, the regular patrols along the river had diminished. Abandoned at one of these outposts were the very boats once used to transport soldiers. They forsook their horses, and, with James at the oars, slipped into the river's grasp, allowing the current to carry them toward the island's southern tip.

The rowboat cut through the icy waters, the city's silhouette emerging in the dawn light. James rowed with determined strokes while Thomas kept his gaze fixed on the looming cityscape. Eliza sat wrapped in her cloak, her mind racing with plans and contingencies.

Thomas broke the silence, his voice barely above a whisper. "The mood must be grim in the city after Yorktown's surrender."

James nodded, his eyes never leaving the shore. "One can only imagine the shock waves when news of the surrender reached its streets. Disbelief, confusion, and fear, I'd wager. If the city was a fortress, Yorktown was its unbreachable gate. And now that gate has crumbled."

Eliza interjected, her voice cutting through the mist, "And the headquarters? With its web spread across the city, how firm can its hold be now?"

Thomas, whose past as a Loyalist officer lent him insight, replied, "Unsettled at best. The officers I served with would now be doubting their future roles. As for General Henry Clinton, he is a seasoned leader who has weathered many storms. He would be fully aware that Yorktown's fall could signal the end. With that in mind, he would be contemplating an orderly withdrawal, orchestrating plans for an evacuation, and perhaps negotiating terms to safeguard what they can as they face the prospect of conceding the city and the war."

James spoke softly. "Cornwallis's defeat transcends the battlefield; it is emblematic. For years, New York stood as the bastion of British might, the very emblem of their imperial strength. But with Yorktown's fall, this city's invincible image is shattered, baring the fragility of British control for all to see."

"And the Loyalists?" Eliza inquired.

Thomas's expression grew distant. "They will be fraught with concern. New York was their sanctuary, a slice of the motherland in this new world. Now, they face a future of doubt, weighing vengeance against the prospect of exile."

James could not resist a wry jab. "I suppose allegiance is a fickle thing for some, is it not, Thomas?" He threw a sidelong glance, the corner of his mouth twitching upward.

Thomas stiffened, the barb finding its mark. "We all have our paths, James. Some of us realize when it is time to change course," he retorted, his voice edged with hurt.

The rowboat rocked gently as James extended an olive branch, his jest giving way to contrition. "Forgive me, friend. War makes jesters of us all at times." Their shared experiences had created a bond, yet the competition for Eliza's regard simmered beneath their camaraderie.

James tightened his hands on the oars as the boat approached the shore. "The British command will be in disarray, but do not expect chaos. They will be pragmatic, calculating their retreat, securing what they can."

Thomas agreed. "The withdrawal will be orderly. It has to be. But the air will be thick with the unease of a coming storm."

Eliza glanced at the two men. "And Cornwallis?"

Thomas met her gaze. "He is a proud man. If he is still here, he will be under the guard of his most loyal officers, likely confused and waiting for orders from home."

James added, "Which gives us an opportunity. In the confusion of defeat, we may find our way to him and to the Solum Codex."

The city, closer now, was a patchwork of shadow and awakening light. Each knew the risks ahead, the narrow thread of hope they followed. Yet within each heart burned the same flame of a cause worth more than their own lives.

CHAPTER THIRTY-FOUR
BRITISH HEADQUARTERS

Thomas trod silently through the labyrinth of New York's streets, with the night enveloping him and his companions like a cloak. The trio's footsteps whispered against the cobblestones. For Thomas, each turn was a reunion with ghosts; here, he had once walked with pride in his British officer's uniform, a defender of the very empire he now sought to undermine.

Headquarters loomed before them. Once a beacon of imperial might, this edifice now seemed a mere specter of authority. Thomas's heart was a battleground of emotions as he faced the fortress that symbolized both his past allegiance and his current betrayal.

They ducked into the protective shadow of an alleyway, the structure's immensity towering over them. Eliza's eyes, sharp and unwavering, met his. In the dimness, her face was an imprint of resolve. "Once you're inside, remember the shadows are your allies. But if something goes awry—"

James, ever the sentinel, completed the thought with quiet intensity. "We will be there. But, Thomas, the mission is greater than any one man."

Thomas felt the weight of destiny pressing upon him. He nodded, his thoughts a tempest. "First, I ascertain if Cornwallis is within. Then I return, and we chart our course forward together."

"What if he is not there? What then, Thomas?" Eliza's voice cut through the night.

Thomas let a breath escape, his exhalation merging with the cool air. "We find another way." His fingers traced the edge of the genuine papers nestled against his chest—a remnant of his life as a Loyalist and, now, his ticket past enemy lines.

With a silent promise etched in his parting nod, Thomas stepped away from the safety of his comrades and into the void, carrying with him their trust and the fate of the mission. The papers he carried were his past and possibly his future—his truth and yet his greatest deception. As he disappeared into the night's embrace, the echo of his resolve lingered in the alleyway, a silent oath to those he left behind.

Eliza's voice, firm yet tinged with concern, reached out to him, "And, Thomas," she said, "be careful. We cannot afford to lose you to the ghosts of your past."

With a fleeting smile, he assured her, "I have no intention of becoming a ghost, Eliza." His hand involuntarily rested on the pistol hidden beneath his coat. "I will return; I hope with the Codex."

James and Eliza, ensconced in the uncertainty of their darkened alcove, were sentinels in the silence, bound to the delicate thread of hope and fear. As Thomas passed through the halls of the British headquarters, his heart hammered against his ribs. His mind was awash with the fabricated tales he had woven as he approached General Clinton's office. The door was ajar, and the voices of the high command spilled out like the light that framed its opening.

Inside, generals were perched like hawks around a table strewn with maps and missives. It was Cornwallis who caught sight of him first, his eyes lighting up with recognition. With a subtle tilt of his head, Cornwallis beckoned Thomas closer, a gesture that cut through the room's tension like a command.

Cornwallis's gaze pierced Thomas, then drifted to the empty space behind him, expectant. "Where is Lieutenant General von Knyphausen?" His tone was even, but the undercurrent of anticipation was palpable.

Thomas inhaled sharply, the deceit he was about to weave thick in his throat. "An ambush, General, out on the road," he fabricated, his voice a melody of feigned sorrow. "It was sudden and vicious. The Hessian fought bravely, but alas, he fell." Each word was a stone in the fabric of his tale, a heavy cloak of falsehood.

Cornwallis's countenance was unyielding, carved from the very stone of discipline and command. As Thomas delivered his report, a flicker of skepticism crossed the general's features. "Von Knyphausen was no novice to the stratagems of war," Cornwallis pressed, his voice tinged with incredulity. "How could such an esteemed tactician be taken by surprise?"

Feeling the weight of scrutiny, Thomas fortified his narrative with the harrowing details of chaos and confusion that befit a sudden ambush. "Even the most vigilant can be caught off guard, General, under the cloak of night and treachery," he asserted, hoping his words would bridge the chasm of doubt.

A tense silence hung between them as Cornwallis deliberated the plausibility of the tale. Finally, the lines of his face softened into acceptance. "Your report weighs heavy on us all, Thomas," he conceded. "But your return has proven your allegiance. It is with this trust that I extend an offer for you to join me in England. Your future lies there now, for remaining here would mark you a traitor to their nascent cause. Let us leave these troubled shores for a position befitting your loyalty."

Thomas nodded, his role cemented in the trust of a man he was here to deceive.

Cornwallis's sharp and probing gaze cut through the room's thick air, fraught with the tension of recent defeat. "Thomas," he declared, "this land you knew is disentangling its loyalties, forging a path that excludes our kind. Your fidelity in these troubled times shines bright. I offer you redemption and a fresh start. Accompany me on the HMS *Charon* as we make for England. There, a position awaits you in London; this is not merely a new chapter, Captain Reddington—it is your deliverance."

A turmoil of emotions churned within Thomas. "General, your offer is a sanctuary I accept with honor," Thomas said, his voice a faint echo of his internal conflict, "but may I settle some urgent matters first?" His mind raced with the need to inform James and Eliza of this sudden change in the winds of war.

Cornwallis studied Thomas intently, a hint of impatience in his stance. "Time waits for no man, Captain. We are set to sail with the tide. We depart at once."

With a heavy heart, Thomas accepted his orders. His resolve to secure the Codex was now entwined with the painful realization that he was leaving his compatriots without a word. He cast a backward glance, hoping against hope that his silent message of farewell might be felt across the distance. Aboard the warship, Thomas faced the irony of his situation—a steadfast escape to a foreign land that promised salvation amidst the ashes of his actions.

CHAPTER THIRTY-FIVE
HMS *CHARON*

From the shadows of an old warehouse, James and Eliza peered out toward the East River docks, the sprawling naval might of the British Empire on full display before them. The warships, anchored with quiet dignity, were titans of timber and sail, their masts like the bars of a gilded cage that had long held the ambitions of men now defeated.

To their amazement, the docks thrummed with orchestrated chaos. Men shouted orders over the din of clanking metal and creaking wood as sailors scurried to ready the vessels for departure. The HMS *Charon*, a ship of the line known for its formidable presence, sat majestically at the pier, ready to bear Cornwallis and his officers away from American shores.

"Look at the size of her," Eliza whispered, a mix of awe and disdain in her voice. The ship, a leviathan of the deep, cast a long shadow over the water, its cannons glaring ominously through the open ports.

James's eyes traced the intricate dance of departure preparations, noting the shipment of trunks and personal effects being hoisted aboard. "They're not just retreating; they're relocating," he murmured.

As they stood in the shadows, James could see Eliza's reflective contemplation, the shifting thoughts that mirrored the ripples upon the river. There was a finality in the sight of the HMS *Charon*, an unspoken acknowledgment that a chapter of their lives was concluding just as another threatened to begin without their authorship.

"It is the end of their reign," Eliza responded, her gaze locked on the warship, "and yet, they leave with such … pomp."

A silent understanding passed between them, a shared knowledge that their own fortunes were inextricably linked to the fate of the man boarding the ship. The *Charon* stood ready to cast off, its sails whispering of distant shores and the inevitability of change. It was a monument to the might and majesty of the British navy—a might that had shaped the world to its design and was now retreating.

The ghostly silhouette of the HMS *Charon* cast a long shadow over the cobblestones, its masts piercing the dimming night. Eliza's eyes were fixed upon the vessel. "James," she implored, her voice a hushed force, "we must get aboard that ship."

In the quiet before the dawn, they stood shrouded by uncertainty as much as the darkness that enveloped them. "To hide in the bowels of a warship is to flirt with death," James countered, his voice low, imagining the dank, cramped quarters where they would be stowaways among cannons and chains.

Eliza's response was swift and sure. "We can slip below in the confusion of their departure, cloak ourselves in the very shadows of their supplies." Her plan unfolded with a clarity that belied the danger. "We stay hidden by day, make use of what rations we can sneak aboard, and at night, we listen, we learn."

"And when they find us? The British are not known for their leniency," James pointed out, the grim reality of their plight chilling the air between them.

"We will be as ghosts, James, unseen and unheard," Eliza insisted, her eyes gleaming with a mix of fear and excitement. "If they catch us, then we face the noose with heads held high, knowing we did all for our cause."

Eliza stood motionless, her silhouette melding with the mist that rose off the harbor waters. Once steely and sure, her gaze now wavered. "James," she whispered, her voice tinged with a vulnerability that the night air carried away, "Could it be that Thomas has deceived us? That his ambition was the hidden compass guiding him all along?"

James looked at her, seeing the shadow of doubt that dimmed the luster of her usual determination. "It is the Codex we seek, Eliza, not answers to Thomas's riddles," he said firmly.

"Yes, the Codex," Eliza repeated, almost to herself, "but the specter of Thomas's possible duplicity haunts me still."

James knew no words could staunch the wound of mistrust that Thomas's actions had opened in Eliza's heart. "Our path remains unchanged," he finally said. "Let us focus on what lies ahead; the truth of Thomas's intent will unveil itself in due time."

Eliza nodded, her decision etched into the firm set of her jaw. Together, they turned to face the HMS *Charon*, a titan of wood and sail that stood ready to carry their destinies into the unknown. They would board the warship, shadowy intruders driven not by the whims of a potentially false ally but by the unwavering pursuit of their mission.

"The heart of the matter remains the Codex," James mused, his mind sifting through their options like a cartographer plotting a course through uncharted seas. "We must board the *Charon*, but how?"

"We could disguise ourselves as deckhands," Eliza suggested. "There is a flurry of activity; we might go unnoticed in the confusion." Her gaze swept across the dock, observing the rhythm of the sailors' movements, the lanterns swaying gently in the brackish night air. "Whatever we decide, it has to be soon," she said with quiet urgency. The ceaseless activity was their ally, a veil of confusion behind which they could vanish.

James's nod was almost imperceptible in the gloom as his attention was drawn to the crane, a looming behemoth of wrought iron and thick cables stark against the inky backdrop of the night. The engineered titan crane creaked ominously with the weight of its suspended load, a testament to human ingenuity and the brute force required to tame the sea's bounty.

The crates dangled precariously from its iron jaws, a pendulous threat hanging over the planks below. "Those barrels," he whispered, his finger barely extending toward the object of their opportunistic plot. "If they were to fall …" James advanced toward the formidable crane, outstretched like the arm of justice in this hour of subterfuge. The somber night air carried the weight of their plan, one that hinged on his next actions. With the stealth of a cat, he moved to the crane's base, his hands finding the main rope with an ease born of necessity. Under his touch, the fibers felt like the sinews of fate, and with a decisive swipe, he severed them.

A cascade of chaos unfurled as the barrels plummeted, crashing with a force that shook the earth and sent men scattering. The clamor rose to meet the night, a violent crescendo that marked their turbulent path to liberty. James's silent alarm galvanized him. Seizing the momentary tumult, he surged forward, ghosting past the guards, their gazes skittering away in the confusion. Approaching the HMS *Charon*'s gangplank, he caught a glimpse of Eliza's silhouette dissolving into the pandemonium, her movement as fluid as the shifting tides.

They ascended the gangplank into the HMS *Charon*, mere shadows slipping through the frenzy. Once aboard, Eliza and James shared a tacit nod before descending into the belly of the leviathan.

The Weather Deck, exposed to the whipping winds and the stern kiss of the sea, was abuzz with sailors scurrying like ants during a flood. They bypassed the ship's wheel and dodged the long barrels of the main armament, their footfalls silent against the din of shouted orders and clanging metal.

Below, the Gun Decks hummed with martial life, heavy with the scent of oil and iron. Cannon muzzles gleamed dully in the dim light, silent sentinels awaiting the command to unleash their fury. James and Eliza moved with careful urgency. Down they crept to the Orlop Deck.

Here, amidst coiled ropes and spare sails, they found the arteries of the HMS *Charon*—provisions, barrels, and the miscellaneous sinews that bound the ship's might. Here they could breathe, albeit shallowly, as the absence of prying eyes lent them a moment's reprieve.

Finally, in the depths of the Hold, they came to rest. Below the waterline, they entered the heart of the ship, a cavernous domain of shadows cradling the precious cargo of water casks and the remnants of the New World. Tucked behind stout crates and obscured by the maze of stored goods, their sanctuary was a coffin of obscurity. Time was marked only by the subtle dance of the ship's body as it responded to the sea's call. A shiver coursed through the HMS *Charon*, signaling anchors aweigh, and hearts aboard set aflutter with the promise of home.

Eliza and James, now but whispers in the wooden giant's hold, listened as the rhythm of the sea wove into the timbers' creaks—a symphony of anticipation and the soft murmur of trepidation. As the HMS *Charon* turned her bow homeward, they receded into the embrace of the deep, their existence aboard as tenuous as the fleeting foam on distant waves.

CHAPTER THIRTY-SIX
THE STORM

Thomas stood on the deck of the HMS *Charon*, his eyes fixed on the roiling horizon where an imposing storm brewed. Towering clouds clashed together, foretelling a natural onslaught mightier than any clash of naval artillery. The sharp scent of ocean brine, interlaced with the raw energy of the impending storm, filled the air, awakening a deep-seated apprehension of the sea's untamed might.

As he scanned the seascape, Thomas's attention was drawn to the outline of a French warship, a faint but persistent presence trailing them. This ghostly adversary ignited a sense of urgency, a primal instinct for battle. Yet the brooding, chaotic skies presented a greater peril than the looming threat of French cannons.

With its swirling mass of dark vapors and howling winds, the encroaching storm offered both a hazard and a hideaway. Thomas understood the gravity of their predicament: the HMS *Charon* must either outmaneuver their persistent foe or brave the fury of the oncoming tempest.

Around him, the ship's officers, including General Cornwallis, gathered in earnest council. Thomas lingered on the outskirts, an eavesdropper to their strategy. The captain's authoritative tones betrayed no hint of fear, only respect for the man he consulted. "A

French ship gives chase, but the storm offers a veil," he heard the captain propose.

Cornwallis, whose visage seemed to mirror the steely gray of the sea, gave a short nod, the lines on his brow as firm as the words he spoke. "We use the storm," he asserted. "It is our shield."

Thomas felt the weight of the decision settle around him. The ship's course charted straight into the heart of the swirling chaos. The salt that lingered on his tongue now seemed a harbinger of the tumultuous journey ahead, the flavor of danger and desperation intertwined.

As the *Charon*'s bow cut a steadfast path toward the burgeoning squall, the French adversary became a specter consumed by the fog, a phantom of war dissolved by the greater threat looming before them. In the privacy of his thoughts, Thomas grappled with the enormity of their gamble. It was a dance with the forces of nature, where the stakes were their very lives.

With a resolve hardened by the certainty of the unknown, Thomas watched as the HMS *Charon* sailed into the belly of the storm, an island of resilience amidst the roar of wind and sea. The tempest's embrace was imminent, and at this moment, Thomas knew they were all at the mercy of the capricious gale. With all its might and mettle, the warship ventured into the abyss; its fate—and his—surrendered to the will of the storm.

From his vantage point on the deck, Thomas watched with a mix of awe and apprehension as the sky turned a menacing shade of gray.

The sea, previously a rhythmic companion to their journey, now reared up in angry swells, challenging the HMS *Charon*'s advance with every wave. The crew, faces set with grim determination, scurried to secure sails and batten down the hatches, their movements a dance of defiance against the coming onslaught.

After a brief consultation with General Cornwallis—who stood as a beacon of resolve amidst the chaos—the captain gave the order to sail into the storm. Cornwallis's firm and commanding voice cut through the rising wind: "The storm may shield us from our pursuers. We have no choice but to go through it."

In the grip of the tempest's fierce clutches, the HMS *Charon* heaved and toiled against the relentless sea. Taking advantage of the mayhem that reigned on deck, Thomas found a rare moment of opportunity amidst the bedlam. His pulse quickened, echoing the thunderous symphony of wind and rain that battered the warship as he made his descent into the vessel's inner sanctum.

Below, the dim corridor to General Cornwallis's quarters seemed a world apart from the battle being waged by man against nature. The swaying lanterns cast eerie shadows, transforming the walls into a spectral theater of light and dark. With a swift glance behind to ensure he was unobserved, Thomas stepped forward, navigating the clutter of naval life that littered the hallway.

His fingers grazed the brass handle of Cornwallis's cabin door, cool and slick to the touch. He paused, his breaths shallow, mind racing with the gravity of his mission. This was the chance to seize the Codex, the fabled repository of knowledge that could shift the tide of their struggle. Beyond this threshold lay answers, power, and perhaps even the fate of nations.

With a resolve fortified by necessity, Thomas pressed down the handle and edged the door ajar, his movements as fluid and silent as the shadows that kept him company. The cabin, an enclave of command and strategy, was absent its master. Thomas's eyes scanned the interior, the polished surfaces and orderly array of maps and instruments betraying none of the turmoil that had taken the ship in its grasp.

Thomas knew Cornwallis would be wholly preoccupied, his attention riveted on the storm's wrath and the safety of the ship. Now was Thomas's moment, a narrow slice of time to act while the general's gaze was turned outward toward the raging elements.

Moving with a mix of trepidation and urgency, Thomas began his search. The Codex could be anywhere—a hidden compartment, a nondescript folio among many, a sheaf of papers disguised as mundane correspondence. He felt along the edges of the desk and probed the bookshelves, his fingers questing for the telltale texture or heft of the ancient tome.

Every crash of wave against the hull, every howl of wind through the rigging above, reminded Thomas of the storm's might, of the danger that loomed so close. But within these walls, amidst the scent of ink and the faint aroma of the sea ingrained in every fiber of the wood, Thomas's fear was replaced by the thrill of the hunt, by the nearness of the prize.

For this, he had crossed an ocean of doubt and peril. For this, he had allied himself with rebels and rogues. With the Codex, their ambitions, their very destinies, might be realized. And as he rifled through Cornwallis's belongings, Thomas felt the weight of history pressing upon him, sensed the breath of destiny stirring in the air, as palpable as the storm that raged beyond the sturdy oak of the *Charon*'s hull.

In the dense quietude of Cornwallis's cabin, amidst the relentless tumult of the storm, Thomas's fingers stumbled upon a texture unlike the others—a subtle ridging that spoke of artisan craft and ancient binding. He drew the volume from its seclusion, and time seemed to still. It lay heavy in his hands, the leather cover cracked and supple, whispering tales of the many fingers that had caressed it over the centuries.

The Codex's presence filled the cramped quarters with a resonance that belied its physical dimensions. The scent of it—a fusion of old parchment and ink, a hint of must from years within sealed chambers— rose to greet him, carrying with it the fragrance of time itself.

Thomas opened the Codex, his breath catching in his throat. Before him lay pages edged in the faintest gilding of gold, a halo of bygone opulence that gleamed in the storm's intermittent flashes. The symbols upon the pages were a mystery, a script of elegance and complexity, rendered in ink that had faded to a dusky hue yet remained striking against the yellowed background. Here in his hands lay wisdom that had traversed eras, a legacy of thought and power preserved against the ravages of obscurity. It was a poignant irony that such enlightenment should be rendered mute to its seeker. The magnitude of the Codex's presence—a testament to the scholars, philosophers, and keepers of truth who had come before—left Thomas momentarily adrift in wonder and awe.

His mind raced. Madison and Jefferson—were they privy to the means to decode these cryptic messages? Could they unravel the arcane linguistics that now lay spread before him? Doubt gnawed at him as the ship continued to buck and pitch, the storm outside a relentless beast.

He steadied himself against the desk, the Codex open in his hands. Each roll of the *Charon* sent a fresh wave of unease through him, not just for the turbulent sea but for the precarious position in which he found himself. The implications were clear: if Cornwallis discovered the Codex's absence, the ship would be turned inside out, and every soul aboard scrutinized.

In a moment of clarity amid the chaos, Thomas knew he could not risk removing the Codex from Cornwallis's quarters, at least not yet. The general's wrath would be swift and certain, and suspicion would cast a wide net. Besides, the more immediate threat of the HMS *Charon* succumbing to the storms might loom over everything—the Codex would be of no use at the bottom of the Atlantic.

With a sigh that carried the weight of his frustration, Thomas closed the Codex and returned it to its hiding place, securing the drawer with the same carelessness as before. He needed time to think.

Slipping from the room as silently as he had entered, Thomas made his way back to the relative safety of his own quarters. In the rocking darkness there, he would bide his time, waiting for the right moment to lay claim to the Codex once more. For now, the secrets within would remain just out of reach, their promise undiminished by his prudence. As the HMS *Charon* groaned and creaked around him, Thomas pondered his next move, knowing the storm was far from the only challenge he would have to face.

CHAPTER THIRTY-SEVEN
THE HOLD

Beneath the waterline of the HMS *Charon*'s hold, within its darkest recesses where daylight was nothing but a legend, James and Eliza were secreted away. This hold was a forbidding cavern, a gloomy labyrinth of supplies and the necessities of seafaring life—among them, barrels of hardtack and water that had become the sustenance for the hidden pair.

The darkness was an entity unto itself, pressing coldly against their skin, a constant oppressive force that weighed on their spirits as much as on the aged timbers of the ship. In this chill, they huddled not for comfort but for the essential warmth their bodies could muster against the creeping cold that the lower decks emanated. "How long now?" Eliza's whisper tore through the oppressive silence, a stark reminder of their isolation.

"Days and nights blur together," James responded, his voice laden with a weariness that spoke of their shared ordeal, "but try to remember the sun, Eliza. Its warmth will find us again."

Their cramped alcove was but a dent in the hold's expanse, a space once reserved for excess rigging and sailcloth. Now, it provided a scant shelter for the two rebels. They had pilfered from nearby barrels—

gnawing on stale hardtack that crumbled at the touch and sipping cautiously from a cask of water that tasted faintly of wood and iron.

"The smell, James," Eliza complained, her voice heavy with distaste as she shifted uncomfortably on the unforgiving wooden floor. The pungent odor from their makeshift latrine melded with the mustiness of the old barrels and the faint tang of spoiled provisions. "It is a torture in its own right."

"It is a deterrent," James retorted with a wry twist of his lips, trying to cast their plight in a strategic light. "Our repulsive redoubt."

A humorless chuckle escaped Eliza as she nestled closer to James, her body aching for relief from the hard surface. "This redoubt reeks of our desperation," she observed dryly. "Yet, if it serves to cloak us from prying eyes until landfall ..."

Surrounded by the ship's provisions, the pair existed on stolen time, each morsel of food and sip of water a stolen treasure, each rustle of the rats that shared their darkened domain a jarring reminder of the nightmare they navigated. In this shadowed hell, James and Eliza waited, endured, and plotted, their hope as fervent as the hunger that gnawed at their bellies, their resolve steadfast.

As the HMS *Charon* began to rock gently, the creaking of her wooden bones was a subtle prelude to the maelstrom that lay ahead. James and Eliza, nestled in their shadowy alcove amidst the provisions, felt the rhythm of the sea shift beneath them. A growing tension in the air, a whispering apprehension that seeped through the timbers, told of the gathering storm.

"The sea is restless today," Eliza murmured, a note of unease threading her words as she felt the first hesitant roll of the ship.

James wrapped his arm tighter around her, trying to offer solace as much as seek it. "I'm sure the HMS *Charon* has weathered worse," he said, though his voice betrayed his concern. They listened as the ship's subtle rocking grew more pronounced, the intervals between the creaks of the hull shrinking. The rolling motion that had been almost comforting in its regularity now quickened, each wave hitting with more force, each dip and rise more abrupt.

"The waves ... they're growing stronger," Eliza noted, her body tensing with each new swell.

James nodded, his own pulse quickening to match the tempo of the sea. "A storm is upon us, but we must have faith in the ship and her crew."

As the hold quaked with the storm's approach, the first true pitch sent a jolt of fear through them. The sound of the tempest above was distant yet menacing, like the growl of a beast prowling just out of sight. They clung to each other as the HMS *Charon* began to protest, her timbers groaning under the strain of the burgeoning gale.

"James, do you think—" Eliza's question was cut short as a wave struck with such might that it seemed the sea sought to reclaim the warship for itself.

"The HMS *Charon* is strong," James insisted, his voice a bastion against the mounting dread. "She will carry us through." But the waves became mountains, each one a titan straining against the HMS *Charon*'s might. The ship, with her proud sails and towering masts, now seemed a mere cork bobbing precariously on the ocean's wrathful surface.

The storm drew closer, wrapping the hold in a shroud of fear. The noise above intensified, the pounding of the rain and the howling of the wind joining in a fearsome chorus. They felt the HMS *Charon* rise and fall, her descent into each trough more terrifying than the last.

"James, the ship will not survive!" Eliza's cry was nearly lost amidst the cacophony of the storm. The hold that had been their sanctuary now seemed like it could become their tomb.

"It must," James insisted, his voice a defiant shout against the roar. "She will, and so must we!"

They braced as the HMS *Charon* was thrown yet again by an angry sea. Around them, the world was a tumult of noise and motion, the ship a living thing fighting for survival. They, too, were caught in the tempest's fury, passengers on a voyage that tested the very limits of their courage.

James, trying to mask his own creeping dread, held Eliza close. "She's a strong vessel, braver than us both. We will weather this as she does."

As the hours stretched on, the assault did not relent. Barrels that had stood like sentinels now rolled and crashed with violence that shook their souls. Their enforced prison became a maelstrom of noise and motion, leaving them reeling, gasping for respite.

"Hold on to me!" James shouted over the din as a particularly vicious surge threw their bodies together with bruising force.

Eliza's response was lost in the cacophony, but her grip on him tightened—a silent pact against the chaos.

"We cannot last like this!" she cried out when the tumult waned for a fleeting moment, her words thick with panic. "We are at the sea's mercy!"

James felt her shivering against him, her body a small, fierce flame in the overwhelming darkness. "The sea has no mercy to give," he confessed, his voice a ragged whisper. "But we have each other, and that is more than the HMS *Charon* can claim. Our will is stronger than this storm."

The words were as much for him as for her, a mantra against the ever-present fear that the next wave would be the one to shatter the mighty warship and send them spiraling into the watery abyss.

"Talk to me, James. Keep talking!" Eliza begged as another violent shudder ran through the ship.

"About what, Eliza?" he replied, his voice steady though his heart was anything but.

"Anything! Everything!" she pleaded. "Tell me about the sun, the warmth … tell me we will see it again."

He complied, speaking of brighter days and open skies, of the feel of sunlight on their faces, crafting a tapestry of words to shield them from the grim reality. Together, they recounted tales of the lands they'd seen and the dreams they still harbored, their voices intertwining to create a fortress against despair.

Hour after hour, they fought the invisible beast, their small world tilting and heaving in ways that defied their senses. With each passing moment, with each shuddering impact and bone-jarring roll, their physical strength waned, but their resolve to outlast the storm solidified into something unbreakable.

Finally, the tempest's rage diminished. The ship's violent dance slowed, her tortured creaking softened, and the battered HMS *Charon* remained whole. As the motion subsided, James and Eliza remained entwined, their bodies and spirits battered yet unyielding.

Exhausted to the core, they lay in the aftermath, their breaths heavy, their voices reduced to whispers. The darkness of the hold remained absolute, but in its suffocating embrace, they found a moment of peace. They had endured, surviving the storm's might through their unwavering support for one another.

"We are alive," Eliza murmured, half in disbelief. "We are still here."

"Yes," James replied, the relief evident in his voice. "We have lived to see the dawn that is sure to come. And we will see many more, my Eliza, many more."

In the depths of the HMS *Charon*, their bond had held fast against nature's fury, just as the stout British warship had battled and bested the raging seas. Together, they faced an uncertain future, but they did so with the knowledge that they had withstood the storm's worst and could face the challenges to come.

CHAPTER THIRTY-EIGHT
PORTSMOUTH

Thomas edged along the gunwale of the battered HMS *Charon*, every creak of her damaged hull a stark reminder of the storm's wrath. The white cliffs of Portsmouth loomed ahead, a beacon of both his salvation and impending peril. General Cornwallis stood alongside the ship's pilot and captain at the wheel, his steely gaze fixed on the harbor, observing the vessel's limp home. This was Thomas's moment.

As the HMS *Charon* inched toward the harbor, the quayside clatter of a city awakening to their arrival filled the air. Thomas knew the labyrinthine streets of Portsmouth would swallow him whole if he allowed it. The bustling port was a tapestry of shadows and light, its alleys and throngs a perfect cloak for a man with no name, allies, or history.

With the ship's crew preoccupied, their energies fixated on the final approach to the dock, Thomas slipped like a wraith into the general's quarters. The Codex, for which he had risked the Atlantic's fury, was concealed within—a prize worth the treachery. The ship's corridors, usually alive with the footsteps of mariners and the commands of officers, were subdued, the crew's attentions ensnared by the work of docking the crippled vessel. Thomas slipped through the shadows undetected, moving with the quiet certainty of a man whose time had come.

Reaching the door to the general's cabin, Thomas paused, his breath steady despite his hammering pulse. He pressed his ear against the cool wood, ensuring the room's emptiness, before easing the door open. The quarters welcomed him with the scent of sea brine and the underlying musk of polished leather—smells that spoke of journeys past and tales untold.

The room was a sanctum of strategy and solitude, with maps and charts adorning the walls. The desk was a testament to the general's command. The Codex was nestled within an open drawer as if it were nothing more than a sheaf of ordinary documents.

Though steady in their task, Thomas's fingers could not help but tremble as he reached for the Codex, his touch reverent. As he grasped the volume for a suspended moment, he understood the gravity of his actions—the theft was not just of a mere object but of destiny itself.

Thomas tucked the Codex into the depth of his pouch, its weight against his hip a solemn reminder of his chosen path. The velvet wrapping was soft, but the implications were not. With a final, sweeping gaze, he committed the quarters to memory—the maps, the inkwell, the scent of sea and wood, the faint echo of Cornwallis's commands—these were the last threads of a former life.

Stealthily, he reemerged into the corridor, moving with purpose yet discretion. The HMS *Charon*'s groans underfoot grew more insistent as the ship neared the dock. Thomas could hear the bustle of the crew above, a chorus of orders and responses, the scuffle of boots on deck, the ship coming alive to berth.

He made his way through the lower decks, a spectral figure flitting through the press of sailors and dockhands. His ears rang with the impending finality of the voyage as he ascended toward the main deck, each step a measured beat in his silent symphony of escape.

Emerging into the brisk air, Thomas paused for a heartbeat, letting the brine fill his lungs and the sound of the harbor's cacophony wash over him. He joined the flow of sailors making their way across the gangplank, just a man among many, but within him, a secret that set him apart.

He crossed the threshold from ship to shore, aware of the Codex's gentle thud against his side, a rhythmic assurance of the power he wielded. Yet, as he stepped onto the solid ground of Portsmouth, the reality of his solitude pressed upon him. Eliza was not there—she was a dream ahead, a dream for which he now bore the key.

He stopped at the base of the gangplank, his gaze drifting over the hustle of the docks, the seafaring dance of arrival and departure. In that fleeting stillness, Thomas felt the swell of his story, the chapter he had just concluded, and the unwritten one that lay ahead. The Codex's weight was no longer just a physical presence; the gravitas of hope, potential heroism, redemption, and reunion with his beloved Eliza pushed him onward into the throng. The Codex was now an extension of his very soul, a relic that would elevate him from a nameless rebel to the savior of his cause. He had risked it all for Eliza, for the promise of a future where they could be free from the shadow of war and live without fear or restraint.

With a breath that tasted of sea salt and a newfound purpose, Thomas stepped onto the quayside, the mist clinging to him like the whispers of destiny. The Codex was his key to new horizons, and Eliza, his beacon, guided him through the perilous waters ahead.

His boots struck the stones of Portsmouth with purpose, his stride confident yet unassuming. The cacophony of the dock—a symphony of curses, commands, and the clang of the industry—provided a cover as he dodged between laborers and past market stalls, beginning to brim with the day's catch.

He slipped through the network of alleys, where the cries of the quay softened, and the smells of salt, fish, and tar became the scent of anonymity. Among the ragged children playing between barrels and the wenches negotiating with sailors, Thomas was just another face, another pair of weary legs striding toward nowhere.

He could not afford the luxury of planning; every moment was a precious gem to be spent on survival. With each step, he distanced himself from the HMS *Charon*, Cornwallis, and the life he had known. The sea offered him countless routes, each as perilous as the last, but it was the path into obscurity that Thomas embraced. For now, the Codex was his compass, and survival was his only destination.

CHAPTER THIRTY-NINE
REUNION

As darkness enveloped the HMS *Charon*, the ship that had been both prison and passage, Eliza and James seized their moment to make their escape. With hearts thrumming against the confines of their chests, they slipped through the ranks of the unsuspecting crew, a dance of shadows amidst the chaos of docking. With its towering masts reaching for a starless sky, the ship groaned and creaked, a leviathan stirring in the embrace of the sea.

Barely a whisper against the wooden deck, they reached the gangplank—an unguarded bridge to freedom. The fog, a loyal accomplice, shrouded their descent, cloaking their movements as they merged with the ebb and flow of Portsmouth's nocturnal life. They emerged from the spectral mist, finding themselves at the threshold of the city, its cobbled streets unfurling before them.

The labyrinth of Portsmouth awaited, a city of secrets cloaked in the guise of lantern-lit pubs and shadow-strewn markets. James felt the pressure of Eliza's fingers intertwining with his, a silent pledge between them as they ventured into the warren of the unknown, their steps hesitant yet determined.

With the HMS *Charon* now nothing more than a shadowy figure in the distance, James and Eliza let the rhythm of the city streets draw them in, guiding them through the labyrinthine alleys. Here, the air was thick with stories. The duo stumbled upon a tavern that promised modest comforts. The worn sign above the door, groaning on its hinges, seemed to sympathize with their plight. They slipped inside, where the warmth starkly contrasted with the night's chill and the clatter of conversation a balm to their isolation.

Once over the threshold of the tavern, the air was rife with the aroma of roasted meat and woodsmoke. James approached the innkeeper, a stout man with a grizzled beard and a gaze that had seen too many weary travelers to count. "We require a bath and whatever meal you can spare," James requested, his voice low and steady.

The innkeeper eyed them with a discerning squint and nodded toward the back. "Bath's that way. Two pence. Dinners are stew or pie. Stew will fill your belly more, if you've got the appetite for it." He leaned in closer, lowering his voice conspiratorially. "And if you want a bit of ale to wash it down, I've got a brew that's been warming by the fire—just the thing for folks fresh off a ship."

Upon hearing the menu, Eliza's face brightened, the weariness around her eyes softening. She exchanged a quick, conspiratorial smile with James, both relishing the thought of a proper meal after long days of meager rations at sea. James delved into the purse, the weight of the coins a reminder of Madison's foresight, and handed a generous amount to the innkeeper, their gratitude conveyed in the firm nod that accompanied the transaction. The prospect of hot water and a full meal was a welcome slice of comfort, a taste of the home they were fighting to protect.

Eliza emerged from the bathing room with her hair damp and her cheeks flushed from the heat of the water. "I had forgotten how it felt to be clean," she confided to James, her voice a mix of relief and newfound vigor. "The sea is a demanding mistress; she takes more than she gives. But this—" She gestured to the steaming tub behind her. "This is a small slice of heaven."

James could not help but chuckle as he watched the tension ease from Eliza's shoulders. "Indeed, two weeks at sea makes a hot bath feel like the greatest luxury in the world."

They settled at a table, the wood worn smooth by countless others who had sought solace in its sturdiness. As they ate the hearty meal before them, a banquet compared to the ship's stolen fare, Eliza sighed contentedly. "To think I was dreaming of a meal like this," she said between mouthfuls. "To actually have it is … well, it's almost enough to make one forget we're so far from home."

James nodded, his own satisfaction evident.

Eliza and James were tucked away in the corner of the tavern, the hum of conversation around them like a cloak of anonymity. They were just another pair of travelers, weary from the road—or so the other patrons thought. But as the tavern door creaked open, admitting another figure into the warm glow of the hearth, their pretense nearly shattered.

It was Thomas who stepped into the room, the wild cacophony of mirth and music momentarily receding into the background like a tide withdrawing from the shore. James felt a jolt of surprise surge through him as Thomas materialized from the sea of faces. His heart raced, and the chair beneath him creaked in protest.

For a breath, there was nothing but their trio in the tavern, a small island of recognition in a sea of oblivion. Thomas's eyes locked with theirs, a flicker of shock passing over his features as well—shock swiftly smothered by the necessity of discretion. He smoothed his expression into one of casual nonchalance as he navigated the maze of tables, though the slightest tightness around his eyes betrayed his controlled alarm.

As Thomas drew near, their circle tightened instinctively. The tavern's clamor rose once more around them, shrouding their reunion. Yet, the air between them crackled with the intensity of their shared astonishment. With an effort that spoke of deep reserves of calm, Thomas gathered his composure as though wrapping a cloak tighter against the chill and began to unfurl the tale of his odyssey.

The tavern's rowdy atmosphere cocooned them from the world outside; the clinking glasses and off-key sea shanties starkly contrasted the gravity of their hushed conversation. As Thomas spoke, James and Eliza leaned forward, their faces a tapestry of shadows and light, etched with the intensity of their mission.

"Cornwallis saw me as a loyal officer, an ally in his ranks," Thomas said, the corner of his mouth turning up in a bitter half-smile.

"That is what we had hoped for," James admitted.

After a moment, Thomas's gaze sharpened with curiosity. "And what of you both? How did you come to Portsmouth? Were you aboard the HMS *Charon* as well?" His questions, casual to any eavesdropper, were laden with unspoken urgency to his companions.

Eliza glanced at James before replying, her voice a whisper lost in the ambient noise. "Yes, we were, hidden in the dark recesses of the cargo hold."

"As stowaways," James added, the word tasting of both danger and pride. "We clung to the shadows, as unnoticed as the rats that shared our cramped quarters."

Thomas leaned back, absorbing the revelation. "A harrowing journey for you both," he murmured, admiration lacing his tone. "It seems fortune favors the bold—or at least the very stealthy." Their laughter was a soft chuckle that blended seamlessly with the tavern's mirth, a brief moment of lightness in the shadow of their perilous reality.

"Well, tell us," Eliza demanded. "Did you find the Codex?"

Thomas's gaze unfurled as he reminisced. "The HMS *Charon* was at the mercy of a wrathful storm, its decks awash with rain and sea foam," he murmured, the candlelight glinting in his distant eyes. "Cornwallis joined the captain on the quarterdeck while his cabin lay vulnerable in his absence."

James's deep voice broke through the memory. "Yes, the ship heaved as if possessed, but in the belly of the beast, we were but ghosts to the crew."

Eliza's nod was solemn. "The storm could have been the hand of Providence itself," she mused, a note of wonder threading through her words.

Thomas's smile was tinged with awe as he brought himself back to the present, drawn by their camaraderie. "When I found the Codex, hidden in a desk drawer like a secret waiting to be told, I could scarcely breathe," he confessed, his words touched by emotion. "Opening its bindings, I was greeted by an expanse of parchment that held the most cryptic array of symbols I've ever seen. They twisted and turned, a dance of ink that seemed almost alive, weaving a narrative I could not decipher but felt in my very soul."

He paused, and for a moment, the tavern fell away as he was consumed by the weight of that moment, the gravity of holding a tome that could change the world—or at least their part in it. Thomas's hands, though now empty, held the memory of the Codex's power, and his heart was full. Thomas nodded solemnly. "I dared only a glance at the mysterious script by the light of a single candle. The text was a labyrinth of unknown symbols, an enigma. Not in any recognizable written words."

"That makes perfect sense," Eliza said, nodding.

His gaze met theirs, his brown eyes burning with the fire of rebellion. "I placed the Codex back, waiting for our arrival in Portsmouth. Then, amidst the bustle of docking—when the hands of every man, including Cornwallis, were occupied with rope and sail—I retrieved it."

Eliza's mouth parted slightly, and she gasped at the audacity of the act. "And then?"

"And then," Thomas continued, "I slipped away with the Codex. As chaos reigned and the men scrambled on deck, I vanished like a ghost."

The tavern seemed to grow quieter around them, the laughter and song fading into the background as they absorbed the magnitude of what Thomas had done. James leaned closer, his voice a whisper lost in the raucous harmony of the tavern. "The Codex, Thomas, do you have it?"

Thomas responded not with words but with a subtle gesture, his hand brushing against the leather pouch that clung to his chest like a shadow. Inside, the Codex nestled—an object mundane to the unknowing eye, yet fiercely coveted by those who understood its true value.

"We need to plan our return to America," James urged, his eyes scanning the room for eavesdroppers. "With the war ... going to France first may be our best chance. They are, after all, allies of our cause."

Thomas nodded, his gaze sharp and calculating. "France is the key, but the journey there will not be easy. We—"

Their strategy was cut short. The door of the tavern swung open with a sense of foreboding, and British soldiers spilled in. The red of their coats was like a flame in the dimly lit room.

In an instant, Thomas understood. They were here for him. The Codex's thief. He slid the pouch off his shoulder and pressed it into James's hands. "Keep it safe," he murmured, just before standing to face his fate.

James watched, the pouch burning against his side, as Thomas casually attempted to walk past the soldiers. But fate, it seemed, had a cruel sense of irony. One of Cornwallis's officers, with a sharp eye for traitors, recognized Thomas. The officer's voice was triumphant as he called out, "That's Captain Reddington! Take him!"

Thomas did not resist as he was ushered away, his head held high, his eyes never leaving those of his comrades. In that look was an entire conversation—of hope, trust, and a rebellion that chains or dungeons would not quell. The Codex was more than mere paper and ink; it was the embodiment of their fight, which was now up to James and Eliza.

CHAPTER FORTY
SHADOWHAWK

Under a sky veiled in the somber hues of dusk, the prison wagon rattled through the English countryside, its wheels carving a relentless path from Portsmouth toward justice awaiting in London. Inside, bound by iron and circumstance, Thomas felt the echo of his past—days spent clinging to the King's favor, nights turned sleepless with the realization that the tides of war favored the bold and adaptable. Now, he sat across from a man who was a legend among both the lawless and the lawful: Captain Elias "Shadowhawk" Bramwell, whose very name conjured images of black sails against the tempest and thunderous volleys upon the waves.

"I was once a staunch Loyalist," Thomas confessed, the wagon's jostling a sharp contrast to his voice's smooth, steady tone. "But as the colonies' resolve hardened and victory became a distant star for the Crown, I hoisted my beliefs upon a different flag."

A smirk spread across Bramwell's shadowed visage as he leaned in, the moonlight lending a sinister gleam. "Adapting your creed to the changing winds? That is a true survivalist's art. It is bold to consort with the devil, then leave him in flames."

Reclining against the wagon's wooden slats, Bramwell's voice took on the rhythm of a seasoned raconteur. "Adaptation has always been my compass," he mused with a glint of reminiscence. "At the height of the Shadowhawk's terror, nightmares were but children's fables compared to my deeds. Treasures uncounted filled our coffers, and we nearly laid hands on the Crown's own riches."

The captain's history was a vibrant tapestry of high-seas adventure, but the present painted a different picture. As Thomas hung on every word, he saw the fierce pirate of yore and a man curtailed by the tightening noose of British naval supremacy. The empire's ships had become vigilant guardians of the seas, their towering masts a permanent fixture on the horizon, ever searching for black sails bearing the ominous emblem of the Nightingale—a symbol that had struck dread into the hearts of seafarers, signifying the approach of Bramwell and his ruthless crew. The valiant ships of the line, bristling with cannons, had imposed a rigid order upon the chaotic waters where the Nightingale once flew with impunity. The open ocean, a domain where liberty and prosperity once beckoned to the daring, was now subdued, the spontaneous rhythm of piracy ensnared by the disciplined march of British naval power.

"And now, the Crown has stopped your dance," Thomas said, his voice a quiet echo in the confines of the wagon, intentionally drawing a line from Bramwell's past glories to the stifling reality of their imperial crackdown. "But what if the dance floor shifts?" Thomas ventured, a flicker of rebellion igniting in his eyes. "In the New World, opportunity awaits, unfettered by the Crown's reach."

A spark of fire seemed to reignite in Bramwell's eyes. "The New World, ye say?" His voice was a hushed growl, a predator sensing prey. "Aye, the tales have reached my ears—lands untouched, seas unclaimed. A place for men of ambition to carve out their destiny. I've been itching to chart a course to those distant shores."

"What life awaits a pirate in waters where the navy's shadow does not loom?" Thomas asked, his words carrying the weight of a man standing at the crossroads of his life. The lantern's flickering light danced across his hopeful features. "But all this is idle fantasy, it seems. Our fates are chained to the dreary confines of an English dungeon."

Bramwell's eyes were not confined to the dim light of their prison; they pierced the darkness, seeing a world uncharted. "Picture it, lad," he whispered with fervor. "Expanses of open water where the Royal Navy's iron grip cannot reach, where destiny is not dictated by the Admiralty but seized by the brave. In those distant, feral waters, a man could reclaim the liberty that has been stolen from him under a boundless, untamed sky."

The sudden jolt of the wagon shattered their exchange. Chaos erupted outside—a symphony of clashing steel and the booming cracks of musket fire. Through the din, Bramwell's voice remained steady, imbued with a note of triumph. "Our saviors have arrived," he declared, his words carving certainty in the tumultuous night.

Shots tore through the night, each blast echoing the ferocious struggle for freedom just beyond their wooden cage. The pungent odor of gunpowder filled their nostrils, mingling with the sharp, acrid scent of spilled blood. The wagon's door flew open, revealing Bramwell's crew—grim reapers, their expressions resolute. They moved with lethal efficiency, cutting away the binds that held their captain and his newfound comrade.

Surveying the lifeless bodies of the English soldiers who had been tasked with bringing them to justice, Thomas knew that his lot was now inseparable from Bramwell's. No course lay ahead but to embrace the path of the renegade.

Bramwell offered his hand to Thomas. "The time has come, mate. What will it be?"

"To the New World," Thomas affirmed, his voice a low vow to the future. "To unfettered horizons and the freedom that beckons beyond them."

Thomas and Bramwell made their escape, the pounding of horses' hooves a desperate rhythm against the earth. They approached a secluded cove where the ship lay in wait, hidden from the prying eyes of the Crown. She was a grand brigantine, her dark hull blending with the night, her masts towering like specters. The emblem of the Nightingale, stark against the black sails, fluttered with the anticipation of the chase.

The vessel herself was a phantom, shrouded in tales of terror and awe. Her decks were silent, save for the muted orders of the crew as they prepared for departure, checking every rope and sail with the meticulous care of men who knew the sea's capricious ways. Cannons, silent for now, lined her sides, sleeping dragons that awaited the captain's command. With dawn's first light, the navy's vigilant watch would resume. Every man aboard moved with quiet urgency, loading supplies, plotting their secretive course, and readying the Nightingale to once again dance upon the waters she knew so well.

Thomas stood on the deck, his life's chapters flipping backward and forward in his mind. He had crossed the Atlantic on a journey of hope and allegiance. Now, as he gazed into the dark abyss that lay before them, he was crossing back into the uncertain embrace of home—a home where the memories of Eliza and James haunted him, their fates an unresolved cadence in the symphony of his heart. His thoughts lingered on Eliza, her image a beacon of light in the overwhelming darkness, her spirit as untamed as the sea they were about to navigate.

Bramwell's voice, gruff with command, broke the solemnity of the night. "Hoist the colors, boys! We plot a course for the New World! A realm where the *Nightingale* will once again reign supreme!" The crew sprang into action, and the *Nightingale* came alive, her sails billowing as they caught the first whispers of the wind. They set forth, a silent specter gliding through the water with lethal intent.

As the shore receded into the distance, becoming nothing more than a shadow melded with the horizon, Thomas felt the chains of his old life fall away. Ahead lay the vastness of the Atlantic, a realm of boundless potential, a blank canvas on which their stories would be etched—where the *Nightingale*'s cry would signal rebirth, a defiant proclamation of freedom.

CHAPTER FORTY-ONE
LE HAVRE

Portsmouth's docklands lay shrouded in mist, a refuge for whispered bargains and fugitive souls. James and Eliza wove through the throng, their features shrouded beneath hooded cloaks, burdened with the knowledge that Thomas's capture could soon entangle them. The British were not fools; suspicion would cast its net once they realized the Solum Codex was not in Thomas's possession. At the inn, overheard mutterings and the innkeeper's willingness to trade their descriptions for coin would set the soldiers in pursuit. With the net drawing tighter, they hastened to the docks, where lawlessness held sway over loyalty, seeking a shadowy vessel to smuggle them across the Channel to France.

The air was thick with sea salt and whispered secrets. Here, at the southern reaches of England, smugglers plied their trade with a brazenness born of necessity. James and Eliza, with ample coin at their disposal, sought out the captain of a vessel known only by reputation—a ship that was more shadow than wood and canvas, a specter that haunted the British navy.

"La Fantôme," the smugglers called her, a ship that slipped through blockades like a ghost through walls. Her captain, a man known as Gaspard, met them in the belly of a dockside tavern, the stench of ale and sweat a pungent cloak around the clandestine proceedings. His eyes, sharp as a hawk's, appraised them, and his voice, when he spoke, was the sound of the sea's own rasp. "Discretion is expensive," he murmured.

With a nod, James placed a heavy purse in Gaspard's waiting palm. The jingle of coins was the key to their silent flight across the Channel. Under cover of darkness, they boarded La Fantôme, a vessel that seemed nothing more than a whisper on the water. The night swallowed their departure, and by dawn, they were but a tale on the lips of the gulls.

The journey across the Channel was silent, the sea calm as if respecting their need for secrecy. As La Fantôme sliced through the waters, Gaspard, the captain whose very presence seemed as ephemeral as the ship he commanded, spoke to James and Eliza about their onward travels. "The New World, you seek?" Gaspard's voice was a low rumble, like thunder rolling in from the deep. "Le Havre will be your crossroads. There, ships bound for the Americas depart with the tide, and captains care more for the weight of your coin than the secrets you carry."

As La Fantôme neared the French coastline, the first light of dawn cast a golden hue over the port of Le Havre. The city unfolded before them like a living painting, a tapestry of masts and sails undulating in the morning breeze. The silhouette of the cityscape was punctured by the spires of cathedrals and the rigid lines of warehouses, a testament to its role as a nexus of commerce and a gateway to the New World.

The ship cut through the Channel's waters, her prow slicing through the waves with the grace of a seabird in flight. James and Eliza stood at the bow, watching as the busy harbor came into view. Fishermen hauled in their nocturnal catches, calling to each other in a rhythmic cadence that matched the seagulls' raucous symphony. The docks were lined with vessels of all sizes, from modest fishing boats to grand merchantmen like the ones they sought.

The air was salty and brisk, invigorating their spirits. They inhaled deeply, savoring the scent of freedom. Le Havre was a bustling port where the world converged through trade, tales, and the constant exchange of ideas. Stepping off La Fantôme, James and Eliza navigated the planks of the dock with an unspoken kinship to the bustle around them, feeling a connection to the French allies who had been instrumental in the Colonialists' victory. The vitality of the port, pulsating with the rhythm of stevedores and tradespeople, resonated with their own pulse of newfound freedom. As they threaded through the throngs on the cobbled streets, the blend of languages and clamor of commerce enveloped them, a tapestry woven from the threads of myriad nations. It was a symphony of human endeavor, and within it, they moved with the buoyant step of those allied by shared aspirations and common cause.

Their path eventually took them to the harbormaster's office, a sturdy building perched at the edge of the waterfront, overseeing the maritime ballet. The harbormaster, a man weathered by salt and years, listened to their request with an impassive face before nodding toward a tall ship anchored at the far end of the quay. *"L'Avenir,"* he pronounced, pointing to the vessel. "She is a sturdy ship with a seasoned captain. She will carry you to the shores of America." Securing their passage required the rest of their coin and surrendering their anonymity, a price they willingly paid for the promise of reaching home.

This captain, a robust man named Lefebvre, conducted his business openly. Here, negotiations were not whispered but declared with the confidence of those protected by a friendly flag. Lefebvre's terms were fair, and they secured a private cabin, small but with a porthole that would grant them views of the horizon and the future that awaited.

The door to the cabin closed with a gentle click, sealing James and Eliza within the intimate sanctum that was now theirs. The world beyond the porthole seemed to pause, the sea's whispers falling to a hush as they turned their attention to the object that had so irrevocably altered their destinies. The Codex lay on the modest table, innocuous in appearance, yet its pages held secrets that had eluded comprehension for eons.

With reverent hands, Eliza opened the cover. The parchment, aged yet resilient, rustled like the wings of a caged dove yearning for release. The symbols and writings, inscrutable glyphs that danced before their eyes, seemed to pulse with an energy of their own. The characters cast enigmatic shadows in the dim light, weaving an atmosphere thick with the musk of mystery and antiquity.

James leaned closer, his breath caught in his throat as if the very air in the room had thickened with the weight of revelation. "Do you realize," he whispered, "what truths might be hidden within these pages?" The enormity of their discovery pressed down upon them, a tangible presence in the room as potent as the salt-laden air that filled their lungs.

Eliza nodded, her eyes reflecting a maelstrom of wonder and fear. "It's more than just knowledge, James. It's a legacy—of civilizations long vanished, of wisdom that might change the world as we know it." Her fingers traced the cryptic letters, a plea for understanding.

They sat together, ensconced in the silence of their cabin, the Codex, a silent sentinel between them. Its secrets lay just beyond the grasp of their comprehension, a riddle wrapped in the enigma of ages past. Yet, as the ship plowed its steady course across the Atlantic, they felt the promise of answers that would unfold with the passage of miles and the turning of pages. At this moment, bound by their quest for understanding, they were no longer mere fugitives but keepers of a truth that had traversed the annals of history to find refuge in their hands.

With a solemn pact to protect the Codex at all costs, James carefully tucked it away within a false bottom of their travel trunk. Once it was hidden from prying eyes, they emerged from their cabin, ascending to the main deck where the world was nothing but sea and sky.

L'Avenir was already slipping her moorings, easing away from Le Havre's embrace with a grace that belied her size. James and Eliza leaned on the rail, the salt breeze tousling their hair as the coast of France receded into a watercolor blur. Their hearts were sailors, too, navigating the tumultuous sea of their own uncertain future.

"What shall we do with it?" Eliza mused aloud, her gaze on the horizon. "The Codex, I mean, once we're home."

"To Madison and Jefferson," James replied, the names of the great thinkers sounding like an incantation. "With their breadth of knowledge and resources … they just might unlock its secrets."

Eliza nodded. "They must have the capability. Otherwise, why send us on such an arduous quest across the ocean?"

James conceded with a small lift of his shoulders, "Indeed, that must be the case."

Eliza's query floated up delicately, a vulnerable blossom on the winds of fate. "But what about us, James?"

A flicker of bewilderment crossed his features, soon replaced by an awakening as if her words were the final piece to a celestial puzzle. "Us," he repeated, the word blooming with the possibility of infinite tomorrows. Amidst the quietude of the morning, with the golden light draping them in its blessing, James's heart found its scripture. "Eliza," he started, his voice now a vessel for his deepest conviction. "As your friend Agatha said, our souls were destined to meet."

Eliza's lips parted gently, a tender correction poised on her tongue. "Not merely to meet, James," she whispered, her voice a soft chime of truth. "But to find each other again, as if we have been dancing through lifetimes just to converge in this one."

In the golden embrace of dawn, the world seemed to hold its breath as James's words wove the threads of countless lifetimes. "Eliza Sinclair"—he spoke with the gravity of a soul echoing through eternity—"will you be my wife in this lifetime?"

The rising sun cast its light upon Eliza, lighting her red hair with a radiant glow and illuminating her face with the tender warmth of morning. "Yes, James," she vowed, her voice echoing an infinite bond. "In this lifetime and whatever comes after, I will."

Their kiss transcended the mere touch of lips; it was the profound union of two eternal souls meeting in the sacred dance of reunion, the sky blazed in celebration, hues of amber and rose painting a scene. They kissed not just for now but for always and forevermore, an endless promise cast upon the waters of the ever-turning world.

CHAPTER FORTY-TWO
A PLAN FOR THE PIRATES

The *Nightingale*, a lone silhouette against the gray, pre-dawn sky, was an icy specter navigating the merciless Atlantic. Her masts, encrusted with a thick armor ice, groaned under the weight of the frozen gale. The sails, once billowing with the breath of the sea, now crackled like ancient parchment, their surfaces glazed with a sheath of frost that shimmered eerily in the faint light. The deck was a perilous expanse, each surface slick with ice that clung with a stubbornness that defied the crews' picks and shovels.

The wind was a slicing blade, cutting through the thickest coats. It was a relentless howl that bore the sting of a thousand needles. It whipped across the ship with fury, a masterful sculptor turning ropes and riggings into bizarre, twisted icicles that clicked and clattered like glass chandeliers in the tumult.

Thomas, ensconced in the inadequate shelter his cloak provided, became a mere shadow amongst the ship's crew. His breaths were visible puffs of white, hanging in the air before being snatched away by the wind; coughs wracked his frame, a harsh reminder of his body's rebellion against the unyielding freeze.

The very planks beneath their feet groaned and creaked, the ship protesting as she was pushed to her limits. The relentless cold was an adversary as formidable as any enemy cannon or fire. This voyage was marked not by the distance covered but by the sheer will to endure, a test of both the spirit and flesh against nature's raw, untamed power.

In the dim belly of the *Nightingale*, where each creak of timber and groan of rope sang of the sea's relentless will, Bramwell and Thomas found themselves deep in the strategy of predation. Lanterns swung to the rhythm of the waves, casting an ominous dance of shadows as they debated the merits of New York Harbor's wealth.

"Plenty a merchant vessel to lighten off their load, eh?" Bramwell's voice was a growl, hungry for the spoils of conquest. A shrewd mariner, Bramwell knew well the rich pickings New York Harbor could offer. The labyrinth of merchant ships, the warehouses groaning with goods, the air of affluence that hovered over the city—it was a pirate's dream.

Yet, his seasoned instincts warned of the perilous guard the King's navy provided. "And the King's navy? They still haunt those waters?" Bramwell asked, his voice as steady as the ship beneath his feet. Thomas, though weakened, perceived the underlying tension. He knew the answer would steer their fate.

"They do," Thomas replied, the weight of his words more burdensome than chains. "The harbor may glisten with gold, but lions guard it." The cabin fell silent, save for the creak of wood and whipping of the winds through the cracks in the wallboards. Bramwell's dream of New York's riches faded like the ghost of a dying man. He paced the floor, his boots thumping a morose rhythm, his mind churning like the stormy sea.

In need of a new quarry, Bramwell sought the tales of men who'd seen the empire's edges fray. "Tell me of your battles, Thomas. Of the places where the red coats faltered," he urged.

Thomas, caught in the web of his feverish memories, began to recount the thunderous clamor of artillery, the desperate cries of men, and the despair of the vanquished at Yorktown. Though tinged with pain, his narrative shone a light on a new possibility—a place stripped of its guardians.

"Yorktown, you say?" Bramwell stopped mid-pace, a spark igniting. Here was a prize left unguarded, a jewel discarded in the aftermath of war. "A place left naked to the eye of predation," he pondered aloud.

Thomas felt a pang of dread despite the fever gnawing at his mind. The images of Yorktown's streets, the homes of his comrades, of Eliza, the lives he had intertwined with—all suddenly vulnerable. Frail as autumn's last leaf, his voice whispered, "No, not Yorktown. There are better places."

But Bramwell was no longer listening. His thoughts raced ahead to the logistics of such an endeavor, the crew he'd need to rally, the arms, and the approach. He envisioned the Chesapeake Bay not as a site of historic loss, but as a gateway to riches untold. "Then it is settled," he said, his eyes alight with the fire of ambition. "We set course for

Yorktown. The British lion may have retreated, but it leaves a den ripe for the taking behind."

As Bramwell left his cabin, Thomas wrestled with the guilt and the fever in equal measure. He had hoped to find refuge and recovery on the *Nightingale*, to escape the horrors of war he had endured. Instead, he found himself complicit in a scheme that might bring ruin to his doorstep.

A grim silence settled over Thomas as the *Nightingale* sliced through the waves. In his heart, a battle raged as fierce as any he had fought in uniform. Would he be the harbinger of doom for his own people, or could he yet find a way to avert the disaster he had set in motion?

He lay in the dim light of the lantern, thoughts adrift on a sea of feverish uncertainty. He pondered the fate of Eliza and James. Were they able to escape Portsmouth as he did? Did they still possess the Solum Codex? Would they find their way back home? And would they speak of his bravery or of his folly?

The *Nightingale* groaned and creaked. Would they reach Yorktown or succumb to the tempest's rage? Would the sickness in his lungs claim his life before he could witness the outcome of his unintended betrayal?

Bramwell, meanwhile, was steadfast amidst the chaos, his figure an unmoving pillar against the wind and rain. To him, loyalty was a currency spent only on the surety of profit. Yorktown, with its undefended treasures, was not a place of moral quandaries but a land ripe for his taking. As the *Nightingale* plowed through the tumultuous waves, edging closer to their destination, the crew battled the elements, their hands as firm on ropes and wood as Bramwell's resolve was on his ambition.

The strife within Thomas's soul mirrored what clawed at the ship's hull—the struggle between the tempest of greed and the still waters of right, as if the gods themselves waited to see which force would prevail: the hunger for gold or the search for redemption.

CHAPTER FORTY-THREE
RETURN OF THE CODEX

As the *L'Avenir* creaked into the welcoming embrace of Philadelphia's harbor, the relief James and Eliza felt was palpable. The sea had unleashed its wrath upon them in relentless winter storms that had turned the sky to an inky blackness and tested their limits. Night after night, Eliza had found solace in the circle of James's arms, her head resting against his steady heartbeat—a rhythm of survival and hope amid the howling winds and towering waves.

With each tempest that descended upon them, their vessel was tossed like a mere plaything of the gods, its masts groaning in protest. The crew battled the elements with a ferocity born of desperation, their faces etched with the salt and scars of the ocean's merciless onslaught. It was in these moments when the world seemed reduced to nothing but the roar of the sea that Eliza's thoughts drifted to the Codex nestled against her. Its presence constantly reminded them of the purpose, propelling them forward through squall and shadow.

When they finally set foot on solid ground, the bustle of the port was a jarring symphony after the solitude of the sea. With its swarm of sailors and merchants, Philadelphia seemed a universe away from the quiet desperation they had faced on the open waters.

Their arrival was marked not with the fanfare one might expect for the bearers of such a crucial artifact but with an unexplained wait that gnawed at their nerves. For two days, the doors to Madison and Jefferson remained closed to them, and the silence sowed seeds of doubt. Their patience frayed like a sail in the storm, but they held fast to the hope that the importance of their mission would soon be recognized.

When they were finally ushered into the presence of the statesmen, the room's grandeur was overshadowed by their tale's urgency. "With our friend Thomas Reddington, we reclaimed the Codex." Eliza spoke, her voice a beacon of fortitude that had weathered much more than the sea's fury.

When Thomas Reddington's name left Eliza's lips, a shadow crossed Jefferson's countenance. His acquaintance with Reddington's repute was tinged with wariness, for the man was a known adherent to the British regime. This affiliation posed a silent question, a riddle of trust and motives. Jefferson's voice, tinged with a hint of incredulity, broke the stillness. "You trusted this man?" he questioned, his gaze piercing, seeking the truth beyond the surface.

Eliza met his scrutiny with the clarity of conviction, her reply resolute and unwavering. "Yes, we placed our faith in him, and he has more than proven his merit," she affirmed. "The Codex is back in our hands—its return speaks volumes of his allegiance and the role he played. Without Thomas, our success might have remained an elusive dream."

Jefferson and Madison listened, the gravity of the situation settling upon the room like a dense fog.

With the Codex splayed open, revealing its cryptic script and enigmatic symbols, James asked, "You've deciphered this?" Madison's response was a shake of his head—a silent but firm denial. "No, this remains an enigma. Your return of it, while commendable, does not advance our cause. It holds no value in its current state."

James and Eliza exchanged a glance, their shock palpable. "What do you mean?" Eliza's voice faltered. "Is this not the very cornerstone of your efforts to finalize the drafting of the Constitution?"

Madison allowed himself a thin smile that did not quite reach his eyes. "Without the means to interpret the Codex, its words are as elusive as shadows at dusk. We permitted its theft, using it as a ruse," he explained. "The British were convinced that devoid of the Codex, our hands would be tied in completing our work."

"So, our mission was a ploy?" James asked, struggling to understand.

"Yes," Madison affirmed. "It was a calculated risk. Harrison was dispatched to Yorktown with the intention of recruiting you under this guise."

James's thoughts swirled, turmoil rising within him. "Harrison … he died for this. And now you say it was for nothing? We—Eliza,

Thomas, and I—we all teetered on the brink of death for a mere diversion?" The betrayal was a bitter pill, and it stuck in his throat, the weight of their sacrifices crashing down upon him like the ruthless waves of the sea.

Jefferson and Madison absorbed the tempest of emotions before them, the stark revelation recasting the room's atmosphere. The Codex was a bridge to the past, cradling secrets that might one day unlock a future bright with promise. Yet, it was also now a symbol of the intricate web of stratagem and sacrifice woven into the very fabric of their burgeoning nation. Their quest had been noble, if not essential, in the way they had believed, and their bravery and resolve were the true guiding lights of the fledgling republic's path forward.

Eliza's stance was defiant, her voice a sharp arrow in the quietude of the chamber. "Why would you ignite a perilous chase for the Codex if its secrets hold no value to you?" she demanded, her gaze locking with Madison's.

Madison spread his hands wide, his fingers tracing the invisible threads of a master plan. "Ah, but that is where you are mistaken," he began with a sly edge. "The very odyssey you embarked upon, braving death for the Codex's retrieval, spun a web of deceit so convincing that the British clung to its supposed significance. Your valiant quest, unwitting though it may have been, has shielded the sanctity of our Constitution's birth. For this, you have the everlasting gratitude of your country."

Eliza's brow furrowed, her thoughts adrift between betrayal and pride. "And what fate befalls the Codex in this grand design?" she pressed, her words heavy with the cost of their journey.

Jefferson, with the care one might afford a fragile relic, pushed it toward the pair, its passage across the table slow, almost reverential. "It is yours to claim," he announced, each word infused with the gravity of history. "Accept it as a testament to your sacrifice, a symbol of our nascent nation's esteem. Let it remind you that the light of liberty emerges stronger from the shadows of intrigue."

James and Eliza were momentarily rooted to the spot. The air felt heavy, laden with the unspoken cost of their journey. Eliza's fingers trembled faintly as they hovered above the ancient artifact, her heart a tumultuous sea mirroring the very waters they had traversed.

"You are … giving it to us?" James asked with wonder and a raw, unmasked incredulity.

Jefferson nodded solemnly, his eyes reflecting the room's dancing candlelight. "Indeed, we are," he affirmed. "Your courage and unwavering dedication have earned you this and so much more. The Codex may not hold the key to our country's laws, but perhaps you will discover new mysteries to explore within its pages."

Madison's demeanor softened as he added, "Consider it not just a relic of your journey but a beacon for future endeavors. In your hands, it may yet reveal secrets that elude us."

Eliza finally allowed her fingers to caress the cover, feeling the weight of generations beneath her touch. Once a mystery that loomed distant and foreboding, the Codex was now theirs—its destiny inexplicably entwined with their own.

James reached out to rest his hand atop Eliza's. They felt the pulse of history in their grasp. Their eyes met, and they understood that this was not merely the conclusion of an arduous quest, but the inception of their next great adventure.

CHAPTER FORTY-FOUR
THOMAS'S RETURN

Through the fevered haze and the relentless grip of his sickness, Thomas's vision swam, the faces around him merging into a tapestry that seemed to float above his prone form. The gentle rocking that had accompanied his fraught journey aboard the *Nightingale* was replaced by the stillness of the earth beneath him, its steadiness a strange contrast to the heaving decks he had come to know. The pirate ship, a silhouette etched against the tempestuous sky with sails that whispered of nocturnal intrigues, now receded into the realm of memory as Bramwell's unlooked-for act of compassion deposited him onto the shores of Yorktown.

Recognition flickered behind the townsfolk's eyes as they beheld Thomas, his form now a mere shadow of the Yorktown resident who had once forsaken their collective cause and Eliza, their cherished daughter. Yet, the bonds of his lineage bore an unspoken obligation. They arranged for his passage with whispers that danced with judgment and mercy. In the solemn dignity of a carriage drawn by horses that tread softly on cobblestones heavy with history, they escorted him to the sanctuary of his parents' home in Williamsburg, where he could convalesce away from the eyes that still remembered.

As the contours of Williamsburg rose to greet him, Thomas felt the weight of history in its unchanging facade. The colonial buildings, proud and dignified, stood as sentinels to the revolution that had churned around them. Yet here, time seemed to hold its breath, the echoes of rebellion lingering in the air like the scent of spent gunpowder, a reminder of the struggles and triumphs that had unfolded within and beyond these walls.

His parents' home stood as it always had—a steadfast monument to the life he had left behind in pursuit of greater causes. As the door opened, the scent of herbs and the warmth of the hearth enveloped him, a stark contrast to the biting cold of the Atlantic winds he had endured.

His mother, her face lined with worry, became the angelic force of his recovery. With a tenderness that only a mother's touch could convey, she nursed her son, her silent prayers weaving through the drafty chambers of the old house, battling the shadow of death that loomed over him.

As health slowly reclaimed his body, so too did the need to unburden his soul. With a newfound clarity that often accompanies one's dance with mortality, Thomas sought his father's counsel. This man had once viewed him through the eyes of disdain as a Loyalist, an unwelcome advocate for the Crown in a family of dedicated Patriots.

In the parlor, where portraits of their ancestors bore witness to the unfolding reconciliation, Thomas sat across from the man whose disappointment had once been as palpable as the chill of winter. Now, the air between them was thick with anticipation and, perhaps, the possibility of absolution. Thomas's confession unfurled, his words weaving a tale as intricate as the secret knots of a sailor. "Father," he began, his voice a mingling of ardor and penitence, "led by the compass of my convictions, I found myself aboard the British warship the HMS *Charon*. It was there, hidden in Cornwallis's very quarters, that destiny entrusted me with the Solum Codex. A tome of such consequence, its secrets could have tipped the scales of war heavily in favor of the Crown."

Thomas recounted his tale, his voice tinged with pain, as low and remorseful as a confession whispered through church lattice. "With the deftness of a spy," he intoned, a solemn gravity pressing down upon his shoulders, "I liberated the Codex from the very heart of the HMS *Charon*, right under the noses of the King's men. It was from the warship's clutches at Portsmouth that I escaped, the precious volume in hand."

The air shifted, a tender nostalgia threading through as his mother appeared like a specter. "I entrusted the hope of our nation into the hands of two of our most ardent compatriots—James, whose resolve is as the oak, and Eliza, whose spirit burns with the fire of liberty." He halted, the heavy thud of his heart betraying his next words.

A curtain of silence fell, pierced only by the rustling of his mother's silk gown. With a soft and reflective voice, as if conjuring the ghost of a memory, she murmured, "Eliza, is it?" The name hung between them, ripe with the unspoken history of a bond sundered by war's divide. Her curiosity was alight, not merely with concern for the fate of the Codex, but for the woman who once lay heart to heart with her son.

Thomas met her gaze, his eyes mirroring the uncertainty that clouded their fate. "Of them or the Codex, I can claim no knowledge. Like whispers in the wind, they have vanished, leaving naught but the legacy of their courage and the echo of their names."

Thomas gathered a quiet breath, steadying the tempest within as he prepared to unfurl the final chapter of his tale. "In the grip of my hands, the Codex became more than a mere object—it became the fulcrum of my fate. With its heavy presence, the scales of loyalty shifted, revealing a patriotism deep within my bones. It was then I knew—I could not bear to be a turncoat to the very soil that nurtured me, to the very people who were a part of my sinew and soul. I delivered the Codex into the hands of our soldiers, a decisive blow to the general's campaign and the ultimate renunciation of my ties to the Crown."

His father listened with a slowly softening gaze. The air, once rigid with judgment, began to thaw as Thomas recounted his harrowing escape, his unwilling alliance with the pirate Bramwell, and his secretive voyage back to American soil.

"I was proud of my journey, for it was fraught with peril and demanded every ounce of courage I possessed," Thomas said, his voice barely louder than a whisper. "But I also regretted it, for I know the pain my allegiance has caused you."

As the father beheld Thomas, it was not the image of the Loyalist he had renounced that he saw; instead, it was a son who had dared to defy the very fabric of his own allegiance for a cause grander than himself. Here stood a man who, in one singular act of valor, had redefined his essence.

Thomas realized that his greatest adventure had not been his escape or his battle with the sea but rather the journey back to his father's heart, to a place where he was not a traitor but simply his son—flawed, changed, and finally home. He recounted the irony that the pirate Bramwell, who had shown him unexpected kindness, was now the scourge of Chesapeake Bay. Bramwell's mercy had been a flicker of light amidst the pirate's usual ruthlessness, a complexity that now haunted Thomas as he convalesced in the cocoon of his childhood room.

Though his body mended, his spirit chafed at the confinement. His mother, wise to the ways of the world, listened and understood the unspoken yearning behind her son's words. She knew that the same winds that had brought him home would soon carry him back to the fray. Her hands trembled with the knowledge that Thomas's destiny was intertwined with the tumultuous birth of a nation.

As Thomas's strength waxed anew, so did his awareness of the storm on the horizon. Bramwell and his men were a looming tempest, threatening to engulf Yorktown and, eventually, Williamsburg in their maelstrom of piracy. A confrontation was inevitable; Thomas would see them ousted from the Chesapeake Bay or defeated permanently. But such a feat demanded allies, comrades in arms. His thoughts drifted to James and Eliza. If they stood by his side, with their combined might, they could turn the tide. Their absence was a gulf in his plans, but hope remained like a steady flame.

CHAPTER FORTY-FIVE
THE CODEX COMES HOME

Under the vast expanse of a sky transitioning from the velvet of night to the first blush of dawn, Eliza and James rode toward Yorktown. The rhythmic cadence of their horses' hooves against the dirt road harmonized with the early morning chorus of the waking countryside. They had been furnished with sturdy horses, supplies enough to see them through, and coins that jingled in their pouches—a token of Philadelphia's gratitude. Their journey had been undisturbed, but the ease of their travel did nothing to quiet the turbulence in Eliza's mind.

The road beneath them stretched on, each mile a quiet companion to their troubled musings. James broke the morning's hush, noting the furrows on Eliza's brow. "You carry a heavy silence," he said, his tone soft as the dawn. "Share with me your burden."

Her eyes, mirrors to a soul in turmoil, met his. "It is Thomas," Eliza confessed, the edges of her mouth curling with a sorrow-tinged smile. "My heart frets over his fate. Does he yet draw breath in a dank cell, or has he met the gallows' embrace for his betrayal of the Crown?"

James reached across the space between their horses, grasping her hand. "Thomas's wits have always been his shield and sword. We must believe there's a thread of hope to cling to—that he's still out there, somewhere beyond the King's reach."

"Should we not seek some word of him? A discreet inquiry might ease this dread or confirm our worst fears."

James pondered, his gaze lost to the horizon. "To inquire is to stir still waters, possibly drawing eyes to our own deeds. Yet, to leave a comrade's fate to the wind …" His voice trailed off, leaving the question to hang between them as they continued on, bound by the past and the shared resolve for the future.

"But hope can be a cruel guest," Eliza murmured, "flitting away just when you need it most. The Thomas I knew—the one before … he became something else—would stand against any storm. But now, after all he's done, I fear he may have been swept away by it."

The air between them was laden with the gravity of their revelation as they approached the crossroads. A silence had settled, a stark contrast to the usually spirited banter that accompanied their travels. The Codex, now revealed as a mere ploy, lay among their provisions.

Eliza's voice was tinged with a blend of disbelief and despair. "To think we wagered our lives, and Thomas perhaps his own, for nothing but a ruse," she lamented, her fingers brushing the deceptive leather with a sense of betrayal. "And Harrison … he paid with his life for this … this artifice."

James regarded her with somber empathy, his eyes reflecting a hard-earned wisdom. "This is the nature of war, Eliza. It is a tapestry woven with the threads of deception and sacrifice. It is not the veracity of the Codex that matters but the hope and the advantage it provided our cause."

Eliza cried, "But at what cost? At what terrible price must we value such hope?"

James's response was measured, his tone imbued with the weight of many such calculations made in dark times. "It is the price of freedom, the currency of rebellion. We weigh the lives given against the lives we aim to free. And in that balance, we find our resolve to continue, knowing that each sacrifice paves the path to a future where such choices are no longer our burden."

Despite the somber wisdom in James's words, a flicker of resistance sparked within Eliza. She clung to a sliver of hope that the Codex held a significance beyond their current understanding. "This cannot be a fruitless endeavor," she insisted, her voice a mix of defiance and desperation. "The Codex hails from Lemuria, a land of legends, where it is said humanity once thrived in an ageless society of enlightenment and harmony. Its wisdom cannot simply vanish into the annals of warfare."

James watched her. "You speak of myths, Eliza. But even myths carry the weight of truth, sometimes."

Eliza's eyes were alight with a fervent glimmer, reflecting the undying hope that the Codex still held value. "There are layers here, not visible to the eye. Perhaps Agatha and her tarot … they could offer us a glimpse into its profound truths."

The idea of consulting Agatha flickered in Eliza's eyes like a stubborn flame, but James met it with a cool breath of cynicism. "Tarot cards, they have their charm, particularly when it comes to entangling the matters of the heart," he remarked with a dismissive edge. "Amusing at a fair, perhaps, but not for unraveling something as momentous as the Codex."

Eliza recoiled at his mocking tone. "When Agatha spoke of eternal soulmates, you nodded, you agreed—was that merely your path to my heart … to my bed?" Her voice was a low tremble of betrayal.

James scrambled for composure, the guilt etching lines of strain around his eyes. "Eliza, my intentions …" he began, his voice a hesitant murmur. "I may have played along with Agatha's readings, but my feelings for you were never a charade."

But Eliza's anger had found its mark, and it held fast. "Convenient, James," she hissed, "to don Agatha's prophecies like a cloak when it suited you. And now, when I seek the same mysticism to guide us, you discard it—and my foolish beliefs along with it?"

James reached out, seeking to bridge the chasm his words had created, but she recoiled from his touch. "It was not … I—"

"No, James," Eliza cut him off, her eyes ablaze with wounded fury. "You cannot dismiss my beliefs as trifles and then claim sincerity. You cannot scorn the tools I choose to fathom this enigma we have bled for."

The rhythm of their horses' hooves against the hard-packed earth was the only sound that filled the air between Eliza and James as they rode side by side back to Yorktown.

Eliza, astride her mount with a rigid posture that betrayed none of the turmoil churning within her, kept her gaze fixed on the road ahead. The landscape's transition from dusk to night mirrored the darkening of her thoughts. Their first disagreement, especially one so rooted in core beliefs, was a wound to the heart that could not be easily salved.

James rode uneasily beside her, his glance occasionally stealing to her profile, seeking an opening, or at least the start of a healing conversation. Yet, he found none. His attempts at bridging the divide had been rebuffed, his words dissolving into the cooling air of twilight.

The Codex, tied securely in the saddlebag between them, might as well have been leagues away. It had been their shared quest, their common ground, but now it lay at the heart of their discord.

As they traversed the final stretch of their journey, the silence was not broken, and the gap that had opened up seemed to grow wider with every mile. The shadows of the night crept around them as if to envelop them in a world where the stark truths of day grew dim and uncertain. They moved forward, together but alone with their thoughts and the unspoken fears of what this rift could mean.

CHAPTER FORTY-SIX
PROBLEM WITH PIRATES

The dock's wooden planks creaked under Thomas's boots, a rhythm that matched the pounding in his chest. It was here, years ago, that he had stood tall and proud as a captain in the British Army. Now, the same dock bore witness to his shame. Thomas's gaze fixed on the dark silhouette of the *Nightingale*, the pirate ship casting a long, ominous shadow on the waters of Yorktown. With its tattered sails dancing in the wind, the vessel was a stark reminder of the chaos he had inadvertently unleashed.

The name of Captain Elias "Shadowhawk" Bramwell struck fear into the townspeople's hearts, and the blame lay at Thomas's feet.

Yorktown, in the wake of the British withdrawal, was a town licking its wounds, its structures scarred from the relentless siege. The captured British and German soldiers had been herded to prison camps far away, and the valiant American and French forces had dispersed. They had been the de facto peacekeepers, but now there was a void where order once stood.

The Continental Army, under the stalwart guidance of General George Washington, alongside their French allies, had been the town's safeguard, the captives' managers, and the peace's enforcers. Their departure had left behind a fragile skeleton of security. The local militia, a patchwork of willing souls, were unprepared for the tyranny of the sea that now threatened their doorsteps. Bramwell knew this, and he exploited it with the precision of a surgeon, each cut leaving Yorktown more defenseless.

Thomas felt that he must forge a new fighting force from the fearful and the weary. The town's survival depended on his ability to lead, transforming farmers and tradesmen into warriors. With each pirate raid, Thomas's resolve hardened. He moved amongst the townsfolk, his voice growing stronger, not with the authority of his former rank, but with the conviction of a man who had nothing left to lose. He spoke of homes and families, of the life they all yearned to reclaim.

He visited the blacksmith, the carpenter, the barkeep—men whose hands were more accustomed to tools of trade than weapons of war. Yet, in their eyes, he saw not the spark he hoped to ignite, but the smoldering resentment of his Loyalist past. Each attempt to rally the townspeople was met with a cold refusal, their memories of his allegiance a chasm too wide to cross.

By day, he found himself alone, drilling in silent futility, his musket the only one rising against the foes. By night, he planned, maps and reports scattered across his table like the remnants of dreams unfulfilled. And always, the *Nightingale* loomed in the distance, a specter in the chilling mist of winter, a cruel reminder of his isolation.

As the moon climbed high and silvered the night, Thomas stood once again on the dock. The *Nightingale*'s presence was felt more than seen, but he knew the dawn would come and, with it, a reckoning. Yorktown's fate seemed to rest on reluctant shoulders, weighed down by the heavy chains of past loyalties.

In the silent hours of the night, when shadows stretched like phantoms across Yorktown's cobblestone streets, Thomas walked alone. The weight of his past—marked by service to a Crown that now felt worlds away, mingled with the present peril, wrapping around him as tightly as the fog that rolled in from the sea. Every whispered conspiracy of the *Nightingale*'s prow haunted his thoughts; every glance from his fellow townspeople, a blend of suspicion and derision, burrowed deep into his sense of duty.

He passed homes darkened by the hour yet unsettled by fear, their once bright futures as dimmed as the sputtering lanterns by their doors. These were the people he had pledged to serve, whose dreams of peace had been dashed not just by war but by his inadvertent betrayal. They slept, not knowing that the man who had once led redcoats through these streets now bore the crushing hope of their deliverance.

Thomas reached a tavern, a haven of hushed voices and dull candlelight, and pushed open the door. The chill of estrangement greeted him. In this refuge for the lost and the weary, he sought solace but found none. As the door swung shut behind him, Thomas realized that this was not a retreat from his troubles but a stark embodiment of them.

Thomas nursed his ale in the dim corner of the nondescript tavern, a stark contrast to the warmth of the Sinclair, where Eliza poured drinks with a kind word. Here, the air was thick with the smell of unwashed bodies and stale tobacco, and the proprietor, a stout man with a look that suggested smiles were a currency he could not afford, gave Thomas only the briefest of nods before disappearing behind the bar.

The door swung open, ushering in a cold gust that seemed to whisper of the sea's ruthlessness. All eyes turned as Captain Elias "Shadowhawk" Bramwell stepped in, commanding the space as the sea commanded its tides. The tavern's dim lighting danced across the silver trims of his coat, and a sneer played upon his lips as his gaze found Thomas.

"Stirring the pot of rebellion, are we?" Bramwell's voice cut through the low hum of conversation, every word dripping with disdain. "Or has the mighty British officer come to drown his failures in drink?"

The tavern fell silent, the tension thick as the patrons waited for Thomas's response. But Thomas did not rise to the bait. His grip on his mug tightened, the knuckles whitening—a stark reminder of his lone stance.

Bramwell leaned in close, his voice low enough for only Thomas to hear. "I saved your life, and this is how you repay me? By rallying these sheep to revolt?"

In the charged stillness between them, Thomas held Bramwell's gaze, a calm clarity in his voice. "I refuse to weigh one life against another," he stated resolutely. "My aim is not to kindle war but to defend what is justly ours."

A cold mirth danced in Bramwell's eyes as he replied, "You talk of rights and justice as though they were bestowed upon you by a Crown that has long since discarded you like an unwanted trinket."

Thomas stood firm, bolstering himself with the quiet determination seen in the downcast eyes around him. "Your barbs are misplaced," he countered, the measured force of his words cutting through Bramwell's cynicism. "I may be a wanderer between worlds, but my allegiance is clear. It's not to a Crown or a creed, but to the enduring spirit of freedom."

Bramwell's laughter was a dissonant note in the tense, sharp, and jarring atmosphere. "Ah, Thomas, ever the lost soul, flitting between loyalties, never truly pledging to one side," he sneered. "But make no mistake; in this realm, the *Nightingale* rules supreme, and I am her master."

With a final glare, Bramwell turned and left as abruptly as he had arrived, leaving behind a trail of whispers and uneasy glances. Thomas looked down at his ale and pushed it away. He could not afford the luxury of intoxication when the *Nightingale*'s shadow loomed over Yorktown.

It was clear that he could not wait for the town to rally. If Yorktown were to have a fighting chance, it would be because he stood and faced

the tide head-on. Thomas would need to become a beacon for resistance,
a harbinger of the town's courage.

CHAPTER FORTY-SEVEN
RETURN TO YORKTOWN

James and Eliza returned to Yorktown and traversed streets etched with the scars of battle, but the town's reconstruction efforts were gradually working. Brick by brick and with cautious optimism, the town was slowly knitting itself back together.

Eliza was besieged by inner conflicts. She had anticipated a serene homecoming, but the restless whispers of the townspeople quickly dispelled that hope. The tales they spun were of a pirate vessel wreaking havoc in the bay, a ghostly presence from a bygone time they had all hoped was behind them. The shadow deepened as they learned of Thomas; that he was home but not only entwined with the very menace that now threatened their shores but also unwittingly responsible for bringing the pirate vessel to Yorktown.

The quest to locate Thomas, fueled by a mix of concern and urgency, had James and Eliza navigating through a network of hushed voices and elusive leads. Their journey led them to a covert stronghold, a vestige left by retreating British forces, where they discovered Thomas. Shrouded in the murky half-light of the concealed armory, among remnants of British might and munitions left for the taking, he stood, a silent figure flanked by the very instruments of war he had beckoned to these shores.

Eliza's heart, which had been heavy with dread, now lifted in a surge of relief as she gazed upon Thomas, who stood before them very much alive. His countenance told of a grim saga survived, lines etched by adversity, by the shadow of the reaper he had narrowly escaped. He looked like a man reborn from the clutches of death, his every word and breath a testament to his resilience.

"Thomas!" she exclaimed, her voice trembling with emotion as she rushed forward. "We feared the worst."

James followed, clapping Thomas on the shoulder with a brotherly force. "Seeing you standing here is nothing short of a miracle."

Thomas met their gazes, a wry smile breaking through the creases of his worn face. "Indeed, it would seem fate has yet some use for me."

His story unfolded with a quiet intensity, a narrative punctuated by the softness of his mother's care—each spoonful of broth, each cool compress—a melody of convalescence. "She nursed me through the fever," Thomas said, his voice thick with gratitude. "And as my strength returned, so did my clarity of purpose."

James furrowed his brow, concern etching his face as he sought the truth amid the whispers that had wound their way through Yorktown. "Thomas, everywhere we turn, the word is of pirates," he began, his voice laced with urgency. "And it seems your name is tied to their cursed sails. How did this happen?"

With its scant light, the storeroom seemed to hold its breath as Thomas's features were carved in a tableau of deep regret. But in the steady flame of his gaze, there was a depth of conviction, a readiness to confront the tempest he had unwittingly called forth. "In my sickness, my mind wandered," Thomas began, his voice a low echo of his inner turmoil. "Delirious with fever, I spoke of Yorktown, not as the home I cherish, but as a mere shadow on a map. I painted an unwitting beacon to Captain Bramwell with tales meant for no other ears—a beacon that has led that fiend and his crew to our very doorstep."

James's gaze lingered on the weapons before Thomas, his expression one of skepticism. "You're preparing for battle alone?" he questioned.

Thomas's hands stilled. "I tried to rally the townsfolk to form a unified front against Bramwell and rid us of this threat," he confessed, his voice tinged with disappointment, "but my past ties to the Crown loom over me still. I am not a defender to them but a reminder of a tyranny they wish to forget. They've turned away, leaving me to stand alone."

With a wrinkle of concern on her brow, Eliza broke the silence. "Is there no one to uphold the law against these marauders?"

Thomas gave a rueful half-smile. "Yorktown stands at the threshold of order, our leadership yet unformed, and our would-be guardians are scattered, each grappling with the war's aftermath." He waved a hand toward the streets outside their dim refuge. "Bramwell exploits this void. He navigates our disorder with the skill of an opportunist, seizing the chance as a predator would a vulnerable prey. Our present state invites his boldness."

James's eyes gleamed with a mixture of strategic thinking and a touch of relief. "We will send Eliza," he said decisively. "Her voice carries weight. As Yorktown's beloved daughter, they will not turn her away as they have you."

Understanding the pivotal role she was to play, Eliza nodded with a resolute tilt of her chin. "Yorktown has been my cradle, and I its steadfast daughter," she affirmed. "I will not let our town fall to shadows and dread. I will gather our people; their hearts will rally to the cause."

Thomas looked from James to Eliza, a silent accord passing between them. "And we," he said, motioning to James and himself, "will craft our strategy. We have armaments aplenty, but wits and courage will carry the day against Bramwell's blades and muskets."

James clapped Thomas on the shoulder, a show of camaraderie and support. "Tonight, then, we will convene at the tavern that Bramwell's eyes have not tainted," he proposed. "It is there we will lay our plans, in the heart of Yorktown, under the cloak of night. We will strike a balance between sword and shield and turn this tide of piracy back upon itself."

With a sense of purpose that lent gravity to the moment, Eliza stepped away from the storeroom's dim confines, her determination a cloak upon her shoulders. She would marshal the townspeople, ignite their will to fight, and forge the disparate spirits of Yorktown into the steel of a militia.

Thomas and James watched her leave, a receding promise of unity and action. They turned their attention to the arsenal before them in the quiet that settled after her departure. Each weapon was waiting to be called into service, and as the shadows lengthened with the approaching night, so too did the necessity of their task.

They would meet again under the veil of dusk in the very heart of the town they sought to protect. There, in the hushed whispers of the tavern, a plan would be born—a plan to cast out the darkness that threatened their home.

CHAPTER FORTY-EIGHT
SECRET MEETING

In the heart of Yorktown, under the cover of night's deepest shroud, Eliza succeeded in calling together a formidable assembly within the walls of the tavern—a place bustling with the raw energy of men and women bound by a common purpose. This place, operated by a rival in the days when Eliza's Sinclair Tavern had been the town's jewel, now served as a cradle for rebellion. Her family's legacy, now reduced to ashes in the siege's aftermath, was a silent testament to the cost of freedom.

It was well past the witching hour when the meeting began. Eliza stood at the forefront, her figure etched against the backdrop of murmuring townsfolk, her presence commanding silence and respect. The room brimmed with anticipation and whispers woven into the air as the door creaked open to admit James and Thomas.

An undercurrent of unrest rippled through the crowd at the sight of Thomas, but Eliza raised her hands, her voice cutting through the murmurs like a beacon dispelling fog. "Friends, I stand before you with Thomas, not as the man of old, but as our staunchest ally," she declared. "He is here to right a wrong, to help us vanquish the specter he unwittingly conjured in his fevered state. It is with his help that we will end Bramwell's torment."

The throng's muttering subsided, and the eyes shifted from Eliza's earnest expression to Thomas's stoic countenance. Eliza's faith in him lent weight to the promise of his redemption. Tonight, they would forge their strategy, not as fragments of a shattered past but as architects of a safer future.

James stepped forward; the hush of the tavern seemed to hold its breath, the very walls leaning in to listen. "Tonight, we end the nightmare," James proclaimed, his voice steady and assured. "We will commandeer the rowboats left behind by the retreating British. We will encircle the *Nightingale* with stealth, silent phantoms upon the water."

He paused, his gaze sweeping over the sea of faces before him. "We are well-armed—with muskets, shot, and blades. Our assault must be swift, our purpose singular: to dismantle the source of our fear, to ensure no tomorrow dawns under Bramwell's shadow."

A murmur of dissent rippled through the crowd, a voice rising above the rest. "Why must it come to bloodshed? Can we not parley with Bramwell, drive a bargain?"

James fixed the questioner with a solemn stare. "To bargain with a serpent is to invite a bite," he answered gravely. "An agreement with Bramwell is as brittle as a dry reed. Even if he were to agree, what then? He sails to the next town, and their nightmares begin afresh. No, we cannot allow the cycle to continue. Our course is clear—Bramwell and his reign must end tonight for the sake of all coastal towns, not just our own."

The room fell silent, the weight of his words settling like cannonballs. Tonight, they would be agents of their own deliverance or perish trying. The fate of Yorktown, and indeed the coast, was in their hands.

*

In a vessel with nine others following, Eliza, James, and Thomas glided across the still waters toward the *Nightingale*, a hulking mass of timber and sail that rested unsuspectingly in the bay. Their boat, the vanguard of a silent assault, cleaved through the water with purpose, each stroke bringing them closer.

Behind them, the other rowboats fanned out in a silent arc, encircling the target like wolves and their prey. In the oppressive silence of the night, only the soft lap of water against wood and the occasional creak of an oarlock betrayed the presence of the townsfolk.

Thomas's hands were firm on the oars, propelling the boat with strokes as silent as night. His attention was focused on the gentle swirl of water around them, each pull a quiet testament to the gravity of their mission. James's gaze pierced the darkness ahead, vigilant for any flicker of light or stir of movement that would signal they had been seen. Beside him, Eliza held her breath, readying herself for the pivotal role she was to play. The tension was a tangible shroud enveloping them all, every sense heightened as they neared their formidable quarry.

As they drew alongside the *Nightingale*, hearts pounding against ribs, not a single lamp shone from the ship, and no voices carried over

325

the water—nothing to suggest they had been anything but ghosts upon the water.

With bated breath, the trio secured their rowboat and began the precarious climb up the rope ladder. Each rung was a silent testament to the audacity of their plan. The air was thick with tension, every silent prayer begging that they remain unnoticed. If they were seen, the entirety of their gambit would collapse around them, a house of cards before the storm.

At last, they crested the gunwale, and the main deck of the *Nightingale* sprawled out before them, cloaked in darkness. Their boots touched down on the wooden planks, their bodies coiled and ready to spring into action or retreat, whichever the next heartbeat called for.

For a moment that stretched like an eternity, they stood, three shadows among many, taking in the vast, silent deck of the ship that had brought so much fear to their lives. It was a canvas awaiting their grim artistry.

Upon the deck of the *Nightingale*, the trio moved with purpose in search of the powder magazine, the very heart of the ship's destructive power and the perfect place to ensure a conflagration that would turn the vessel into a blazing pyre.

The darkness below decks was an entity unto itself, a thick veil that clung to Eliza, James, and Thomas as they descended into the bowels of the *Nightingale*. The only light was the faint luminescence of bioluminescent algae clinging to the sides of the ship, casting an eerie glow that seemed to watch them unblinking.

Each step was carefully negotiated with the shadows, a silent dialogue with the unknown. The wooden floorboards moaned beneath their weight, a symphony of ancient timbers that spoke in groans and sighs, the language of the sea-borne and the secrets they keep.

They moved as part of the darkness, shadows among shadows, a trio of fates threading through the heart of a slumbering beast. The ship itself was alive with the deep, resonant pulse of the bay's breath against its hull, the rhythm of waves that could turn treacherous with the slightest shift of wind or current.

Thomas guided them through the veiled darkness. He strained to remember the ship's intricacies, the layout of her decks, and the turn of her corridors before the fever had clouded his senses and confined him to his cabin.

With each step, fragments of memory pieced together like a puzzle. Although fraught and feverish, his history with the *Nightingale* had unwittingly prepared him for this moment.

Eliza's senses were alert, picking out the soft whisper of conversation—pirates, perhaps, unaware that death crept near. James, a silent sentinel, kept their retreat secure, his every sense attuned to the ship and its deadly cargo.

Finally, they found the magazine filled with barrels of gunpowder. With careful hands, Thomas withdrew the flint and tinder from his pocket and struck until one caught, and the kindling they'd placed began to smolder, then flame.

They wasted no time retracing their steps and emerging as the first tendrils of smoke rose. Before long alarms sounded, and the crew of the *Nightingale* woke to fire in their midst.

Panic ensued as the crew scrambled to douse the flames, buckets of seawater passing from desperate hands to futile ends.

Realizing the futility of their efforts, the pirates began to leap overboard, hoping the bay's cold embrace would be a safer haven. But the waters were far from safe; the ring of rowboats that encircled the burning ship was a gauntlet through which none would pass unscathed.

As the doomed pirates hit the water, the men of Yorktown took aim. Musket fire rang out, a grim chorus to the crackle of flames, and the sea became a watery grave for those who had brought so much fear and suffering to their shores.

Amidst the burgeoning chaos, Thomas, Eliza, and James remained steadfast on the deck of the *Nightingale*. As flames began to devour the ship's bowels, spreading their furious appetite for destruction, a chilling realization dawned upon the trio. In the meticulous orchestration of their assault, they had neglected one critical element—their own exit strategy.

The water surrounding the ship was a deadly perimeter, a zone of no reprieve where their compatriots, armed and tense, lay in wait for any escaping pirates. Leaping into the murky depths meant risking the deadly accuracy of their own allies, who could not be expected to distinguish friend from foe in the smoke and confusion.

Their minds raced. "We must signal the others," Eliza hissed, the orange light casting deep shadows across her determined face.

In the fervor of their escape plan, a menacing figure emerged from the smoke like a specter of the past—Bramwell himself, pistol in hand, his eyes alight with fury and disbelief. The raging fire painted him in strokes of madness as he fixated on Thomas, and then he turned to Eliza. "This must be the woman you spoke of?" Bramwell's pistol trembled as he aimed it at Eliza. The memory of Thomas's feverish rants about his beloved Yorktown, interwoven with mentions of a woman he held dear, now taunted him. "Should I take what you cherish most as my final act of revenge?"

The crackle of the flames roared in their ears. Thomas's eyes locked with Bramwell's. He had no words left. As Bramwell's finger tightened on the trigger, Thomas moved with a speed born of desperation and love, thrusting himself in front of Eliza.

The shot rang out, a thunderous echo that would forever resonate in Eliza's heart. Thomas stumbled back, his body recoiling from the impact as a scarlet bloom spread across his chest.

Eliza and James were at his side in an instant, their hands pressing against the wound in vain. Thomas's gaze found Eliza, and in that fleeting moment, time ceased its march. "I love you, Eliza. I always have. I'm so sorry." His eyes closed, and his spirit slipped away, leaving behind the shell of a hero whose love had proven boundless.

In the chaos that followed, Bramwell, his face a mask of shock and satisfaction turned horror, failed to notice the ominous creaking above. The mast, aflame and weakened at the base, groaned under the strain of the fire. With a deafening crack, it snapped, hurtling downwards like the vengeful spear of fate itself. Bramwell's moment of triumph was cut short as the mast struck him with brutal force, pinning him to the deck amidst the roaring inferno. His screams were lost in the crackle and hiss of the flames as the ship continued to burn around him, sealing his fate just as mercilessly as he had sealed Thomas's.

There was no time for grief, no moment for goodbyes. James, his heart heavy with loss and urgency, grabbed Eliza. "We must go now!" he shouted over the roar of the fire. With a shared look and a nod that conveyed the pain of their sacrifice and the necessity of survival, they leaped from the *Nightingale* into the dark embrace of the waters, leaving the fire and Thomas's sacrifice behind.

CHAPTER FORTY-NINE
REST IN PEACE

In the quietude of the Williamsburg cemetery, a hushed assembly had gathered to pay their respects to Thomas. It was a winter day that seemed to mourn with them—the skies a tapestry of somber grays, the ground beneath their feet hardened by the cold embrace of frost. Where Thomas's headstone would eventually mark his final resting place, now there was only a small wooden cross and the raw silence of recent loss.

James and Eliza stood side by side as family and friends formed a circle of solemn remembrance around the grave. Their breaths materialized in the chill air, mingling with the whispered condolences that drifted among the mourners.

The priest had yet to arrive, and in this interlude, those gathered leaned on one another, seeking solace in shared memories of a life so fiercely lived. James, clearing his throat, recounted the final act of bravery that defined Thomas's last moments—how he had stepped in front of danger, a shield of flesh and bone, to protect the woman he loved.

Eliza, her face a portrait of sorrow etched with gratitude, told of Thomas's sacrifice. Her voice trembled but did not break as she painted a vivid picture of the burning *Nightingale*, the air thick with heat and desperation, and Thomas's decision that saved her life at the cost of his own.

Amid the crowd, Thomas's mother wept, her body wracked with sobs that told of a heartbreak only a mother could know. Yet, in her tearful eyes, there was a glint of understanding—a recognition of the depth of Thomas's love for Eliza. She acknowledged the rupture between them when Eliza had ended their courtship over Thomas's allegiance, but now, all was overshadowed by the profound finality of sacrifice.

Thomas's father, his voice a steady current beneath the raw winds of sorrow. "How," he asked, his tone threading through the frozen stillness, "did you elude the wrath of such inferno?" His eyes, seeking an anchor in the tempest of his grief, looked upon Eliza and James for answers, his question a quiet echo amidst the collective heartache.

James answered, his tone both heavy and hollow. "We had but one choice—to leap into the bay with the Yorktown forces encircling the *Nightingale* raining justice upon those who tried to flee the blaze."

Eliza added, "Dr. Wellington saw us—recognizing me in the water amidst the chaos. He's been my safeguard since the day I was born."

The mourners listened, hearts heavy, as the tale unfolded—the demise of the pirate ship, the end of Captain Elias "Shadowhawk" Bramwell and his diabolical crew, and the salvation of two souls amidst the turmoil of war and flame.

A somber peace settled over the group as the final words were spoken. Thomas's life, love, and end were now part of the lore of Yorktown—a story of valor and loss that would be whispered through the annals of time. The priest arrived, his robes fluttering in the frigid breeze, and the ceremony began. Beneath the gray expanse of heaven, as words of prayer and passages of scripture wove through the air, they all stood to honor the man who had wrestled with his conscience, fought for redemption, and died a hero. Thomas would rest in peace, his legacy etched not in stone but in the hearts of those he left behind.

As the priest concluded his solemn benediction, a stillness settled over those gathered. Into this hush, Eliza stepped forward. Her silhouette was steady against the gray winter sky, her voice clear and resonant as she began her tribute.

"Thomas was a constellation of contradictions—a man who held my heart and then broke it, a man who walked a path that diverged from mine yet found his way back to stand for a cause greater than us all." Eliza spoke softly, her voice steady and laden with emotion. She scanned the gathering, making a brief, heartfelt connection with those who had come to honor a man represented by the unfilled space before them—a grave holding no more than memories.

"He was a soul torn between two worlds, yet in his final moments, he chose to be the shield that protected me from harm." Her voice wavered. "Thomas's sacrifice was the ultimate testament of his courage—a courage that now whispers to us, urging us to hold fast to our convictions, to love deeply, and to live in a manner worthy of the time we are given."

As tears brimmed in the corners of her eyes, Eliza concluded, "He gave everything for the Colonial cause, for my life, and for that, we owe him our unwavering gratitude. May his spirit soar in the peace he has earned, and may we never forget the price of the freedom we cherish."

*

The journey back to Yorktown was silent, James and Eliza lost in their own thoughts, the carriage wheels crunching on the frozen road. James broke the silence, his voice uncertain. "Eliza, what now? For us?" They spoke of Thomas, his final act of love—a subject as delicate as it was raw. James watched her closely, the question unspoken yet hanging between them like a fragile frost. "Do you still love him?"

Eliza's reply was soft but sure. "I will always harbor love for Thomas. How could I not? But, James, you are my constant, my eternal soulmate." Her hand found his.

James gazed at Eliza, his countenance etched with contrition. "Eternal soulmates," he murmured, the words resonating with a humility that had eluded him before. "Agatha had clarity, which I blindly rejected. I was churlish, and I regret my arrogance."

Eliza's eyes softened, the last vestiges of their old dispute dissolving in her gentle response. "We all have moments of folly, James," she said, her voice warm with forgiveness. "Your apology means more than you know. Let's look to the future, not the past." Her smile sealed the unspoken promise of a new beginning for them both.

James smiled, a hint of relief in his features, but it quickly gave way to a more practical concern. "As a soldier and a spy, it would seem that I'm at loose ends," he confessed.

Eliza's eyes brightened with a mixture of ambition and affection. "Let's rebuild the Sinclair Tavern, James. Not just as partners in business but …" She trailed off, leaving the possibility hanging in the air.

"In marriage, too," James finished for her, the idea settling around them like a promise. "I want all of that with you, Eliza—all of life's ventures, shared side by side."

As the carriage rolled on, they spoke of a future, of rebuilding not just a tavern but their lives. They envisioned a family, a union of hearts and purpose, a new beginning carved from the ashes of the past.

Then James's thoughts turned to another mystery. "And what of the Codex?" he inquired, the words laced with curiosity and the thrill of the unknown.

Eliza nodded, her mind already turning over the possibilities. "For that, we need to see Agatha. Perhaps she's the key to whatever secrets it holds."

As Yorktown's familiar outlines came into view, they were united in purpose and heart, ready to step forward into a shared future that honored the past but was vibrant with the promise of what was to come.

CHAPTER FIFTY
THE SOLUM CODEX

The door to Agatha's home creaked open, admitting Eliza and James into a realm that felt removed from reality. The chamber, shrouded in shadows and whispers, welcomed them with an air thick with the scent of incense and mystery. With solemn faces and hearts still heavy, they approached Agatha, the Solum Codex cradled between them like a newborn from another age. They set the text upon the worn wooden table that had seen countless secrets unravel.

Agatha, her presence as much a part of the room as the ancient tomes that lined the walls, moved forward. Her fingertips danced over the cover with a deference that spoke of awe and familiarity. Her eyes, dark pools of knowing, met theirs. "I've heard whispers of your trials," she murmured. "The skirmish with darkness on the seas … and the price paid in blood and bravery."

Eliza nodded, her throat tight with emotion as memories surged like tides within her. "Thomas …" she began, but no more words would come.

"He sacrificed himself," James finished, his voice a low rumble of storm clouds held at bay. "For the sake of all of us."

A solemn pall hung briefly in the air. Agatha acknowledged the weight of the sacrifice with the silence it deserved. Her breath seemed to draw in the sorrow and fortitude that lingered around them, an invisible shroud that was both comfort and reminder of what had been lost. With reverence, she shifted the atmosphere from one of mourning to one of purpose. The air itself seemed to respond, the subtle energy of the room awakening with the turn of each page as she began to delve into the Codex's pages. Her fingers traced the ancient lines of text, and she leaned closer as if to confer with the very essence of the Codex, seeking the wisdom that would illuminate their path forward.

Agatha hovered over the tome, her fingertips brushing the ancient parchment with a touch lighter than a whisper. "These symbols," she murmured, her voice barely more than a breath, "are more than mere marks. They are the legacy of lost wisdom, keys forged in the fires of time and memory."

James and Eliza leaned in, their eyes drawn to where Agatha pointed. Intricate sigils and glyphs sprawled before them, a complex tapestry of lines and curves that beckoned with a silent promise of secrets. They saw characters that resembled the unfurling fronds of ferns, spirals reminiscent of galaxies, and geometric shapes that hinted at mathematics far beyond their understanding.

"See how this swirl here seems to mimic the flow of water or perhaps the spiral of life itself?" Agatha traced the looping design with a reverent finger. "And this one," she continued, moving to a symbol composed of interlocking triangles, "speaks of the union of opposing forces, the harmony of balance."

James's eyes were drawn to a series of vertical lines intersected by horizontal ones, like the strings of a harp. "What of these?" he asked, his voice hushed.

Agatha smiled, a knowing glimmer in her eyes. "Ah, that is the rhythm of the universe made visible. The cadence of stars and the dance of fate."

Entranced by the unfolding revelation, Eliza pointed to a sequence where characters seemed to cascade one after another, each connected yet distinct. "It is as if they're telling a story."

Agatha nodded, her gaze deepening. "Indeed, Eliza. It is a story of epochs and ages, of the rise and fall of a civilization that breathed in rhythm with the earth."

The air around them seemed to pulse with the weight of discovery, each symbol a doorway to an era shrouded in the mists of legend, each page a map leading them through the labyrinthine corridors of history. With the Codex as their guide, they embarked on a journey to unlock the long-closed doors of Lemuria, stepping across the threshold into a realm of forgotten lore.

Agatha then reverently pushed the Codex aside and her old and worn tarot deck came into view, the cards sliding from their resting place with ease. "Let us see what truths we can unveil," Agatha said, her eyes locking with theirs. "For in the echoes of Lemuria, through trials and tribulations, your path has led you to this nexus of fate and time."

As they settled around the table, the world outside faded, leaving only the flicker of candlelight, the thrum of ancient energies, and the promise of revelations. The cards slipped through her fingers like fragments of destiny as she shuffled them. With grace, she fanned the cards into a spread that mirrored the stars under which the lost continent once flourished. Eliza and James leaned in, their breaths held, as Agatha slipped into a trance. Her voice, not entirely her own, chanted rich and strange cadences, narrating the legacy of a civilization long ago swallowed by the sea.

"The Fool," she said, tapping the card featuring a young man on the precipice of a journey, "represents the courage to step into the unknown. He is both of you, James, Eliza—stepping into the mystery of the Codex without fear, embracing its puzzles with a heart willing to learn."

She then revealed the next card, the image of a woman crowned with a crescent moon and flanked by pillars. "The High Priestess," Agatha continued, her voice taking on a reverent tone, "guards the secrets that lie beneath the surface. She urges you to look deeper, to understand the hidden layers of meaning within the Codex."

Then, Agatha presented a card portraying a stalwart emperor seated upon a throne, the symbol of steadfast authority and structured power. "The Emperor," she explained, her fingertips caressing the card's edge, "represents the structure and order that underpin the Lemurian ethos— the methodical nature of their society and their language. It is through understanding this order that you can begin to unravel the intricate tapestry of the Codex."

Each explanation she offered was a thread in the tapestry of understanding they hoped to weave, a narrative that spanned beyond the cards and into the essence of the Codex itself. As the reading unfolded, a revelation dawned that the tarot itself held the keys to the Codex. The imagery on the cards, adorned with subtle Lemurian inscriptions, was a lexicon, a cipher that unlocked the manuscript's language.

Agatha spoke of a collective unconscious, a tapestry of human memory where Lemuria's essence lingered, dormant yet accessible. Decoding the messages of the cards was to awaken a slumbering remembrance, to rekindle the spark of an ancient consciousness embedded within humanity's soul.

As Agatha concluded her oracular recitation, the cards spread before them like a star chart, James and Eliza leaned closer, the flickering candlelight casting long shadows across their earnest faces.

"Agatha," James started, his voice tinged with the gravity of their quest, "we came here seeking more than understanding. We seek a vision that could shape the very foundations of a nation."

Eliza nodded, her eyes alight with the fervor of their mission. "The Codex indeed holds a wisdom, a utopian ideal that was realized in Lemuria," she said passionately.

James nodded vigorously. "Yes, and we desire this wisdom."

Agatha listened, her eyes reflecting the flames that danced before her. "You seek to prevent a darkness that looms in the threads of time," she intuited, her gaze piercing through the veils of possibility. "The answers you seek, the guidance to ward off an era of despotism, lies entwined within Lemuria's legacy."

"The draft of the Constitution is taking shape," James said, a sense of urgency threading his words. "Madison and the others are penning what will be the law of the land. But we feel it lacks the foresight to prevent the calamities that may come decades or even centuries hence."

Agatha's eyelids fluttered closed, her spirit extending tendrils through the mists of time. In a whisper that seemed to weave the very fabric of the ages, she imparted, "The spirit of Lemuria was woven from balance, a tapestry where every voice found harmony and power served the many, not the few. Enshrine these principles within your Constitution, and you will forge a shield against the shadows of tyranny you dread."

James, his brow furrowed with the urgency of their cause, pressed her for deeper truths. "These are but the foundations," he insisted. "There is more, I know it—more we must understand."

James's plea for profound insight hung in the air, a testament to their shared resolve to unearth the deeper layers of Lemurian wisdom. Understanding the weight of James's demand, Agatha allowed a serene silence to fall, a meditative pause that seemed to gather the room's energies before releasing them in her reply. When she spoke, her voice carried the resonance of a truth that transcended time, her words flowing into the space James's question had opened. "In Lemuria," she said, "the governance was a living organism, each part synchronized with the whole. Decision-making was a tapestry woven by many hands, each thread as crucial as the next, creating a governance that breathed with collective purpose."

She spoke then of the cultivation of the mind and spirit. "In this ideal land, every child's curiosity was kindling for the fire of wisdom. Education was a river that nourished every mind, ensuring the growth of enlightened stewards of democracy."

With a somber tone, Agatha described a system of justice and equity that shone like a beacon. "Lemurian law was the very embodiment of fairness, a justice that extended its arms equally to embrace every soul, standing as an unyielding pillar against the divides of inequity."

Her hands, moving with a rhythm that traced the ebb and flow of an unseen ocean, spoke of an environmental consciousness that transcended time. "Lemurians lived in sacred communion with the earth, guardians of its legacy, vowing to preserve its riches for those yet to breathe its air or walk its paths."

Agatha painted the marketplaces of Lemuria as forums of exchange, where wealth was shared, ensuring that no one was left in want. "Prosperity was a shared song, and each voice in the chorus contributed to its harmony. In the Lemurian heart, culture and faith were woven into a vibrant tapestry of inclusion. Temples stood not as fortresses of singular truths but as gardens where a thousand flowers of belief bloomed. Peace was a practice, the very cornerstone of a civilization that held diplomacy as its most sacred art."

Agatha concluded with a call to action, "To interlace these principles within your Constitution," she urged, "is to cast a spell of preservation, to lay down a foundation strong enough to withstand the tempests of time."

Her gaze locked with James and Eliza's. They absorbed her words, each one a seed that, if properly sown, might one day yield a nation resilient against the storms of power and ambition. They knew the work would stretch beyond their lifetimes, a gift to the future they would never see. But in this room, under Agatha's gaze and Lemuria's watchful legacy, they felt the first stirrings of hope for a nation dedicated to the proposition that all beings are truly created equal.

James and Eliza sat in contemplative silence, Agatha's words settling over them like a mantle. They were custodians of knowledge that could seed a nation's ethos, guardians of a vision that might safeguard society from the tempests of tyranny and greed. Their path was now clear, their purpose steadfast. Before they would lay the cornerstone of their future—the rebuilding of the Sinclair Tavern—they would journey to Philadelphia.

In the burgeoning heart of a nation still in the throes of its making, they would bring the wisdom of the Codex to those who toiled over the

Constitution. They envisioned a contribution to the drafting process that might shape the very soul of the country. They sought to infuse the foundational document with Lemurian insights, ensuring that the seeds of liberty, justice, and equality would grow to be as enduring as the stones upon which they stood.

Only after ensuring that the essence of Lemuria was interwoven into the fabric of the burgeoning United States would they return to Yorktown. There, amidst the familiar ashes and memories, they would build anew. The Sinclair Tavern would rise again, as a place of merriment and solace and as a testament to their journey, love, and unyielding hope that a new and just world could be birthed from the old.

THE END

ABOUT THE AUTHOR

Neil Perry Gordon has made his mark on the literary world with the force of a tempest, bringing a fresh and dynamic energy to historical and metaphysical fiction genres. Embracing the notion that fiction lays bare the obscured truths of reality, his impressive repertoire, which now includes the highly acclaimed "Eternal Patriots: The Crusade for a More Perfect Union," demonstrates this conviction across over a dozen published works.

Neil's passion for storytelling was nurtured and refined in the fertile grounds of the Green Meadow Waldorf School. Here, the arts were not just taught but experienced with every sense, unlocking the profound truths beneath our everyday lives. This unique education has undoubtedly shaped his approach to storytelling, making his narratives rich and immersive.

Neil Perry Gordon's storytelling is a form of alchemy, where he transforms words into vivid images. His prose is a palette where the colors of humanity are painted in stark, gripping detail. He has a unique ability to bring the metaphysical and historical to life on the page, making them pulse with the same vitality as the present.

Neil's steadfast commitment to the art of storytelling, coupled with his innate ability to render rich, immersive narratives, has earned him a hallowed place among literary connoisseurs. Neil pulls back the curtain on reality with each story he crafts, revealing the underlying truths beneath. He serves up generous helpings of literary fare that celebrate the intricate, wondrous expanse of human experience.